jF SKYE Obert
Apprentice needed /
Skye, Obert

WITHDRAWN

MAY 2019

D0454892

Wizard for Hire

Wizard for Hire

Apprentice Needed

Obert Skye

Shadow Mountain

© 2019 Obert Skye

Interior illustrations by Brandon Dorman

All characters in this book are fictitious, and any resemblance to actual persons, living or dead, is purely coincidental.

All rights reserved. No part of this book may be reproduced in any form or by any means without permission in writing from the publisher, Shadow Mountain®, at permissions@shadowmountain.com. The views expressed herein are the responsibility of the author and do not necessarily represent the position of Shadow Mountain.

Visit us at shadowmountain.com

Library of Congress Cataloging-in-Publication Data

Names: Skye, Obert, author. | Skye, Obert. Wizard for hire ; bk. 2.
Title: Apprentice needed / Obert Skye.
Description: Salt Lake City, Utah : Shadow Mountain, [2019] | Series: Wizard for hire ; [2] | Summary: Ozzy thinks his life is finally becoming normal until someone delivers a mysterious plane ticket, and Ozzy, Sigi, and Clark find themselves in dire need of a wizard again.
Identifiers: LCCN 2018039672 | ISBN 9781629725291 (hardbound : alk. paper)
Subjects: | CYAC: Friendship—Fiction. | Wizards—Fiction | Magic—Fiction. | LCGFT: Fantasy fiction.
Classification: LCC PZ7.S62877 Ap 2019 | DDC [Fic]—dc23
LC record available at https://lccn.loc.gov/2018039672

Printed in the United States of America
Publishers Printing

10 9 8 7 6 5 4 3 2 1

TO MY BROTHER MIKE

a wizard of words.

PROLOGUE

THIS IS A GOOD INTRO

The phone in the study rang as Ozzy sat in the room reading *The Dark Is Rising.* The ring was an alarm, indicating to the senses that a response of some kind was needed. Ozzy leaned over and looked. The caller ID read:

Unknown Caller

Ozzy sat up straight—there was only one person he knew who fit that description. He dropped his book and picked up the receiver.

"Hello?"

"No time for small talk," the voice on the other end said. "You know who this is."

"Rin?"

After a few moments of silence, Ozzy spoke again.

"You know I can't see you if you're nodding yes."

"I forget you're limited in your abilities as a non-wizard."

"Where are you?"

"Not important," Rin said kindly. "You need to know that things are happening."

"What things?"

"Again, we don't have time for small talk. Just know that the time has come."

The phone went dead. Apparently, the wizard didn't even have time to say goodbye. Ozzy held the receiver in his hand for a few moments before placing it back on the base. It was the first he had heard from Rin since he had disappeared in the mountains of New Mexico, and it had gone about as well as he could have expected.

"Things are happening," he whispered to himself.

Ozzy jumped up and walked quickly from the study toward Sigi's room. He had some good news to deliver. According to Rin, the time had come. Of course, it was unknown just *what* time had come, but for the moment that didn't matter. The wizard was returning.

CHAPTER ONE

THROUGH THE DARK

The day had departed, dashing off like a frightened child as the first slender fingers of dusk gripped the sky. In its absence, darkness arrived at 1221 Ocean View Drive. Like a large visitor whom nobody had invited, the inkiness came early and in force, its arms filled with fatigue and exhaustion. It sat down on everything and moaned like an old man with tired legs and no intention of getting back up anytime soon.

Amidst the black, the home struggled to keep its glow.

The windows of the large manor were lit, and dozens of porch lights circled the abode, trying their best to remain seen. A strong wind twisted through the air and began to push around anything weak or loose that it could find.

Through the bay windows of the kitchen, a person with nerve or audacity or a desire to be intrusive and out of line could easily peep in and see what was going on.

Inside, sitting around a large table, there was a boy, a girl, and a bird.

The boy, Ozzy, was tall even sitting down. He was fifteen and possessed brown hair that came down over his ears. He was handsome in a way that he wasn't aware of, with grey eyes that typically did a fine job of matching his emotions. His nose was straight, but his head was tilted as he looked at the playing cards he had in his hand.

"Come on," the girl said.

Ozzy looked across the table and his eyes settled on Sigi. Her mop of curly hair was tied back, the overhead chandelier spotlighting her face. Her dark skin was beautiful to Ozzy—something he thought he'd seen in a giant box of crayons. She had turned sixteen two weeks before, but she carried herself with an unusual confidence that made her look years older.

"Seriously," Sigi said with a smile of teeth and tease, "you're slower at this game than Monopoly."

"You should see him play Pictionary," a small bird chirped in.

Clark was no ordinary bird. Quite the opposite. He had been created by Ozzy's father many years before to aid him in his scientific endeavors. Clark was mostly made of metal. His body and wings were black, but his tail was tin, his beak was gold, and the tips of his talons were copper. He was sentient, sarcastic, and something to behold.

"I'm not that bad at Pictionary," Ozzy said defensively.

"It took you like an hour to draw a rock," Clark reminded him. "You're a good drawer, but you shouldn't add shade and dimension while playing Pictionary."

"I do," Ozzy said. "Rocks are important."

"You sound like Rin," the bird said without thinking.

Ozzy stared at Sigi and Clark as an awkward silence dropped in. The truth was they all wished Rin were there, but the wizard was gone. He had slipped away after the great fight at the top of the stormy mountain in New Mexico. Rin said he was going to Quarfelt, a place for wizards that may or may not exist. He had vanished like a ghost, and all three were constantly looking over their shoulders (or wings) in hope that he would reappear. The only contact any of them had received was a short phone call to Ozzy two weeks before, on Sigi's birthday. Even though he had made no mention of his daughter's birthday, the call had still filled them with hope—but since then, nothing.

"Rin does like boulders," Ozzy said.

Clark hopped off the table onto the top of Ozzy's head. Hoping to make the hair more nest-like, the bird began clawing at the boy's scalp with his copper-tipped talons.

"Ouch."

"I bet people would pay good money to have their heads scratched like this," the bird pointed out.

"I don't think they would."

"Well, then, it helps my feet," Clark said. "I get restless talons if I don't move them around."

"It's been two weeks since he called," Sigi complained. "I'm surprised he's not back."

"Me too. He said something's happening."

"I don't know about that phone call," Clark said, being the chirp of reason. "Mr. Wizard was probably just talking about getting a haircut. Or maybe he's gained weight and that's his way of telling you."

"I don't think so," Ozzy said.

The three of them had discussed the short phone call many times over the last two weeks. All their thoughts and theories were pointless, though, because there was no way to predict what a wizard like Rin ever meant, or to know what someone like him would do.

Sigi yawned. "You know what? I'm sorry, but I think I'm done for the night." She tossed her cards onto the table. They'd been playing a slow game of cards for an hour, but the dark wind outside made it feel like the world was shutting down. And Sigi, it seemed, felt the same way. "I'll see you two in the morning."

Ozzy set his cards down. "Good. I was about to lose anyway."

"Goodnight, Ozzy," she said with a smile.

He smiled back, and Sigi slipped off to her first-floor room near the home's library.

"Is your face okay?" Clark asked once she was gone. "I mean, is that supposed to be a smile?"

"Yes," Ozzy said as he stood up.

"Human mouths are so messed up. I like a straightforward beak."

"We can't all be perfect."

"Your smile just proved that point."

Ozzy put away the cards and moved out the side door of the kitchen. Outside was a short breezeway and a steep set of wooden stairs that led up to a room above the garage. It was dark and windy as he climbed the stairs to the second floor. Clark fought the wind and flew beside him.

"What's the deal with you and Sigi anyway?" the bird asked.

"What do you mean?"

"In all the movies I've seen, people fall in love much quicker than you two. They go bowling together, maybe sing something at each other, and then get married."

"What movies are you watching?"

"I just saw the one about the magic pink elixir."

"That was a commercial for Pepto-Bismol."

"Well, it had a happy ending—isn't that what everyone wants?"

"How would I know? I'm not sure what a happy ending feels like."

Clark hovered inches away from Ozzy's nose.

"Really? You can't take a guess?" the bird asked. "I think it would feel like owning the motor of a 1968 Mustang."

Clark had been binge-watching a lot of videos about engines lately.

"You and I have different definitions of happy," Ozzy said. "You love things that are metal, like engines, and I'm looking for an ending that feels complete."

"Well, if Rin was here, you know what he'd say."

"What?"

"I don't know—I'm a bird, not a wizard."

Ozzy stopped three stairs from the top. His left hand began to buzz and he could feel the sensation rattle through his entire body.

Clark fluttered in front of Ozzy's face. "Are you okay?"

"I think I'm just tired."

Ozzy climbed the last three steps and opened the door into his room. Clark flew in and glided over to the desk in the corner. He hopped into a nest he'd made from a small pile of orange yarn.

"Keep the desk light on," Clark said. "With Sigi's mom gone, I want to make sure I stay powered up. I promised Patti I'd keep an eye on things."

Three hours before, Sigi's mom, Patti, had taken a shuttle to the Portland airport. She was on her way to be the keynote speaker at a five-day conference in Seattle. She had been hesitant to leave Sigi and Ozzy, but Clark had promised to act as chaperone and guard-bird. He took the task very seriously.

"Thanks for keeping us safe," Ozzy said kindly.

"It's what I've done from the start."

Clark was right—the bird had kept an eye on Ozzy from the moment they'd met. And now, even though things were calm, they both knew trouble had not ceased to exist in the world. What they had gone through months before had been dangerous and life-changing. It had involved people who would stop at nothing to get what they wanted. And knowing that made it hard for them to ever feel completely at ease. Having to have a guard-bird was just a sign of the times.

"Goodnight, Clark." Ozzy patted the bird on his small head.

"Really?" Clark said. "It seems too windy outside to be good."

"Okay. Night, Clark."

The bedroom above the garage was small with two large windows that ran from floor to ceiling on the west wall. The windows overlooked the backyard and the beach that spread out in front of the Pacific Ocean. At the moment, however, they simply overlooked darkness.

The wind rattled the windows.

Inside the room was a bed with an iron bedframe, its mattress covered in white linens and topped with four white pillows. Next to the bed was the small desk Clark slept on, along with a chair and a trash can with pictures of seashells painted on it. Across the room from the bed was a door that led to an attached bathroom and an open closet. All the doors in the room were painted blue, while everything else was white.

Ozzy washed up in his bathroom and then turned off the overhead light. He left the desk lamp on for Clark, who was lying still in his nest, his eyes closed. Ozzy sat down on the edge of his bed and tried to calm his mind.

His left hand buzzed again, and the soft vibration felt uncomfortable.

He held his hand in front of him and stared at his digits in the dimly lit room. The pointer finger on his left hand had a birthmark that wrapped his entire finger like a purple sheath.

"Is this what you mean by 'Something's happening,' Rin?" he said aloud.

The wind outside howled, but the question went unanswered.

At the age of seven, Ozzy's parents had been taken from him—ripped away in front of his own eyes. He'd been left alone in a small house in the middle of an isolated forest to raise himself. When he had grown old enough to begin looking for answers, the quest had been long and filled with some less-than-happy endings, one of which was coming to know that his father and mother were no longer alive. That ending had also included Rin's disappearance. The wizard had become an important part of Ozzy's life, and now he too was gone.

The wind chuffed and stuttered against the glass.

Ozzy lay down on his bed and closed his grey eyes. For the first time in many years he had a place where he belonged with people who loved him. But even with nice sheets and soft pillows, sleep didn't come easy. He missed the cloaked house he had grown up in—his attic bedroom with its round window was a part of him that he'd given up to live as the lawyers and guardians in his life saw fit. Now he had things like electricity and warm showers—but he missed the forest.

His finger buzzed again.

When Ozzy was younger, he had believed the strange birthmark meant something. He thought it might be a powerful sign, an indication of some great ability. But it wasn't until his struggle on the mountain that his finger began to feel like anything more than just a finger. That night, he had felt it trigger something in his mind, something strong and confusing. Since then, however, nothing had happened until tonight—when his finger had begun buzzing.

It took a while, but eventually Ozzy fell into a sort of half-slumber, a fitful sleep, his body twitching like the whiskers of a worried cat in the throes of curiosity. His breathing fluctuated between shallow and deep. Sweat ran down his forehead and covered his sheets. He closed and opened his fists as his back arched and he shivered from hair to soles.

Ozzy gasped.

Struggling to get air, he shook. Then, as he relaxed, his lungs did a spot-on imitation of a boiler slowly bellowing.

"Ooooooooooom."

Ozzy's head rocked back and forth, but his dark hair stayed fixed, plastered to his top like a puddle of muddy tar.

"Sig—!" he tried to yell, but his mind wouldn't let him.

The wind outside pressed its stormy face up against the glass, rattling the panes, curious to see what was happening.

Ozzy stopped shaking and sat up in bed. His blankets fell to the floor. The birthmark on his finger buzzed like a reminder had been set by his soul to wake up his body and cause great alarm.

With his eyes closed, he swung his legs over the edge of the bed and stepped on the floor. His bare toes grabbed at the carpet. He wasn't asleep, but his mind was not his own.

The wind thumped against the house like the bass line of a harrowing song. Ozzy blinked and opened his eyes. He shuffled to one of the huge windows that were facing west toward the ocean. He pressed both of his palms up against the glass. His hands shook as they touched the shivering window.

Turning slowly, he walked back to the bed. The iron bedframe had four decorative bedknobs at each corner, each a little larger than a billiard ball.

Ozzy grabbed a bedknob on a post at the foot of the bed. He closed his eyes and unscrewed the iron bedknob. The metal sphere squeaked until it came loose in his hands. The weight of the round knob pulled his arm downward. He swiveled, and with one smooth motion, threw the heavy object at the closest window.

Crasshck!

The bedknob hit the center of the glass, creating an ear-splitting sound and thousands of veiny fractures that covered the entire window with a webbed pattern. After hitting the glass, the metal bedknob dropped to the floor with a thud.

Ozzy just stood there, his mind feeding him messages he didn't want to obey. Without warning or reason, he ran across the room, barrelling directly into the already fractured glass with his right shoulder.

The second-story window burst outward in a thousand shards as Ozzy flew through it.

The boy didn't scream or flail, he just hit the grassy ground behind the garage, rolling toward the trees at the edge of the yard. His body crumpled up into a heap of human as it came to a stop near two large boulders.

He stood up.

The wind was thrilled to have full access to him now. It enveloped Ozzy, buffering him from side to side and tossing his dark hair every which way but neat. The lights on the back of the garage and house swayed wildly, creating jittery shadows that danced rhythmically around the boy.

Still more asleep than awake, he started to walk away from the garage. His body was covered with small cuts and tiny splinters of glass.

His face, however, was expressionless.

Ozzy walked over the grass, past some boulders, through the trees, and between a stone bench and a metal railing. He stepped onto a thin sandy path winding past the long grasses down toward the beach.

His expression remained the same.

Wind smacked and shoved him around like a pushy

bully who had no understanding of how a person should act. Sand blew through the air like errant pieces of glass—stinging his arms and head and eyes, adding to the cuts and scrapes he'd already gathered.

Still, he kept walking.

A small dot of blackness competing with the night moved in behind the boy and spoke.

"What are you doing?" Clark chirped loudly from behind him.

The bird's small voice was barely audible over the raging wind. And the strong gusts were making it difficult for Clark to catch up.

"Hey!" Clark screeched. "What gives?"

The wind tossed the bird back toward the house.

Clark righted himself and fought the air. It was dark, and the electric charge he'd accumulated before shutting down dropped quickly as he used his full strength to push against the elements.

"Stop walking!" he tweeted. "Ozzy!"

Hearing his name, the boy stopped for a moment, blinked twice, and then kept moving. The momentary pause was just enough for Clark to catch up and dig his claws into the back of Ozzy's T-shirt.

"What are you doing?" Clark scream-tweeted. "I like the ocean as much as you, but it's the middle of the night and the wind has lost its mind!"

In the distance, massive mounds of water crashed down, pummeling the shore with their heavy bodies.

"Seriously," Clark yelled as he tried to climb up Ozzy's shirt onto his left shoulder. "I . . . I . . . I'm wearing down. I can't . . ."

Clark was out of power; he let go. His left talons raked Ozzy's shoulder as the wind violently flipped him back toward the house like a wad of unwanted paper.

Ozzy continued toward the water.

Now something was different. The deep scratch from Clark's talons had awakened something inside the boy. His head thrashed from side to side and his feet moved slower as he began to fight whatever was happening.

The elements pushed him closer and closer to the water; mist from the waves rose up and over him, soaking his body and clothes.

He tried to yell, but his mind was not his own. Something was moving him—his legs, his arms, and his body were being manipulated, working together to lead him directly into the raging sea.

His feet reached the shore as waves taller than most hills crashed down around him. He fought the wind and water but it was pointless, because even as he struggled mentally, his body continued to walk.

Ozzy stepped into the waves.

The sea pushed him backwards, but his body kept him surging forward.

In a moment the water was up to his waist, then his chest.

He moved deeper, as wave after wave came thundering

down on top of him. His being shook from the cold and relentless ocean. Water filled his mouth and blinded his eyes. He could taste the salt and the unsavory realization of what was happening.

Death seemed like the most likely next step.

The sea ripped his legs out from under him and Ozzy sank below the wet and deadly surface.

CHAPTER TWO

TEARING ME APART

Sigi's brown eyes flashed open and her heart was racing—something had woken her up. She laid in her bed trying to figure out what it had been. A dream? The wind? A troublesome metal raven that was trying to be a chaperone/guard-bird but was failing at being quiet?

The wind, she decided.

As if to verify her thoughts, the wind outside of her curtain-covered windows screeched, making it sound like Mother Nature hadn't figured out how inappropriate catcalls were.

Sigi closed her eyes, sighed, and then sat up.

Her room was dark, but the light from a small clock on her desk lit up the space just enough to enable her to walk around without bumping into things.

The wind whistled louder.

"Knock it off."

Sigi stood up and walked to the lightswitch. She pushed the button and her world became brighter.

Glancing around, everything appeared to be in order, but from somewhere far away she could hear something banging repeatedly. Wearing an oversized T-shirt and shorts, she stepped out into the hall.

"Clark?" she called out.

There was no answer.

Sigi walked down the hall and the thumping grew louder.

"Clark? Ozzy?"

The noise was strongest in the kitchen. It seemed to be coming from the direction of the garage. Sigi opened the kitchen door and looked across the breezeway at the wooden stairs. Something clapped and slammed. She looked up the dimly lit stairs and saw Ozzy's door blowing open and closed in the heavy wind.

"Ozzy?" she shouted. "Clark?"

Something was wrong.

Sigi ran across the breezeway and up the stairs. She grabbed the handle of the slamming door and flipped on the overhead light. There, like a bad surprise, was Ozzy's empty bed and a shattered window. Wind poured into the room and around her like a fat clumsy ghost. Bits of orange yarn were blowing everywhere.

"Ozzy?"

Stepping up to the window, she stared out into the windy darkness. Her hands were shaking; her knees felt loose in their sockets. Her curly hair twisted in the wind. What Ozzy and she had already been through was dangerous and unsettling. The thought of new trouble made her stomach queasy.

As she stared out what was left of the window, something came flying in and hit her in her uneasy stomach. Sigi fell backwards onto the bed and rolled to the floor. She reached for what had struck her and squeezed.

"Stop it!" Clark squawked. "You're going to break my wings."

Sigi sat up on the floor, holding the bird in front of her. "What's going on?"

"It's Ozzy," Clark answered. "He's freaking out." The bird jumped from her hand and positioned himself near the lamp on the desk. "He's down on the beach, walking toward the waves. I couldn't stop him. I had to ride the wind just to get back here. You've got to get him. I'll come as soon as I'm charged."

Sigi didn't waste time with questions or comments. She turned quickly and ran out of the room and down the wooden stairs. She ran into the kitchen and grabbed a small red aluminum flashlight. Switching it on, she ran back out onto the breezeway and across the yard toward the beach. She passed the boulders and trees.

"Ozzy!" she screamed, tossing the small beam of light from side to side. "Ozzy!"

She ran over the sand toward the ocean as fast as she could. And when she reached the water, the waves were angry and deafening. Turning in a circle, she shone the flashlight across the waves and the sand.

"Ozzy! Ozzy!"

Clark powered through the wind and landed on her right shoulder. He clawed at her T-shirt.

"He's in the water!" the bird yelled.

Sigi ran into the ocean as if she knew what she was doing.

"Where?" she screamed.

"I don't know," the bird screamed back. "But he was . . . there!"

Clark shot off of Sigi's shoulder toward a spot twenty feet to her left. Sigi aimed the flashlight and marched farther into the water. She saw Ozzy's wet brown hair bobbing up in the distance.

"Ozzy!"

Sigi dropped the flashlight and dove under the water. The ocean was as black as the sky, but after only a few strong strokes and kicks she ran directly into Ozzy. Sigi wrapped her right arm around his listless body and pushed her head up to get a lungful of air.

"You got him!" Clark yelled as he fluttered above, the wind making it hard for him to fly in place.

With her right arm around Ozzy's chest, Sigi began to swim back toward the shore. Under normal conditions the act of dragging a six-foot frame through the torrid water would have seemed impossible. But Sigi had adrenaline coursing through her body. Plus she was being cheered on by a metallic bird with strong vocals.

"Don't let go!"

Sigi's feet finally found the bottom of the ocean. She used her legs to help pull Ozzy the rest of the way through the surging water and up onto shore.

Clark dropped from the sky and started clawing at the boy's wet shirt. Sigi gave one last yank and then dropped Ozzy on the sand just out of the reach of the waves.

She collapsed next to him.

"Is he alive?" Clark screamed above the wind.

Sigi rolled over onto her hands and knees and took a few moments to cough and gasp for air. The intense darkness and continuous wind were relentlessly stealing her breath.

"Is he dead?" Clark asked. "He looks dead. Kiss him!" the bird chirped. "That's what they do in movies."

Sigi ignored Clark and put her hand on Ozzy's chest to see if he was breathing.

"That's not how you kiss," Clark squawked. "Smash your face against his."

"It's okay," Sigi said. "He's breathing. I can feel his chest moving."

"Oh." Clark sounded almost disappointed. "I just thought a kiss would be more dramatic. Besides, if he's alive, why isn't he moving?"

"He's unconscious." The night was so dark that Sigi

could barely see the bird she was talking to. "We need to get help."

"What about the flashlight?" Clark asked in a panic.

"What about it?"

"I really liked that light."

"Forget about that. I lost it in the ocean. We have to get him . . ."

Sigi stopped talking because Ozzy had suddenly sat up. The relief on her face was visible even in the dark.

"You're okay!" she said, throwing her arms around him as they sat next to each other on the sand.

Ozzy didn't reply.

"He's probably mad about the flashlight," Clark said.

"He's not—"

Ozzy stood up without saying anything.

"What are you doing?" Sigi asked. "You should rest."

The boy wasn't listening. He turned around twice, and then began walking back toward the house. Sigi scrambled to get up and Clark darted onto Ozzy's left shoulder, grabbing his wet T-shirt with his talons.

"What's the deal?" Clark tweeted. "What are you doing?"

Ozzy kept walking.

Sigi caught up and put her arm around him as he walked. Together they moved through the trees, past the boulders, and across the yard. The lights on the back of the house were still swaying in the wind, doing their best to light things up. The tiny scratches covering Ozzy's arms and legs were visible for the first time.

"What happened to you?" Sigi asked.

Ozzy didn't answer.

Sigi looked up and saw the shattered window in the room above the garage. The light from the room shone down. "Did you *jump* from there?"

Ozzy blinked and kept walking.

"Your mom's not going to be happy about this," Clark said to Sigi. "She said to keep things in order."

"You're the chaperone," Sigi argued.

Ozzy walked through the breezeway and started climbing the stairs to his room.

"What do we do?" Sigi asked the bird.

"Maybe he wants to jump out the window again," Clark suggested. "Some people live for the thrill of dumb things."

When they got to Ozzy's room he walked directly to his bed and climbed in. Reaching down, he pulled the blanket up from the floor, covered himself with it, and closed his eyes.

Clark perched himself on the remaining bedknob at the foot of the bed. The wind coming in through the broken window caused him to sway.

"Should we call a doctor?" Sigi asked.

"You think *she* could find the flashlight?"

"The flashlight's gone, Clark."

The small metal bird shivered. “Maybe Ozzy just needs sleep?”

“Maybe.” Sigi didn’t look sure of anything. “One of us needs to stay here and keep an eye on him. We need to make sure he doesn’t do something else like that.”

Sigi’s words fell on deaf metal—Clark had already shut down.

The wind rocked Clark some more and he fell off the bedknob and onto the mattress near Ozzy’s feet.

“Some guard-bird.”

Sigi moved the desk chair nearer the bed and out of the direct path of the incoming wind. She took a seat. She sat looking at Ozzy—her hair was wet, her mind was a mess, and the wind wouldn’t shut up. She knew very well that what had just happened was caused by more than just a blustery night. Something terrible was brewing. Something was happening, and she had never felt more anxious to have her father back.

Unfortunately, anxiety does nothing to help the cause.

CHAPTER THREE

SLIPPING THROUGH THE DOOR

The wizard moved up the street quietly and with speed. His eyes took in the dark night before him as he searched for any potential hazards or obstacles ahead.

The scene was still and the town was sleeping.

He dashed in a fashion befitting a wizard, making it across the empty road and over to his destination. Gazing at the front of the building, he felt a sudden and surprising sense of guilt. There was some reason to worry, but he knew what was at stake. Finishing the task was all that mattered.

He reached out and tried the knob—the door was locked. The wizard pulled his wand from his robe and spoke softly.

"*Sintabio afinisha.*"

The door opened, and he stepped inside.

The dark interior was void of people but contained

some obstacles. He could see the shadows and outlines of the areas he needed to search.

"*Resped umidino.*"

The words caused a small flame to burn in his hand and light the space.

He quickly and carefully searched the room.

Finding nothing, he unlocked another door and moved into the inner chamber. His hands and eyes looked over everything, taking care to leave things as undisturbed as possible. A locked drawer offered some difficulty and resisted his initial spells.

"A staff would be nice," he whispered, knowing how magical leverage could be.

Having no staff, he found a closed umbrella in a bin by the wall. He placed the tip of it under the top of the drawer and pried it up. The locked drawer popped open, and inside it he found a few items of interest, but not what he had come for.

"Quite disappointing," he muttered.

A weak light came into the room through a small square window at the back of the inner chamber. The wizard looked out and saw lights moving in the distance.

He turned and walked back through the two doors and out into the dark night.

Once outside, the wizard pulled his robe tightly around him and walked quickly and undetected through the wind—acting as if he were simply a part of the strong breeze, blowing back to where he had come from.

CHAPTER FOUR

SCARED OF WHAT THE MORNING BRINGS

Sunlight poured into Ozzy's room and applied a sugary white glaze to everything. The air was cool and smelled like the ocean—salty, with a hint of sulfur.

Ozzy had slept peacefully and soundly through the night, and hadn't taken any additional strolls into the ocean. Sigi had slept in the chair at the foot of his bed all night. When morning arrived, Clark had woken up, allowing her to take a shower and dress in clean clothes.

Now Sigi was back in Ozzy's room. She and Clark were standing at the edge of the bed, staring at Ozzy as if he were something so delicate that even speaking too loudly might harm him.

"So . . . you think he's okay?" Sigi whispered.

"I don't know," Clark chirped softly. "It depends on your definition of okay. I think he's alive, but his hair looks awful."

Ozzy's hair was messy, his eyes were closed, and his chest was rising and falling slowly as he continued to sleep.

"I'm not worried about his hair," Sigi said.

"Sad." Clark shook his small metal head. "Birds are very particular about their grooming."

Sigi smiled at her fowl friend.

In all honesty, Clark was much more than any fowl—he was a creation, an unexplainable wonder, and completely devoted to Ozzy. He was also occasionally briefly devoted to other birds and random metal objects.

Clark was powered by light hitting a thin strip of silver paint on his back. His body was mostly black and he identified as a raven, though he could easily be mistaken for a crow. His head was topped with wiry feathers; his wings were metal with bits of leather holding them together. He jumped up and glided onto Ozzy's right shoulder. He looked up at the boy's face and the wire feathers on his head bristled.

"He could have died," Sigi said.

"He almost did," Clark replied. "You saved his life."

"It wouldn't have been possible without you."

"That is completely true," Clark admitted. "Make sure when you're telling other people what happened that you mention that."

Sigi smiled as she turned to look at Clark. Her brown hair moved like a spray of curly flowers. She had changed into a red T-shirt and black shorts.

"What was up with that weather last night?" Clark asked her. "The wind was so strong I could barely fly."

The two of them glanced out the big missing window in Ozzy's room. The wind had gone, and the dark night had been replaced by sunshine and clouds so new that they looked like they were still in their cellophane wrappers.

"Why would he walk into the ocean?" Sigi asked.

"Why does anyone do anything?" Clark asked. "I saw a man in town carrying a skateboard."

"Why is that weird?"

"Who *carries* a skateboard when you can use it? Seems like he didn't think it—"

Ozzy let out a small moan.

Both bird and girl glanced at him, concerned.

Ozzy's hands twitched and his grey eyes opened for a moment before quickly shutting again.

Sigi sat down on the edge of the bed.

"Hey," she said softly, "are you okay?"

There was no immediate answer, but before Clark could fill the silence with more skateboard talk, Ozzy replied.

"What happened?" he asked, his eyelids still closed.

"We're trying to figure that out," Sigi said. "It looks like you threw a bedknob at the glass, jumped out the window, and then went for a midnight walk into the ocean. You almost drowned."

"I saved your life," Clark chimed in.

Ozzy opened his foggy eyes. "Just like a real guard-bird."

"I don't like to tweet my own beak, but *exactly* like a real guard-bird."

"So you don't know what happened?" Sigi asked. "Or why you did . . . any of that?"

Ozzy shook his head. His eyes were clearing and some color began to push up from his neck into his face.

"It's like those tapes," Clark said. "The ones with the brainwashed people your dad experimented on."

Ozzy and Sigi exchanged a pair of worried glances.

"What?" the bird tweeted. "Am I wrong?"

Ozzy's parents, Emmitt and Mia Toffy, had been brilliant scientists. They were wise beyond their years, clever beyond all belief, and intelligent to the point of their own destruction. They had discovered a way for humans to control their own will power—no more harmful decisions or erratic behavior.

But the formula had problems.

If it was administered the wrong way, the formula gave control to someone other than the intended person, making it possible for that someone to dictate the other person's actions. Ozzy had heard the experiments on the tapes his parents had left behind—a woman had climbed onstage at a play and started to sing, a man had jumped into a polar bear exhibit and almost died. And now, it seemed as if Ozzy, as well, had done something he had not chosen to do.

"But I don't get it," Clark said, sounding bothered. "Who's controlling you? And why would they have you walk into the ocean? That's so pointless. I'd make you gather a bunch of random metal things and have them do my bidding."

"You want random metal things to do your bidding?" Sigi asked.

"The way you say it makes it sound evil," Clark complained. "I just need a few nice pens or tin cups to place around my nest. What's wrong with that? Maybe some salad tongs to, you know, just be there for me. I saw a really nice pair in that store in Otter Rock."

"Okay," Ozzy said, "next time I lose control of my mind I'll bring you a frying pan."

Clark looked pleased. Sigi did not.

"This isn't a joke. You almost *died*. *I* almost died. And the window's broken. My mom's not going to be happy."

Ozzy's finger buzzed as Sigi spoke. He moved it under the covers.

"I didn't die," he reminded her. "Maybe I was just sleepwalking."

Sigi rubbed behind her ears as if a headache had just come on.

"I don't think you were sleepwalking."

"I don't either," Ozzy confessed.

"It's too bad my mom's not here." Sigi leaned in closer to examine a few of the small cuts on Ozzy's right arm. "I think we're going to have to take you somewhere to get you looked at."

"I love to be looked at, too," Clark said.

"Sorry, Clark, that's not what I meant." Sigi stood up. "We need to get him to a doctor."

"I don't think we do." Ozzy sat up in the bed. "No doctor is going to know what to do with me."

"So we just wait and see if it happens again? You know, the next time could kill you."

Ozzy shook his head. "Your mom's gone till Wednesday, and I know Rin's not here, but I still don't want a doctor."

Clark looked happy.

"Mr. Wizard would be so proud," the bird sang, putting his wings on his hips. "He was all about waiting around to see what happens—fly onto a train, eat lots of breakfast, wait and see where the magic will strike. And no offense," Clark said passionately, "but I don't trust medical professionals. I've gotten some really shady advice from Dr. Seuss."

"The author?" Sigi asked confused.

"Dr. Seuss is an author?" Clark said perplexed. "I'm talking about the short guy in town who sells colorful drinks that are too cold."

"Well, Ozzy isn't talking about any Dr. Seuss." Sigi blew an errant strand of curly hair away from her face. "I'm happy to wait around for proof that the world is as magical as my absentee father insists it is, but I feel like your life's in danger. It would be dumb to just wait to see what happens."

"Who's to say?" Clark asked.

"People with brains," she replied.

There was a small moment of silence as they wondered what to do. Clark was mere moments away from suggesting something that wouldn't have helped, but before he did, the sound of chimes rang out.

They all looked at the intercom embedded in the wall near Ozzy's door. Most rooms in the house were on the intercom network, and so when the doorbell of the main house rang, there weren't many places you wouldn't hear it. Now it was ringing, and the sound gave all of them goose (and raven) bumps.

There are numerous occasions when the sound of chimes can be comforting, but thanks to the uneasiness already in the room, this wasn't one of them.

CHAPTER FIVE

NO CARS

Girl, boy, and bird all looked shocked, their eyes the size of saucers.

"That's weird," Clark said. "Do you hear bells?"

Sigi nodded.

"Were you expecting anyone?" Ozzy asked.

"No," Sigi said whispering needlessly. "The gardener comes today, but he never rings or comes inside."

Ozzy got out of the bed.

"What are you doing?" the bird chirped.

"We should answer it."

"Should we?" Clark looked at Sigi for support, but she just shrugged. "Sometimes it's best to just ignore things. Seriously," he insisted, "I read that online. It was in an article about mockingbirds."

"I always wanted a doorbell at the Cloaked House," Ozzy said. "I think I thought my parents would return and ring it someday. Or that someone would drop by and deliver me warm food."

"That never happened," Clark reminded him. "In fact, the only people to come by were the ones who took your parents. It wouldn't have made it any better if they'd rung the bell first."

They left Ozzy's room and its shattered window and walked down the wooden stairs, across the breezeway, and into the kitchen. As they reached the foyer, the doorbell rang again. They took a moment to silently contemplate going any farther.

"It's probably just a package," Sigi whispered. "My mom gets stuff all the time."

"I know she does," Clark complained. "And yet she refuses to buy me a label maker."

"You have stuff to label?" Sigi asked as she stared down the hall at the front door.

"No," the bird chirped softly.

Ozzy took Sigi's hand and, with Clark fluttering by their side, they crossed the foyer and stood in front of the large front door.

The doorbell rang a third time.

"Someone's impatient." Clark flew behind Sigi's curly hair to hide.

Ozzy pulled open the front door. A man of regular height stood on the porch, wearing brown trousers and a faded green shirt. He was difficult to describe because he was extremely average, almost completely unremarkable in his appearance. He had short light-brown hair, shoulders, arms, everything that average people have. Unremarkable.

"Hello," he said, showing teeth that were neither too straight nor too crooked. "I have a package for Ozzy Toffy."

"That's me."

"If you'll sign here." The unremarkable man reached out and handed Ozzy a small tablet. "Just use your finger and sign above the line."

Ozzy stared at his fingers as if he had just discovered something new they could do. He dragged the pointer finger on his left hand over the screen, forming his signature. The delivery man stared at his birthmark.

"That's interesting," he said. "My sister has a birthmark on the left side of her face."

Ozzy wasn't sure how to respond to that. So he went with, "Tell her hi."

The man didn't smile.

Ozzy gave him back the tablet and the unremarkable man handed him a small package.

"Have a nice day," the man said with no distinctive inflection.

After thanking the man, Ozzy closed the door and turned the lock. He sat down on the small padded bench in the foyer. Clark crawled out from the back of Sigi's hair, struggling to free his right talon. With a solid jerk, he worked himself free, falling from her shoulder onto the floor. He hopped up quickly, pretending he'd meant to do that.

Sigi sat down next to Ozzy. Together they stared at the small cube in his hands. The box was five inches wide, tall, and long. It was covered in brown paper and almost as nondescript as the man who had delivered it. Ozzy's first and last name were written on one side in black marker. There wasn't an address or any other kind of markings.

"Wait," Sigi said.

Without elaborating, she jumped up, unlocked the front door, and pulled it open. She dashed out onto the porch. Sigi stopped and glanced around. She then ran past the fountain in front of the house and down the sidewalk.

Ozzy exited the house and raced to catch her.

"What are you doing?" he yelled.

"Did that man have a car?" she yelled back.

"I don't remember." Ozzy stopped to better think. "I didn't hear one drive off."

"I'll find out." Clark shot up into the air and flew down the driveway.

"How could someone deliver something to you without an address?" Sigi asked, walking back.

"I'm not sure," Ozzy admitted. "Is that weird? Because it's probably just something my lawyer sent over."

Ever since Ozzy and Sigi had returned four months before, Ozzy had spent a good deal of time with his lawyer, a man by the name of Ryan Severe. Ozzy's parents had left him a lot of land and other possessions, and there had been issues of guardianship and trusts to set up. Living with Patti and Sigi had been one of the conditions the court had insisted on.

"Your lawyer just drops things off in plain packages?"

"Maybe," Ozzy said, still holding the box.

"I think hanging out with you has made me suspicious of everything."

Clark was back now. He landed on Ozzy's left shoulder, chirping loudly.

"I couldn't see anything," he reported. "No cars for miles. Maybe Mr. Blah walked here."

"Maybe I should just open this up and find out what it is," Ozzy suggested.

Sigi and Clark looked on as Ozzy tore open one side of the package. He reached in and pulled out the only thing inside, a small metal flash drive.

Clark was instantly infatuated. "Well, *hel*-lo."

"What is this thing?" Ozzy asked.

"A flash drive," Sigi replied.

"Even the *name* is exciting," the bird crooned.

"Let's find out what's on it," Sigi said.

Sigi and Ozzy walked back into the house, Clark flying alongside, and to the kitchen. Sigi's laptop was at the end of the bar, near the largest refrigerator. She flipped it open and it came to life.

Ozzy handed her the flash drive and she stuck it into the USB port. The machine dinged and whirred for a moment as they kept their eyes on the screen, waiting for something to happen.

The file opened and displayed three attachments. The first was an electronic boarding pass.

"It's an airplane ticket," Sigi exclaimed.

"It's got my name on it."

Sigi took a closer look at the screen. "And it's to New York."

Ozzy shook like a quaking leaf. New York was where he'd been born, and where he'd lived with his parents until they had moved to Oregon. He was seven when they had left, but he still had a few foggy memories of being there. Now someone unknown had sent him a way to return. The thought was knee-buckling and confusing.

"And the flight's for tomorrow out of the Portland airport," Sigi said excitedly. "There's a return ticket for the day after. This other attachment is a ticket for a shuttle to the airport."

"That's great," Clark said. "But maybe I should hold onto that flashy drive until we figure this all out."

The bird was ignored.

"This feels like something," Sigi said seriously. "Someone appears out of nowhere and leaves you a plane ticket? That's not something that usually happens."

"I still don't have a good idea of what is and isn't usual," Ozzy admitted.

"This isn't," Sigi insisted. "Nothing about your life is. Why would someone give you this flash drive?"

"I didn't even know what a flash drive was until right now," Ozzy admitted.

The last file on the flash drive was just an address:

Resort in New York
11234 Avenue Ingracias
New York, NY 10010

"Am I supposed to use that ticket and go to this address?"

"No one can expect you to just fly off to New York." Sigi rocked back and forth on her feet. "People tried to kill you, remember? What if the ticket's a trap?"

"I don't think it's a trap," Ozzy replied. "Look at the name of the resort."

Sigi read it off the screen again. "So?"

"'Resort in New York'?" Ozzy said. "The letters spell R-I-N."

"Actually, they spell R-I-N-Y," Clark pointed out. "Which, if you ask me, is a more interesting name."

Sigi's worry was replaced by happiness. "You think it's my dad?"

"I do," Ozzy answered her. "He called, said something was happening, and then this showed up."

Clark jumped down from Ozzy's head and stood on the end of the bar. "Yes," he tweeted excitedly, "why *wouldn't* it be Riny? I mean, it would be just like him to do something this way. Then, when you get there and find him, he'll say something confusing and claim it was magic that brought you there."

Ozzy looked at Sigi and shrugged.

Sigi stopped rocking on her feet and took a moment to look confused. She half-smiled and then sat down on a barstool and began typing something on her laptop.

"What are you doing?" Ozzy asked.

"Hoping that Clark's right," she replied. "There's no way you're going to New York by yourself. I'm going with you."

"I'll be fine," Ozzy insisted. "I used to live there."

"You were seven." Sigi typed quickly. "I hope I can get on the same flights as you."

"*Now* can I have the flash drive?" Clark asked.

"No," Ozzy said kindly.

Sigi kept typing as the mopey bird hopped back up onto Ozzy's head and settled in his hair. Their day had begun with fear and confusion, but now it felt as if it was stuffed with possibility.

CHAPTER SIX

THE FOREST BEFORE THE CREEP

Jon had delivered the package, then returned to the forest quickly to hide. From behind a stand of trees, he watched the girl come outside to look for him. He also saw Ozzy Toffy following her. Witnessing both those events was relatively unsurprising. What surprised Jon most was the small black bird that shot up into the sky and disappeared temporarily.

The man who had hired Jon had told him stories about the bird. Most of what he'd been told seemed too farfetched to believe, like that the bird had taken out a fleet of SUVs on a New Mexico freeway, or that it had been shot and left for dead on a mountaintop. But now it looked like the bird was very much alive.

The man who had hired Jon, a man named Ray, had given Jon specific orders—orders that hadn't mentioned the bird being alive. Jon had been in Georgia, finishing another task, when this new job had shown up as a text on his burner phone. While most of the jobs Jon did for Ray were complicated and unpleasant, this one seemed simple. Ray needed Jon to help him get Ozzy to New York. The text to Jon had read:

> Deliver the package to the boy in Oregon.
> Make sure the boy gets on the plane in Portland.
> Don't contact me unless absolutely necessary.

Jon wasn't sure if spotting the bird was something Ray would think warranted contact. But if the stories about the strange creature were true, then it seemed like a detail worth passing along.

From behind the trees, Jon saw the bird return to the boy and girl. He watched them open the package and hurry back inside.

Jon was a decorated former solider. He had served in the military for years before realizing that he could make much more money doing unsavory things for wealthy people like Ray. He didn't always feel good about what he did, but the pay was outstanding.

He smiled. This case seemed so easy that it felt like a break. After all, how much trouble could a couple of kids be?

Jon took out his phone and texted:

> Item delivered. There is a bird.

Then he slipped farther into the trees to wait patiently for a reply.

CHAPTER SEVEN

COMPACT YET SPRAWLING

There was some discussion about calling Patti and letting her know what was going on, but Ozzy and Sigi were pretty certain what she would say about them going to New York.

No way.

In the end they agreed that it would be best to leave her a note. It should be further noted that when Patti left for Seattle, her parting words had been, "I'll check in, but my schedule is stuffed. So if you don't hear from me often, remember that no news is good news."

Ozzy and Sigi decided to keep the good news flowing by providing Patti with no news. Besides, if things went as planned, they'd be back from New York with news about Rin well before Patti returned.

Using a debit card attached to her savings account, Sigi had purchased a ticket on the same outbound flight as

Ozzy and a return ticket for the day after. She purchased her tickets online using her mom's profile.

"We're lucky," Sigi said. "This airline lets people fifteen and older fly without supervision."

"I've flown by myself for years," Clark bragged.

The phone in the kitchen rang. For a moment they thought it could be the wizard, asking them if they had received the package. But when Ozzy looked at the caller ID he saw:

Severe, Ryan

Ozzy picked up the phone and talked to his lawyer. It was a short conversation in which Ozzy said *yes* twice, *no* once, and *okay* four times. When he hung up, he told Sigi,

"I need to go sign some things at my lawyer's office."

"How are you going to explain all the little cuts you have?" Sigi asked.

"I'll tell him the truth. I cut myself on a window."

"Tell him about New York," Clark suggested. "People love to hear about other people's travel plans."

"I don't think I'll bother him with that information."

"Should I go with you?" Sigi asked.

"I think I'll be fine."

"Oh," she replied, "I get it. Let me guess—you won't be walking there."

Ozzy shook his head, smiling.

He ran to his room and changed into a blue T-shirt with long sleeves and black jeans. He then reluctantly put on the pair of black Doc Martens Sigi had bought him.

"I miss the days when I never had to wear shoes," he said to Clark.

"I miss the good old days where you and I didn't do anything besides hang out at the ocean and build sandcastles."

"We did that just two weeks ago with Sigi."

"Still, you always like the things *she* builds better. I could do just as well if I had hands, or one of those building uniforms she wears."

"That's a swimsuit."

"I think you mean *swam*suit," Clark corrected Ozzy. "She's already used it a bunch of times."

Ozzy climbed down the wooden stairs and opened the side door to the garage below his room. Ozzy missed a lot of things that had been in his life—the cloaked house, days and days of being alone with nothing but books and his thoughts, his parents. But there were some parts of his new life that helped ease the pain—Sigi, Patti, warm food, and his newest form of transportation.

Patti owned a few motorcycles. Some of them were big, bulky, and made for the street. But one was older and nimbler than the others. Its tires worked well on dirt and gravel and sand. Patti had been kind enough to give Ozzy permission to use it whenever he wanted, but only if he rode in places she approved and only if he wore a helmet.

He was supposed to stick to the forest and land around the house. He could ride on the beach if it was empty, and down to Forget-U-Nots, the convenience store at the end of the paved road by the house that sold things like milk, toilet paper, and zebra cakes.

For the most part, Ozzy had always been the kind of person who tried to do as he was told. But the feel of the motorcycle at full speed was too enjoyable for him to not do more than he was allowed. So through trial and error and some consulting of online maps, he found back roads and old cow paths that enabled him to travel to the spot he missed most—the cloaked house.

It was a ride he took almost every day. It was also something he planned to keep doing. This afternoon, however, he was heading the other direction. The lawyer's office was in town and he knew a couple paths that would get him almost all the way there without having to drive on the paved roads or risk being seen.

Ozzy had a small portable CD player with headphones that Patti had given to him. He would soar through the woods listening to Ben Folds and feeling as if he were flying. Clark enjoyed the motorcycle as well. He liked its engine, and he liked that, for the first time, Ozzy could keep up. They would race across the landscape, bird and bike competing for who could go faster and look cooler.

Ozzy rolled the motorcycle out of the garage and sat on it.

"You should name that thing," Clark suggested.

"Really? Like what?"

"How about *Slow*?"

Clark took off, and Ozzy kicked the bike to life. He

turned his music on, then raced off the edge of the driveway and back behind the huge house. When he got to the trees he weaved through them skillfully, a dark bit of metal speeding along in front, taunting him.

There was a break in the trees and the bike shot out into an empty field. Clark flitted around the boy's head.

"How's it feel being stuck to the ground?"

"It feels—"

Clark didn't stick around to listen. He threw his wings back and shot like a bullet into the next run of trees.

It took very little time to reach an old grove of pine trees huddled in a tight group a block from Main Street. The spot was not far from Ryan Severe's law office.

Ozzy turned off the bike and hid it behind the trees. He set his helmet and CD player on the bike seat.

"Stay here," Ozzy instructed Clark. "I won't be long."

"What do I do if someone tries to steal your engine?"

"Are you kidding? They'd be fools to take you on."

"Damp straight!" the bird said. "Wait—am I saying that right?"

"You're asking the wrong person."

Ozzy left the bird and bike and walked out of the old trees and over to Main Street. He walked along that for two blocks and then turned right and onto a road called Sprig. A block down he could see the law office of Ryan Severe squeezed between a fast-food joint called The Windy Burrito and a store called Runner's High. Ozzy began to jog toward it, hoping to get the visit over with.

He reached the law office and pushed open the front door. A woman he knew as Susan was sitting behind a big desk, shuffling a messy stack of papers on her desk. She had a pale face with overly groomed eyebrows. She also wore a tight linen scarf around her neck that looked as if it was cutting off the flow of blood to her head.

"Hello, Ozzy," she said.

"Hello, Susan."

"You got here quick."

"I'm a fast walker."

Susan looked perplexed, but not perplexed enough to question Ozzy any further. She pressed a button on her desk and then smiled.

"You can go on in," she said, as if she were granting him a wish.

Ozzy entered the office of Ryan Z. Severe, a boring room that lacked any imagination or wonder, a room that looked like the kind of room an adult thought other adults might enjoy. Ryan was sitting behind his desk flipping through a stack of papers. His dark hair was neatly styled and he was in the early stages of growing a goatee. Ryan smiled, showing off his white teeth and affable personality.

"Ozzy, how nice to see you. Please sit down." Ryan laughed like he'd told a joke. "Sorry about the mess—someone broke in last night and rifled through our things."

"Someone what?"

"I don't think anything was taken," Ryan said. "Probably just some kids messing around."

Ozzy was confused. "Kids who like to break in and shuffle papers?"

"Yeah, it doesn't make a lot of sense."

Ozzy shivered. The thought of someone breaking in brought back bad memories of what others had done to the cloaked house in the past.

"No matter," Ryan said, trying to lighten the mood. "How are you doing?"

"Good."

"Patti and Sigi are treating you well?"

"Of course."

"Good. Any plans for the weekend?"

"Nothing out of the ordinary."

"Well, you're not an ordinary kid." Ryan picked up a leather briefcase and opened it. "I have something for you. It arrived yesterday at my house."

Ryan pulled an old, large yellow envelope out of his briefcase.

"It seems your parents had a safety deposit box at a bank in Portland," Ryan said. "Someone who heard about you and your parents' deaths notified the bank. Anyhow, once some forms were filled out and requests were made, it was sent to me as your lawyer."

"My parents had a lock box?"

Ryan smiled. "Don't get too excited. There wasn't much in it."

Ryan opened the yellow envelope and pulled out a

small piece of paper. He slid it across the desk. Written on the paper was a string of numbers:

1189–1922914–229523–121145

"What is it?"

"Not sure," Ryan said with a shrug. "It's not a phone number, and when we ran it though a number of search programs it didn't seem to coordinate with any account or registered number anywhere. I would have just thrown it away, but that's for you to decide."

Ozzy took the paper and put it in his pocket.

"Was that it?"

"No, there's this."

Ryan handed Ozzy a photograph. The image was of his mother and father sitting on a blanket in a park. In between them was a much younger Ozzy. Seeing the picture felt like an emotional ambush. Ozzy's lungs and heart began fighting with his stomach.

He grabbed the photo as if he were scared that it would disappear.

"I thought you'd like that," Ryan said kindly. "I'm so sorry they're gone, Ozzy. They'd be very proud of you."

Ozzy wondered how Ryan could know that.

"Anything else?" Ozzy asked, wanting to leave the office and study the picture somewhere private.

"Yes, a CD." Ryan pulled a CD case out of the envelope. It was in a plain case with a clear plastic cover. Inside the cover was a silver disc. Written on the disc in blue marker were the words "The Cure."

Ozzy looked at it with awe. For months, he and Sigi and Rin had been looking for the formulas and cures that his parents had discovered. Now, here was someone making things simple by just handing him what he wanted.

"It's a music CD," Ryan told, him. "I had Susan listen to it."

"What kind of music?"

"I'm not familiar with it," Ryan admitted. "I'm guessing your parents liked the band. Not sure why they would keep a copy in the bank, but I've seen stranger things. Back when they put this away, they might have thought CDs were valuable—or were going to be. Now, I'm not sure how you'll even listen to this."

"I'll find a way," Ozzy said, grabbing the CD.

"Great," Ryan said sincerely. "Then I just need you to sign this document saying that you received the three items."

Ryan pushed a paper toward Ozzy. He handed the boy a pen and smiled.

Ozzy looked the form over for a moment.

"It says there are *four* things. The paper, the picture, the CD, and the envelope."

Ryan handed over the envelope the items had been in. "It's all yours."

Ozzy signed the paper and left the office as quickly as he could. He walked down the street like someone who'd just stolen something and needed to get away.

When he got back to the motorcycle, Clark wasn't there. He whistled for the bird twice, but there was no reply.

Ozzy picked up his small CD player and hopped on his bike. He switched out the Ben Folds CD for the new one. Then Ozzy took the photograph of his parents out of the envelope and slipped it into the clear cover. He put the piece of paper with the numbers on it behind the photo and closed the case. Then he slipped it all back into the envelope and put the envelope in a leather saddlebag on the side of the motorcycle.

"Clark!" he called out.

Only a few real birds squawked back.

Ozzy turned the key and kickstarted the bike. He pressed *play* and headed west with a head full of new thoughts, emotions, and songs.

CHAPTER EIGHT

LEFT BEHIND

When Ozzy got home, Clark was already there waiting for him. The bird had left to follow a plastic bag drifting in the wind.

"It was mesmerizing," Clark said. "You don't see many plastic bags around here."

Ozzy had taken the long route home so that he could listen to the entire CD. His hope had been that there might be something hidden in the words, but that didn't seem to be the case. It was a collection of songs that made him miss his parents and that he instantly loved.

Sigi wasn't too impressed with the contents of the envelope. She saw value in the photo, and the music on the CD, but the random numbers on the paper and the old envelope seemed unexplainable and unimportant.

"My mom's got a drawer full of envelopes. Would you like a few of those?"

"I just think it would have been nice for your parents to leave behind another bird," Clark complained.

"No way," Ozzy insisted. "The world couldn't handle that."

While he was gone, Sigi had packed a small bag for tomorrow's trip. They wouldn't be in New York for more than twenty-four hours, so they didn't need much.

"You know what bothers me?" Clark asked. "Why did Mr. Wizard only send us one ticket? Sigi had to buy ours."

Both the boy and girl looked at the bird.

"What?" Clark asked.

Ozzy patted the bird on his back. "Sorry, Clark, but you're not coming."

"I think I am," Clark said adamantly.

"You don't understand how airports work," Sigi told him. "Metal isn't something they like."

Clark shivered. "What a horrible place. Well, then, I can fly alongside the plane," he suggested.

"There's no way you can go that far *or* that fast," Sigi said. "It's all the way across the United States, and tens of thousands of feet above the earth."

"She's right," Ozzy said, sounding much more sympathetic to the bird's plight than Sigi. "We're going to be on an airplane for most of the trip. We're just going there, checking out the address, and hopefully bringing Rin back."

"You could pack me in your luggage," Clark argued. "I've always been good at being packed away."

"They inspect the luggage," Sigi informed him. "Who knows what they might think of you. You're not something people see every day."

"Don't butter me up," the bird protested.

"What if the suitcase got lost, or something happened?" Sigi added. "You could end up being packed away forever."

"That does sound dark."

"Airports are notorious for losing luggage."

"They hate metal and lose people's *stuff*?" the bird said with disgust. "I don't know that I *like* airports."

"See," Ozzy said, "you'll be better off here."

"Besides, you have to hang around in case my mom comes back early," Sigi begged. "She's going to need an explanation."

"I am good with moms."

"And protecting houses," Sigi added.

"Fine," Clark conceded, "I'll stay here and work on getting that copper mailbox down the road to notice me. Someone still needs to show that they care for metal."

"You're like the anti-airport," Ozzy said.

"Just doing my part," Clark chirped. He then added in a whisper, "Of course, I'll be doing it reluctantly."

"What?" Ozzy asked.

"Nothing, just thinking about that grocery bag."

Ozzy and Sigi left it at that.

CHAPTER NINE

OBJECT

Ozzy slept on the couch in the study so that if he acted up again in his sleep, Sigi would hear.

Fortunately, the night brought no further incidents.

At four in the morning, they said goodbye to Clark, left a note for Patti in case she returned before she was scheduled, and then took the shuttle bus between Otter Rock and Portland. The ride took about two and a half hours, and each mile they traveled came with a stronger and stronger feeling of uncertainty about what lay ahead.

"This is good, right?" Sigi asked.

"I think so," Ozzy replied.

"I thought we were past all this crazy stuff. I guess I was thinking life would be calm for a little while longer."

"The last seven years I've been alone in a quiet forest. I think I'm due for a little more uncertainty."

Ozzy watched as the miles passed by like wet streaks of green paint Mother Nature was smearing across the windows. The clouds in the sky resembled naked bits of canvas that had yet to be colored in. And when the outskirts of Portland finally came into view, the buildings and river were a beautiful distraction from the green. The structures rose up, giving the landscape sharp lines and squared-off silhouettes.

It was early, but the Portland airport was steadily busy, with buses and cars running everywhere. The shuttle dropped them off and Sigi took Ozzy's hand to pull him through the crowd. They entered the ticketing area and printed out their boarding passes. Then they went directly to the security line.

"This is to keep us safe?" Ozzy asked as he looked at everyone waiting.

"Something like that. Just don't make any jokes or say anything crazy. An airport isn't a place for humor."

"I wasn't planning on telling any jokes."

"Well, then, this is the place for you."

The line moved slowly, but in time they arrived at the front. A TSA agent with an unfortunate hairline asked for their boarding passes and IDs. Sigi and Ozzy stepped up to him together. Sigi gave the man her boarding pass and the passport that she had gotten when she had traveled to Paris with her mother a few years back.

The TSA agent looked it over, scanned the boarding pass, and then handed her items back to her. He looked at Ozzy and held out his hand.

Ozzy gave him his boarding pass and the ID he had been issued just weeks before by the state.

"Name?" the TSA agent asked.

"Ozzy."

"What happened to your hands?"

Ozzy had on a green, long-sleeved T-shirt and long trousers, but there were still some small visible scratches on his hands and a few on his face.

"I fell out the window in my bedroom," Ozzy answered, his voice sounding less steady than he had intended it to.

The TSA agent stared uncomfortably.

"Do you want to talk to my dad about it?" Sigi said. "He's already through security."

The TSA agent stared at Ozzy for what felt like a long afternoon and a short evening combined before he waved them on.

Ozzy got into line behind Sigi in front of a long silver scanner. He watched her take off her shoes and place them on the conveyor belt.

Ozzy did the same thing.

Sigi put her bag on the conveyor belt next to her shoes.

The items moved forward on the belt while another TSA agent motioned for them to keep moving. Sigi stepped into the body scanner and held her hands above her head. A bar moved from right to left scanning her body. Then she stepped out the other side.

Having spent so many years alone and away from

civilization, Ozzy still found wonder in things and places that most people had grown tired of. He liked the post office and what they did. He found the grocery store mesmerizing in its sheer selection and precise organization. But he wasn't sure yet how he felt about the airport. People were stiff and uncomfortable, and nobody appeared to be happy about where they were. Some of the TSA agents smiled, but it was the kind of smile that said *I'm here to make things hard for you.*

Ozzy stepped into the weird chamber and placed his feet on the two yellow footprints.

"Face forward. Arms over your head," a female TSA agent instructed him.

He raised his arms up and the scanner passed in front of him. As it moved two thoughts struck Ozzy. One: his finger was burning. And two: he didn't like airports.

"Step out," the woman told him while pointing to a spot near her. "Stand there for a moment."

Ozzy stood where he was told until he was told he could go stand somewhere else.

He chose to stand near Sigi, who was near the end of the conveyor belt. She was putting on her shoes and waiting for her bag.

"I've decided I don't like airports," Ozzy whispered.

"I think that makes you human."

A tall TSA agent with tight curly brown hair and a stiff upper lip was standing behind the belt scanner. He held up Sigi's bag.

"Is this yours?" Stiff Lip asked.

"Yes," Sigi replied.

"I need to take a quick look inside."

Ozzy's shoes had made it through the scanner and he picked them up and put them on. His head began to feel light, as if it were loosely attached to his neck, as two TSA agents whispered about Sigi's bag. The one with the stiff lip stepped back to where Ozzy and Sigi were standing.

"We found this in your backpack." There, lying lifeless in his hand, was Clark.

Both Ozzy and Sigi groaned.

"What is it?" Stiff Lip asked.

"It's a bird," Ozzy answered.

"I see that, but you can't bring an object like this through security."

"Why?" Sigi said with force. "It's just a toy."

"It's not like any toy we've ever seen. We can't open it up to see if there is anything in the body, and it has a bunch of sharp points and edges and wires. I'm sorry, but it will have to stay here."

"Can't we just mail it back home?" Sigi asked.

"You can," the agent said. "Just leave us your address and we will send it back after we've checked it over."

"That's not right," Ozzy protested.

"Or," the TSA agent said with a smile, "we can detain both of you until it's properly inspected. You might miss your flight, and you'd still have to mail it home."

Ozzy stared at the bird wondering if he should grab

him and run. But as he stared, Clark winked his right eye. Nobody but Ozzy saw it. The bird winked again and subtly nodded his tiny bird head. Ozzy winked back.

"Are you okay?" the agent asked.

"Fine," he replied.

"Good, now you two need to move on. And don't worry, we'll get your *toy* back to you."

Sigi didn't want to go, but Ozzy pushed her away from the agent and out of the security area. Once they were around a corner she spoke.

"I can't believe he stowed away in my bag."

"Not his finest move, I agree."

"We can't just leave him."

"I think we can," Ozzy said in hushed tones. "He winked at me."

"What's that mean?"

"Well, it kind of looked like the sort of wink he gives right before he does something stupid."

The two of them walked as quickly as they could toward their gate. There was no worry of them missing their plane, but the winking bird made them both want to get as far away from security as they could.

After all, Clark had a reputation, and it wasn't good.

CHAPTER TEN

TOSSING AWAY GREATNESS

The security area inside the Portland Airport was busy. Ozzy and Sigi had walked off, but the TSA agent with the stiff upper lip continued to carry Clark by his talons. Stiff Lip moved over to a white cabinet near a metal table.

Clark looked around cautiously.

The world was upside down, which meant he needed to right some things. The gears inside his head began to plot his escape. However, before those gears had time to get moving, Stiff Lip surprised him by grabbing him tightly around the middle, pinning his wings up against his metal body. Then, without any hesitation, Stiff Lip wrapped a piece of wide yellow tape around Clark. In a moment the poor bird looked like a tiny jaundiced mummy. His head and beak were uncovered, and his talons stuck out at the bottom, but the rest of him was completely confined by the sticky yellow tape.

Stiff Lip held the bird tightly.

Clark was in the mood to peck and kick, but he kept his beak and feet to himself. There would only be one chance of getting out, and that was if he played dead and waited for someone to unwrap him.

Stiff Lip went directly to an office located on the south side of the security area. He rapped confidently on the frame of an already open door.

A frustrated sounding woman answered the knock.

"Come in," she said. "Come in."

Stiff Lip stepped in.

Sitting behind a wooden desk in the corner of the room was his supervisor, a woman with the last name of Wicks. Wicks was a human being, which meant that the chances were good she possessed a first name, but nobody ever called her by anything but Wicks. And since Stiff Lip didn't want to be a nobody, he followed suit.

He cleared his throat and said, "Wicks."

She looked up from her work, showing off her wide-set eyes, small nose, and big mouth. Wicks had been working at the airport for fifteen years, and for the most part, she was well respected. She was known for having a cool head and being able to talk down anyone who was on the verge of disturbing the peace. Unfortunately for Stiff Lip, ten minutes earlier, Wicks had received some very bad news about a very bad investment, the kind of news that meant she had lost a lot of money. She was also suffering through a massive toothache that her dentist couldn't fix until the next day.

"What is it?" Wicks asked in a huff.

"Sorry to bother, but I wanted to show you something."

Wicks sighed and sat up in her chair. She rubbed the right side of her jaw and looked at Stiff Lip.

"A passenger came through security with *this*."

He handed Wicks the mummified Clark. She took it from him, looking more bothered than pleased.

"What is it, a toy bird?"

"It's unusual—and its claws are sharp."

"Really?" she snipped. "Do you think we should stop and stare at *everything* unusual we find? Last year a woman came through security with a doll she'd made from a tennis racket. She claimed that racket was her child and she wanted it to have its own seat on her flight. *That* was unusual. This here," Wicks shook Clark in her hand, "this a toy."

"I thought that because its feet were pointy . . ."

Wicks stared at him.

". . . and its beak is sharp . . ."

"This is a weird toy that I didn't need to see. Have them mail it home and thank them for visiting PDX."

Stiff Lip's lip didn't look as stiff as it once had. "Actually, I sent them on their way and told them I'd send it to them after you looked at it." He took out the address that Sigi had written down and set it on Wicks's desk.

She stared at the piece of paper and winced, acting as if the address was the very thing that had caused her to lose her money and had given her a toothache.

"So—you've given our team an *errand*?" she asked. "Something to mail? Now we get to take our time *and* budget to send this back just so you could show me a toy?"

"I just thought—"

"I'm not sure you did." She winced. "Now go."

Semi-Stiff Lip left the office and returned to his post as quickly as he could. Wicks, on the other hand, sat at her desk feeling defeated, angry, and overwhelmed. She put Clark down on her desk and returned to what she was working on.

Thirty seconds later, an airport custodian named Ned came into her office to empty her trash can. As Ned collected the trash, Wicks stopped what she was doing and picked up Clark.

"Don't forget this." Wicks tossed Clark to Ned. "It would have probably gotten lost in the mail anyway."

Ned caught the bird in the trash can and then emptied the can's contents into a large black trash bag that was attached to the back of his cart. He returned the empty can to its spot by Wicks's desk and moved on down the terminal.

It's not hyperbole or overexaggeration to say that Ned's cart had never contained a more amazing piece of trash. It is also no exaggeration to say that Clark was in trouble.

CHAPTER ELEVEN

BOARDING BUT NOT BORED

The airport was a cluttered mess of too many humans with too many places to go dragging too many suitcases and bags around. Things seemed to get more chaotic the farther Ozzy and Sigi walked down the terminal. They watched a man running, witnessed a woman crying near a vending machine, and saw a store that sold nothing but candy and neck pillows. But amidst all the bustle and bodies, things still felt sparse because the scene was lacking a metal bird.

"You're *sure* he winked at you?" Sigi asked as they walked.

"Positive."

They reached their crowded gate and looked around for a place to sit. There were no open chairs. They opted to lean on the wall between a shoeshine station and three massage chairs while waiting for their flight to begin boarding.

Sigi looked into Ozzy's eyes. "Are you nervous?"

"I'm not worried about flying," he said. "I've read enough books on aerodynamics to know how it works. I'm nervous about Clark . . . and your mom . . . and the shattered window . . . and Rin. Also, I hate wearing shoes—even if they're clean."

A man brushed past them, talking loudly on his phone.

"I'm not too nervous about my mom," Sigi admitted. "I mean, she's in Seattle talking to rooms full of people. That's what she loves. I am nervous about Clark and my dad. They're missing and that makes me feel like I'm missing something myself."

"I like that," Ozzy said.

"That I feel incomplete?"

"No, that you're aware of the things that make you whole."

Sigi stopped looking at Ozzy and took a moment to glance around the turbulent terminal.

"I like being aware of the good things," she said. "I like knowing how I got where I am."

"By shuttle bus."

"Funny," she said without laughing. "You think you can say dumb things like that because you have such a straight nose and nice eyes?"

"No, I say things like that because I still don't know how normal society acts."

"I can tell you that they wouldn't wear that shirt with

those trousers," Sigi said, looking Ozzy up and down. "Orange and green are not a good combination."

"I'll never be good at matching."

"It does make you interesting," Sigi consoled him. "You make a lot of things interesting. I don't think I would have done anything like this before I met you."

"I'm a bad influence?"

"For sure. The worst thing I did before I met you was hide in my closet and eat a whole package of Oreos that my mom was saving for a picnic."

"Oreos are good."

"I hardly ever saw my father until you showed up. I never battled people on mountains, or purchased plane tickets to New York, or worried about dumb metal birds that should have listened to me and stayed home." Sigi's voice was growing loud. "Birds that may or may not be about to cause trouble."

The nearby shoeshine man glanced sideways at Sigi.

She lowered her voice. "The point is—you've made things interesting and made me feel even more out of place than I used to."

"I seem like someone you should avoid."

"Possibly," she agreed. "I used to try to hide the fact that my dad thought he was a wizard. I've never liked being singled out for something I have no control over. It used to be the color of my skin—now it's because Jungle Boy lives at my house."

"I've never been in a jungle."

"Forest Boy, then."

The overhead speakers came on and announced that their flight would be boarding soon.

They left their spot against the wall and walked to where the other passengers were beginning to line up. Ozzy looked over his shoulder a dozen different times, hoping to see a small black dot making its way toward them or to hear the sound of chaos the bird was creating.

But there was no dot and no sound of trouble.

The line began to move, and in no time they had boarded the plane and found their place—Ozzy had a window seat, and Sigi had managed to get the middle seat next to him. After sitting down and putting on their seatbelts, Sigi took Ozzy's hand and leaned into him to speak.

"Hey, Forest Boy, don't worry about Clark. He's done this kind of thing before. I bet he's flying back to the house right now to look for that flashlight I dropped in the ocean."

"He *was* pretty broken up about losing it."

They watched the other passengers board the plane and take their seats. There was every reason for them to feel nervous about what lay ahead. But as they sat side by side, that nervousness was mixed with some excitement. There were birds to worry about, questions that still concerned them, but also the possibility of seeing the person they most wanted to see.

CHAPTER TWELVE

DEEP INSIDE

For once in his life, Clark was okay with his inability to smell. Wedged between a half-eaten tuna sandwich and something wet and sticky, the small bird began to question his decision to have stowed away in Sigi's sack. The trash bag he was in jostled slightly as the cart it was attached to bumped over the tile floor of the airport terminal. Still wrapped in yellow tape, his wings pinned, he thrashed around trying to free himself. After Ned had dumped him in the bag, he'd emptied another can into the bag, and so Clark was buried in a couple inches of trash. He wiggled around, trying to see the bag's opening above. If he rolled his body one way and craned his neck the other, he could just see the top of the bag. The poor bird was about a foot below the top of the janitor's cart.

Clark pushed downward with his talons and tried to thrust himself up through the trash toward the opening.

His left foot pierced an empty water bottle and the bird squawked in frustration.

"Don't people know to recycle?" He kicked until the bottle came off his foot. The kick rolled him into a damp tissue. "For bird sake, that better be water."

As far as predicaments go, Clark had been through worse. But this situation had an additional element of concern. As a metal bird, he didn't require oxygen, food, or water to live—but he did require light. And the silver stripe on his back was covered with tape, which meant that time was of the essence. He needed to get out of the bag and get free of the tape so he could soak up the light he'd need to get out of the airport. He had made sure he was fully charged before he hid in Sigi's bag, but he knew that his new condition would require exertion, and that meant he would need to find a charge soon.

Biting the trash above him and pushing it below him, he tried to scoot his way up to the top, but the effort was draining. It was also slow going, and this was a life-or-trash situation, so there was no time to waste.

"Forget this," Clark said. "I'm going down."

Clark twisted and rolled his body until he was facing downward. Then, using his talons, he pushed up, thrusting himself deeper into the trash. It was much easier to move down than up and he dove quickly through the rubbish until he reached the bottom of the bag.

"This should be interesting," he said to himself.

Twisting until his talons were touching the bottom of

the bag, Clark stuck his copper-tipped toes into the plastic and ripped.

The result was impressive!

The rip shot all the way to the top of the bag, letting all the trash, including Clark, fall out and tumble across the tile floor.

People yelled and complained as the sound—and smell—of spilling garbage filled the airport air. One man tripped and slid across the floor screaming.

Ned stopped the cart abruptly and a woman carrying a packaged rice bowl ran into him, dropping the bowl from her hands. It burst open, sending rice, chicken, and vegetables everywhere.

People tried to walk around the mess, but because the airport was so busy, some were forced to walk directly through the trash. Clark, like the rest of the rubbish, was kicked around and across the floor by rogue feet and luggage.

Suitcase after suitcase rolled over him.

One gigantic shoe sent him spinning like a top. Clark bounced off the wall and back across the floor, stopping only when he hit the bottom of the stalled cart.

When he stopped spinning, Clark saw that the beating he was taking was also loosening up the tape wrapped around him. He rolled an inch to the right so that he could be hit straight on by the wheels of an oncoming suitcase.

"Walk around the mess!" Ned yelled at everyone. "Walk around the mess!"

Additional airport personnel appeared and tried to help Ned with the trash. A man with a tie shouted, "Walk to the side of the terminal! The side of the terminal!"

No one obeyed.

Clark was stepped on and rolled over a few more times before he came to a rest against the wall. The yellow tape on him was frayed and ripped in numerous places.

"I hope this . . ."

His words were slurred as his energy diminished. But using his last bit of strength, he flexed his wings and pushed out.

The tape gave way.

He stretched his wings and most of the tape pulled off. Unfortunately, a big piece was still stuck to his back, and that piece covered the silver stripe.

Clark's energy was going fast.

Looking around, he saw gate twenty-three. People were in line and getting on the plane. There was no sign of Ozzy or Sigi, but the bird knew what he needed to do.

A mean-looking woman wearing a fancy pink hat sitting on a nearby bench began to gather her things and stand up. Clark couldn't be sure, but she appeared to be preparing to get on Ozzy and Sigi's plane.

His power was almost gone.

The clever bird looked at the lady as she turned and headed toward the line.

It was a long shot, but he had no other choice.

CHAPTER THIRTEEN

BLAND BUT NOT BOARDING

Jon had seen Ozzy and Sigi get onto the early morning shuttle bus. He had expected to see the boy, but for reasons unknown the girl had joined Ozzy. Jon calculated the new information in his head. It was possible that Sigi was only going along to keep Ozzy company till he reached the airport. It was also possible that she had done something foolish like deciding to travel to New York even though she hadn't been invited.

Jon slipped back into the trees and jogged down the road to where a beige compact car was parked. He climbed in and drove onto the highway.

A couple of minutes later he had caught up to the shuttle bus and was keeping a good distance behind it. Ozzy and Sigi were on their way to the airport and he wanted to make sure they made it there. He was a thorough thug with an excellent dirty-work ethic.

The shuttle bus traveled to the Portland airport without

any incident or problem, and Jon had followed without being detected. He parked his car in short-term parking and strode casually into the airport. He'd purchased a ticket for a flight he wouldn't be taking, but the ticket allowed him to get past security and go directly to gate twenty-three. Once there, he took a seat on a bench near a drinking fountain. The spot was perfect, providing him with a good view of anyone coming into the gate area.

Jon only had to wait a few minutes before he spotted Ozzy and his foolish, uninvited traveling companion.

Once Ozzy and Sigi were on the plane, Jon stood up.

He considered sticking around a little longer, but the sound of a commotion in the terminal bothered him. Someone was hollering about something, and Jon never liked to hang around anywhere there was trouble, unless he was the one causing it. He was a professional who always finished his jobs in the most efficient way. He had no patience for people who made mistakes.

The bland man left the gate and walked down the terminal.

There was trash littered all over the floor and people scurrying around to either clean it up or avoid it. Jon walked straight through the debris, stepping on garbage as he worked his way toward the airport exit. His mind was already switching from the job he had just finished and beginning to wonder when the next one would arrive.

Jon liked downtime, but he also liked having a purpose. He had grown up poor and he knew what it was like to have nothing. Now Ray paid him obscene amounts of money to do things that came easily to him.

When he reached his car, before he drove out of the parking garage, Jon texted the man who had gone to all the trouble to get Ozzy to New York.

CHAPTER FOURTEEN

THE SUN RISES SLOWLY

The plane was close to full. The aisle was full of people shoving their bags into the overhead bins and shuffling to their seats. Ozzy and Sigi had tried to not worry, but their thoughts were on what awaited them in New York—and Clark's current condition and whereabouts.

"He's okay," Sigi said. "Think about it. At the very worst they'll mail him back to us. I'm sure he'll enjoy being mail."

"It feels wrong to fly off."

"*He* always does."

Sigi wasn't being mean; she was making a point. Clark had flown off countless times without letting Ozzy know where he was going. Just yesterday he had flown away from the motorcycle to follow a plastic bag.

The two of them watched the last three passengers get on the plane and come down the aisle. The first two weren't terribly interesting, but the very last passenger on was an older woman who instantly caught their attention. The woman was wearing a pink wool blazer and had broad shoulders and an unhappy face. She also had on a stiff pink hat shaped like a pill with a brim. It was unusual enough to see someone wearing a hat like that, but it was even more unusual to see Clark stuck to the top of it, frozen in an unflattering pose. His head and wings were bent at strange angles and his talons were twisted.

Ozzy and Sigi let their jaws drop.

As the pink woman walked down the aisle, a flight attendant complimented her on her lid.

"What a beautiful hat," the flight attendant said. "So unusual."

The woman didn't like the compliment. "I suppose having the decency to dress well *is* unusual these days."

Everyone she passed stared at her head. It's not every day you see a grown woman wearing a hat with a strangely positioned metal bird taped to it.

Ozzy and Sigi were so shocked they were unable to close their mouths. The woman walked closer and closer. They stared in awe as she arrived at their row and stopped. She looked at the empty aisle seat next to Sigi and then looked at Ozzy by the window. She sniffed in an elegant and passive-aggressive way.

"Seated next to children," she mumbled. "I *should* be in first class."

With another sniff she reluctantly sat down.

The two children stared at the top of her hat. Clark

was staring upward, and it was easy to see the yellow tape stuck to his back that kept him in place. To most of the passengers the hat looked like something an unusual but creative person might have made from odds and ends at home. But to Ozzy and Sigi it looked like Clark was up to something.

The woman tucked her purse under her seat and put on her seatbelt.

Ozzy looked at Sigi and shrugged.

"Is he crazy?" Sigi whispered into Ozzy's ear.

"I don't know what he was planning," Ozzy whispered back. "But he could be out of power."

"How can she not know he's up there?"

They stopped whispering to turn to look at the woman again.

"Do you mind?" the woman asked. "And knock off the whispering. It's very rude."

Ozzy and Sigi looked away and kept quiet.

With everyone on board, the crew prepared for takeoff. The woman with the hat reached up and pressed the call button above her. As it dinged, one of the flight attendants came down the aisle to see what she wanted.

"I need to get up to stow my hat," the woman said. "My head feels warm."

"You need to stay seated—we're taxiing. Let me stow it for you."

The woman grumbled something and then took off her hat. Without looking at it, she handed it to the attendant.

The flight attendant opened an overhead bin and carefully placed the hat inside.

"I hope you didn't crush it," the woman scolded.

"Not at all," the attendant said. "Your lovely bird is safe and sound."

The pink woman looked confused as the flight attendant returned to her seat and the plane rolled closer to the runway.

The woman turned in her seat and stared at Ozzy and Sigi. "Did that woman say 'bird'?"

"That's what kids call hats," Ozzy lied.

The woman swore in an inelegant and snobby way. "Just like kids to go changing perfectly acceptable words. I'm too old for this. If first class wasn't sold out I'd be up there now."

"I wish you were," Sigi said.

Thinking the girl was agreeing with her, the woman said, "Thank you." She then turned her gaze away from Ozzy and Sigi and scowled in the other direction.

Ozzy wanted to whisper something to Sigi, but he was too polite. His hope had been to snatch Clark from the hat during the plane ride, but now his bird was caged up above them. Sigi leaned in closer to whisper to Ozzy, but the pink woman turned her head quickly and gave her the stinkeye.

The plane took off, reached its cruising altitude, and flew east. The flight attendants passed out snacks and drinks. The captain said a few standard things over the intercom. And the now-hatless woman next to them fell asleep and began snoring.

Ozzy watched other passengers get up from their seats and use the bathroom or retrieve items from the overhead bins. An idea struck him.

"I'm going to use the bathroom," he whispered to Sigi.

"Congratulations."

Ozzy pointed to the woman sitting on the other side of Sigi. "Should we wake her up?"

The hatless, snoring woman mumbled something in her sleep.

"I'm sure she'd love that."

Ozzy reached across Sigi and tapped the woman on her broad right shoulder. She didn't respond. He tapped her harder. Still nothing. He tapped her hardest while saying, "Excuse me."

The woman turned her head and gave Ozzy two stink eyes.

"Sorry," Ozzy apologized, "but I need to use the bathroom."

The woman huffed and moaned. She was not pleased about being woken up. Still, she reluctantly stood so Sigi could move and Ozzy could get out.

"Next time you might have the courtesy to wear a travel diaper like I do."

Both Ozzy and Sigi grimaced.

Leaving Sigi alone with the woman and her travel diaper, Ozzy walked down the aisle to the back of the plane.

He didn't need to use the bathroom, but he did need to play the part. He stood inside the tiny lavatory for a minute or two and then came back down the aisle. Sigi and the woman were back in their seats and facing forward. Ozzy stopped just before his row and reached up to open the bin.

The overhead compartment opened to reveal the woman's ugly hat with Clark resting on top of it.

Glancing around casually, he saw that nobody seemed the least bit interested in what he was doing. Ozzy reached up and wrapped his hand around the bird.

With a soft tug, he pulled Clark off the hat.

Then, as calmly and discreetly as he could, he brought his hand down and slipped the bird into his right front pocket.

Ozzy snapped the overhead bin shut and stepped up to his row.

The hatless, heartless—but not diaper-less—woman had already fallen back asleep.

"Excuse me," he said while slightly shaking the headrest on her seat.

"Ugh, you again."

Grumbling, the woman got up and let him in.

"Youth," she said with disdain.

Once Ozzy was seated, the pink woman decided she needed to complain to the flight attendant about something and walked down the aisle, leaving Ozzy and Sigi alone.

"How was the bathroom?"

"Small," Ozzy whispered. "I got Clark. He's in my pocket."

Sigi smiled. "So now all we have to worry about is everything else."

"Like sitting next to someone wearing a diaper?"

Sigi didn't answer, because the woman was back.

"Apparently there are no empty seats on this flight," she said as she reluctantly sat down. "I guess I'm stuck here. If you've had enough jumping around, don't bother me again."

"Neither of us were jumping," Sigi said firmly.

"Who knows what you call things these days."

The woman shut her eyes and went back to snoring.

Knowing that Clark was safe made the remainder of the flight much more enjoyable. They flew through the sky at thirty-five thousand feet and stared out the window. In the distance, they could see the morning sun shining above a thick blanket of clouds. Ozzy and Sigi shared headphones and listened to the CD he had gotten from his parents. The music was an escape from the hum and buzz of the plane's engines.

When the plane landed, the hatless woman told a man standing in the aisle to get her hat. The man retrieved the hat, but he was surprised to see that there was no longer a metal bird attached to it. He, along with many of the other passengers, had witnessed the odd hat being stowed away by the attendant. He checked around in the bin to see if it had fallen off.

"Where's the bird?" the man asked as he handed the hat to her.

"It's called a hat," she insisted.

"Right," he said looking confused. "But what about the bird that was on top of it?"

The now-hatted woman looked bothered. "I think you've had too much to drink."

Nobody asked her any more questions about her hat.

Eventually the plane door opened, and everyone got off.

Ozzy stepped off the jetway and into the busy airport with a sense of awe. It had been years since he had been in New York—he had been seven and his parents had still been alive. His life had been full of darkness and confusion since then. He had been frightened, lonely, and lost. Hiring a wizard had helped, but it had also come with some hard truths. The realization that his parents were gone was not a happy ending. The loneliness still lingered, but there were good moments as well—Clark, Sigi, motorcycles. But it felt like he hadn't been complete since the day before his parents had been taken, and the life they'd once had in New York.

"You okay?" Sigi asked.

Ozzy's finger buzzed.

"I hope so."

They walked away from the gate holding hands and were swept up in a wide stream of people heading for the exits.

CHAPTER FIFTEEN

THE MAN IN CHARGE

Ray walked swiftly, keeping his eyes on the boy and girl as they walked through the airport. For the most part things had gone as planned. Getting Ozzy to New York had been simple—send someone a plane ticket and an address and *voila*, they appear. The addition of the girl didn't please Ray, but her presence wasn't something he couldn't overcome.

Ray kept his distance from Ozzy and Sigi, being careful not to spook or lose them. They continued through the terminal and down the escalators completely unaware someone was watching them. Ozzy looked remarkably similar to his father and mother. The boy's appearance almost made Ray feel sentimental.

Almost.

Ray Dench had known Emmitt and Mia Toffy very well. Ray's father had funded their first experiments. And Ray himself had been the money behind the creation of the Discipline Serum—quite possibly the greatest discovery any living scientist had ever found. The serum was the power to control one's will, and the ultimate power to control the will of others if needed.

Soon after Ozzy's parents had created the formula, they were awakened to the ugly realization of what Ray wanted to use it for. Without notice, Emmitt and Mia had packed up everything they owned and moved to Oregon with Ozzy. They were hoping to hide away, but with the help of his most trusted partner, Charles Plankdorf, Ray had found them and kidnapped the doctors. In doing so, they'd left Ozzy for dead. But science demands sacrifice, and Ozzy's demise was a sacrifice that Ray and Charles had been willing to make.

They had taken Ozzy's parents to a hidden compound where they tried for years to get them to recreate what they had once discovered. But Emmitt and Mia were unwilling to cooperate, and after years of failure and disappointment, Ray had done away with them. And with their deaths, his dream of having control over all others who walked the earth was shattered.

He had believed that Emmitt's and Mia's child had died in the forest years ago. Which is why he was taken by surprise when the boy had turned up four months before in Charles's New Mexico office, asking questions about his parents, accompanied by Sigi and a man who claimed to be a wizard.

When Ozzy had told Charles that he had a tape from

his parents, Charles had called Ray and the race to get the tape began. But in in the end, the tape had been destroyed and Charles wound up dead. Ray was no closer to the prize he so desperately deserved.

There was some hope, however.

Knowing that Ozzy was alive, Ray had sent Jon to fetch him. It's a job Ray would have done himself, but as he had grown older, he found it difficult to venture out from where he lived. There were few people in the world wealthier than Ray, but leaving New York was something he couldn't do any longer.

He ruled his massive empire from a penthouse apartment in the heart of the city. He had many companies and interests, but the Harken Company had been the one that had paid for the Toffys to discover the formula, and it was the Harken Company that had also failed to get it back. Charles had run the company and now Charles was gone.

It was time for Ray to step in. Because, according to Ray, when you want something done right, you have to hurt and manipulate the sources yourself.

He watched Ozzy and Sigi as they left the airport and got in line for a taxi. Ray walked out behind them and climbed into an idling black town car waiting for him at the curb.

"Follow them once they get a taxi," Ray told his driver.

"Of course, sir."

Ray breathed calmly. He had dealt with powerful people all around the world. Two kids didn't concern him in the least. There were a couple things he was curious about, however, and those things were the mysterious and destructive bird and the interfering wizard. He believed that the bird was most likely the fabled creation Emmitt had made many years ago. He'd never set eyes on the invention, but he knew it had been a passion project for Emmitt. As for the wizard, Ray didn't believe. It was obvious that, whoever he was, he was misguided and needed professional help.

"A destructive bird and someone professing to be a wizard. I'm going to enjoy this."

"Excuse me, sir?" the driver asked.

"Ignore me, Gelt," Ray said. "I'm talking to myself again."

Ray watched out the nearly opaque side window as Ozzy and Sigi moved slowly forward in the line of people who were waiting for taxis. He smoothed his dark red hair back with his small hands. After years of failure and dead ends with the serum, something was finally happening. Charles's death wouldn't be for nothing. His demise had provided Ray with one of the most promising leads.

"Ozzy Toffy," he said with a hushed reverence. "Who knew I would ever see you again? And to think *you* have the mark."

Ozzy and Sigi got into their taxi and Ray followed.

CHAPTER SIXTEEN

WAKING THE BIRD

Ozzy was in awe—the size of his eyes betrayed his feelings. He held Sigi's hand as they sat in the back seat of a slow-moving taxi. New York was larger and louder than he remembered. It was a landscape of metal and stone mountains with a river of humanity flowing around the base of everything, people washed up against the structures and over the sidewalks. Cars filled the roads like futuristic icebergs drifting slowly to their destinations.

The taxi driver's name was Dane. Not only had he told the kids that, but it was printed on a large sign taped to the dashboard. He was wearing an ill-fitting toupee and chewing on a thick stick of beef jerky.

Ozzy had given the driver the address from the flash drive, and now Dane was driving, honking, and swearing at other vehicles as he transported Ozzy and Sigi to their destination.

The backseat of the cab was private enough for Ozzy

to carefully pull Clark out of his pocket. The bird was completely still, his wings folded up against himself, his feet spread and bent. Ozzy held the bird down behind the seat so that Dane couldn't see him. Then Ozzy pulled the tape off Clark's back, exposing the silver paint stripe.

"Here," Sigi said, holding her hands down next to the bird. "Let me hold him."

Ozzy handed Clark over and she positioned him near the side window, still out of sight of the driver. It didn't take long before the unusual configuration of metal blinked his eyes and clicked his beak.

A few moments more and the bird shivered.

Thirty seconds later, Clark spread his wings as Sigi held him.

"Did that actually *work*?" he tweeted softly. "The hat trick?"

The sounds of the city were loud enough to keep Dane from hearing the new voice.

"It worked perfectly," Sigi said.

Clark hopped up and stood on her right knee. He shook his tin tail and pawed at her leg like a cat on a carpet. After shaking his metallic head feathers, he turned and looked directly at both Ozzy and Sigi.

"Who's driving?" he asked.

Sigi pointed at the back of the driver and held her finger to her lips. "That's Dane."

Clark bent his head to glance up over the front seat and get a better look at Dane's head.

"Right," Clark chirped quietly. "Why is he wearing a nest on his head? Is he some sort of dignitary?"

"That's a toupee," Ozzy said.

"Smart man," Clark said. "Carrying around a nest for emergencies. You two should do that."

The taxi came to a sudden stop and a bird, a girl, and a boy slammed into the back of the front seat. Clark fell to the floor and Ozzy and Sigi smashed up against each other. There were a half-dozen angry honks exchanged between their taxi and another car that had cut it off. Then Dane yelled a few undignified things at the other vehicle and pressed on the gas.

Ozzy and Sigi sat back and buckled up.

Looking up from the floor, Clark tsked. "What does Rin always say? Seatbelts first. I know a lot of the things he says seem . . . well, questionable, but that seatbelt thing makes sense."

Ozzy and Sigi didn't reply.

"Are you both still feeling good about this?" Clark tweeted quietly. "I mean it seems pretty reckless to fly out here by yourselves and visit an address that somebody you don't know gave you."

Ozzy and Sigi remained quiet. The bird wasn't wrong. There were a number of things about what they were doing that were concerning.

"But," Clark added, "I like reckless."

The taxi sped on as clouds began to gather overhead and the temperature dropped ten degrees.

CHAPTER SEVENTEEN

ARRIVING WHERE ONE SHOULD

The wizard flew through the sky, his robe and beard blowing in the air as he raced to get where he was going. The quest had summoned him, and as a committed member of the lost arts, he could not ignore the summoning.

"I'm almost there," he said slowly, as if the words were a spell his mind needed to hear.

The wizard was ready for what was coming. It was time. There was no one and no way that anything could stop the course he was now flying.

Descending from the sky, he reached the ground and walked with purpose to the small shack near the not-so-distant river. There he bartered with a fat, smelly, scoundrel named Victor for passage and a driver to where he needed to travel.

"Why don't you just fly the rest of the way by yourself?" Victor asked.

"I'm a wizard. I don't need to explain myself."

"Right," Victor said, "then hop in."

The short ride was fraught with peril and uncertainty, but eventually Victor, with his lifetime of experience, navigated the wizard safely to his destination.

When they arrived, Victor looked at the destination and whispered, "Are you sure you want to be dropped off here? I don't think the folk here will have much patience for your type."

"My *type*?" the wizard said seriously. "I don't think you know what you're talking about. You see, there are only two types of people, those who do, and those who complain about doing. I am the former. And I am confident that there are some here who are most definitely also my type."

"Well, then, have at it," Victor said. "I only care about your payment, and I don't care for the way you're talking to me."

"Then let me talk to you like this, it is a fool who laughs at the odd. Different is just an understanding you have not yet grasped."

The scoundrel laughed and went on his way, leaving the wizard to deal with whatever type of trouble lay ahead by himself.

CHAPTER EIGHTEEN

ALL THAT GLIMMERS IS NOT GOLD

The Resort in New York was old. It had been built in 1922 by a man who had made his fortune manufacturing soap. It was eleven stories tall and had ten large, ornate, and gold-painted columns on the front of it. There was a big revolving door with four regular glass doors on either side.

Most people who stayed at the Resort in New York were old, as in older—or maybe oldest. They were wealthy socialites who had stayed at the hotel in the past and remembered it from when they weren't quite so oldest.

Ozzy and Sigi walked out of the cold and into the hotel through the revolving door. It was filled with people who looked as stiff as if they had been warned that any quick movement would cause an explosion. The theme of the lobby appeared to be *You Can Never Have Enough Gold.* Everything was a brash, shiny yellow—the couches, the counters, the fixtures, and the walls. There was a man in one corner of the lobby playing a gold-painted piano, and a gold-plated fountain in the center that gurgled and dripped.

"Who designed this place?" Sigi said with disgust.

"Someone who hates silver?" Ozzy suggested.

They took a slow stroll around the lobby, scanning the nooks, the crannies, or any other area where a wizard might be waiting for them. Clark stuck his head out of Ozzy's pocket and did some looking himself.

"There!" the bird said excitedly, "there, by the stairs."

"That's a woman," Ozzy informed him, "and she looks a hundred years old."

"Well," Clark said defensively, "she moves like Rin. Besides, wizards can shapeshift. There!"

"That's a fern," Ozzy said.

On their second time around the lobby, a friendly woman at the front desk greeted them as they passed. Aside from Ozzy and Sigi she was the youngest person in the place. She had perfect deep-brown skin, tight pulled-up hair, and a loose smile. The nametag on her shirt said Margo.

"May I help you?" Margo asked.

"We're just looking," Sigi answered her cautiously. "Waiting for someone, actually."

"A guest here?" she questioned. "If you know their name I can ring their room."

"That's okay," Ozzy said. "We like walking around this place. It looks like the inside of a treasure chest."

Margo let her smile shine. "That's an interesting way of putting it. You know, I've worked here for fifteen years and I've never thought of that." From her post behind the front desk she glanced out at the lobby. "And you're right, it does."

"Of course, most treasure chests I've read about don't have pianos in them," Ozzy pointed out.

"That's true," Margo agreed. "Well, if you get tired of walking around, there's a restaurant on the second floor. It doesn't look like the inside of a treasure chest, but the food's good."

"Thanks," Sigi said, trying to move Ozzy away from the front desk and over to a spot where they could discuss their next move. "We're not hungry."

"I am," Ozzy admitted.

Sigi stared at him.

Ozzy had grown up alone in the woods and because of that, his social skills were still a bit unrefined. There were times when he was more honest than normal people were used to. This was one of those times. Sigi pinched his arm, the international signal for *stop talking.*

"Right," Ozzy added. "Now that I think about it, I'm *not* hungry."

"Well," Margo said as they moved away, "if you change your mind, the restaurant is just up that wide set of stairs. They specialize in all-day breakfast."

Ozzy and Sigi froze—an audible gasp came from

Ozzy's right front pocket. Both he and Sigi slowly swiveled their heads back around to look at Margo.

"All-day breakfast?" Ozzy asked.

Margo nodded. "But you can also order things like a cheeseburger and fries if you'd like."

"I think we're both hungry now," Sigi said.

They left the front desk and walked directly to the wide staircase. Taking the steps two at a time, they climbed to the second floor and stood at the entrance of the restaurant. The place was called Egg Up, and it looked as old as the lobby, but with a touch less gold.

"This has to mean something, right?" Sigi asked Ozzy as they stood staring.

Clark poked his head out of the pocket. "You think Rin the Yellow is in there?"

"I think we should find out," Ozzy replied.

The three of them entered the restaurant through a wide wooden door and glanced around, hoping that the presence of breakfast food would be the good omen they were after.

"Or at the very least, a good omelet," Ozzy said.

"Is that a joke?" Sigi asked.

"I don't think so," he answered honestly.

"It definitely wasn't," Clark chirped in. "I've heard jokes before, good ones even, and that wasn't one."

The door closed behind them and a woman with small hips and wide shoulders approached.

"How many?" she asked.

"Two," Ozzy replied.

His pocket grumbled—Clark hated to be left out.

The woman showed them to a table as their eyes searched the dimly lit restaurant for any sign of a wizard. They couldn't see one, but wizards are a tricky bunch. It's not easy to know where or when they might show up. But both . . . all three of them were hopeful and hungry for not only omelets, but answers.

CHAPTER NINETEEN

MONEY MAKES THE MADNESS

Ray knew the Resort in New York very well because he owned it. As far as hotels go, it was one of the smaller ones he had in his portfolio. But it was a landmark, and it drew a certain clientele—an older, wealthier clientele—that some of his more modern hotels didn't.

Sitting in an overstuffed golden chair near the massive golden fireplace, he had watched Ozzy and Sigi walk around his golden lobby. He was relieved that Ozzy was now under the roof of a building over which he had ultimate control.

Ray observed the boy and girl talk to Margo and then ascend the stairs.

It should be noted that Ray Dench was an organized, driven person. He was also disgustingly selfish. He had been born with money, raised with wealth, and now basked in the obscene fortune he had established. He was eccentric, but not in a good way—he wasn't interesting or quirky, just spoiled and angry. His goal was to gain more of everything. In his mind he didn't have enough because he did not yet own it all.

Ray's only struggle was his inability to leave New York. The anxiety he felt at the very thought of it made him feel weak and damaged. If he were to make a list of his personal pros and cons, his need to never leave New York would be the only item on the *con* side. Whereas the *pros* would be a list longer than most arms (plus an additional leg) could contain.

Charles had made a mistake by not capturing Ozzy when he took the boy's parents years ago. But Ozzy had hidden from their captors and was presumed dead. That had been one of Charles's biggest missteps. Of course, Charles was dead now, and Ray had plans to finish something that had begun many years before.

Ray stood up from the chair and walked across the gold tiles to the front desk.

"Margo."

"Mr. Dench," she replied coldly.

"I saw you talking to those children."

"Yes." Her answer was flat and lifeless.

The staff at Resort in New York did not like Mr. Dench. It was always a bad day when he came around. He talked to people in a way that made it feel like he was fishing for something that he could use to punish them later.

"What did they want?" Ray asked, while knowing perfectly well why Ozzy and Sigi were there.

"Nothing. They're waiting for someone."

"Did they say who?"

"No."

"Children don't come in here very often."

Margo wasn't sure what Mr. Dench wanted her to say. So she went with, "That's true."

"Well, no bother. They're just children."

"Interesting children," she said, hoping he would go away.

Margo shifted and stepped back a couple of inches from her spot behind the counter. Her body language was shouting to any within eyesight that Mr. Dench made her very uncomfortable.

"Really?" Ray asked. "Interesting? How so?"

"The boy has a birthmark on his left hand."

Ray just smiled. He was aware of the mark. Charles had told him about it shortly before he died. It was much more than a birthmark and considerably more interesting than Margo could possibly understand.

"Are you okay, sir?" Margo asked nervously.

Ray looked her in the eyes. His expression gave her the creeps, gifted her the willies, and delivered a whole shipping container full of concern.

She stepped back another inch.

"Have you ever been so close to something that it took your breath away?" he asked her. "You know, there's a sort of beautiful fear that comes with knowing that you will soon be risking it all for something unimaginable."

"I'm not sure I understand."

"You don't need to," Ray said with a grin.

Margo didn't return the smile.

Mr. Dench walked away from the front desk and took the wide stairs up to the second floor three at a time.

The moment he had been waiting for had arrived.

CHAPTER TWENTY

HOPE

The Egg Up restaurant was far fancier than any eating establishment Ozzy had ever been in or seen before. There were windows around two sides, giving the diners a remarkable view of the streets of New York. It had dimly lit chandeliers above all the tables, and the wait staff were wearing yolk-colored skirts and vests. The utensils on the table were gold, and they had been polished to a fine gleam.

Clark was quite taken with Ozzy's fork.

The bird poked his small head up over the edge of the table as he stood on Ozzy's lap and gazed at the cutlery.

"I thought I knew what forks *were*," he chirped breathlessly.

Hoping that it would quiet Clark, Ozzy picked up his fork and placed it on his lap so that the bird could gaze at it better.

"Okay," Sigi said as she glanced around the room. "We're here in a hotel, whose initials spell out RIN—"

"RIN-*Y*," Ozzy reminded her.

"Close enough. We're also in a restaurant that serves breakfast all day. So where's my dad?"

Outside the windows, snow began to fall.

A man with a yolky vest and blond mustache stepped up to their table and handed them both menus. He had tiny hands and shook just a little, as if he were nervous or over-caffeinated—or perhaps uncertain how to serve anyone under the age of eighty.

"What would you like to drink?" he asked.

"Water," Sigi said.

"Sprite," Ozzy said.

The man turned like a top and walked away.

Outside the snow fell harder.

"Isn't it a little early in the year for there to be snow?" Sigi asked as she looked out the windows.

"I don't know," Ozzy replied. "I haven't been here since I was seven."

"But I'm sure you have a concept of seasons."

"Actually, I'm still not great with months and years. Things were always just cold or warm growing up."

The waiter returned to drop off their drinks and take their order. He suggested a few fancy things, but they both settled on pancakes, scrambled eggs, hash browns, and bacon. After they'd ordered, the waiter walked off again.

"He seemed disappointed with what we ordered, didn't he?" Ozzy said.

"He seems like the kind of person that would be disappointed regardless."

Clark stuck his head up over the table. "Um, are you guys using your spoons?"

Ozzy picked up his spoon and set it on his lap.

The restaurant was filled with the sound of classical music coming from the speakers overhead. The music was soft and mixed well with the din of people talking and eating. Ozzy watched the snow outside for a few moments and then glanced around. About half the tables were occupied, and the elderly patrons picked at things like hardboiled eggs and fluffy omelets. Everybody besides Ozzy and Sigi looked wealthy and bored.

Ozzy's finger buzzed. He moved his hand under the table so Sigi wouldn't see.

It buzzed again.

"Whoa," Clark chirped as he sat perched on Ozzy's lap, still staring at the cutlery. "I think I felt something."

Ozzy's finger buzzed again.

"Wait," the bird tweeted. "That's coming from your finger."

Ozzy moved his hand from his lap and made a fist to stop the vibration.

"What's happening?" Sigi asked in a panic. "You're not going to jump out another window, are you?"

"It's nothing." Ozzy's neck was turning a light red. "It's just my finger. Can I use your phone?"

Sigi pulled her phone out of her bag and handed it to Ozzy.

"If you're calling who I think you're calling, he's not going to answer."

Ever since Rin had disappeared four months before, Ozzy had dialed his number hundreds of times, hoping that the wizard would answer. Sadly, he never did. It was the same number Ozzy had originally found in the Otter Rock Visitors Guide. The same number he had called from the Chinese restaurant. And the same number Rin had once answered.

Sigi was right, there was no answer—just seven rings followed by the sound of Rin inviting the caller to leave a message:

> You've reached the phone of a wizard. I sense you are in need. Leave a meaningful message and I will try my best to travel through time and space to get back to you. If you're calling about the microwave I listed on Craigslist, I've decided to keep it. Until we speak in person, remember that all life is more than a bunch of colors carefully arranged. It is—*beep*.

The recording cut off at the same spot it always did. Usually, Ozzy didn't leave a message, but as his finger buzzed he felt compelled and desperate.

"Hello, Rin," he said into the phone. "Sigi and I are in

New York waiting for you. It would be very helpful if you answered your phone."

"Say *please*," Clark chirped.

"*Please*," Ozzy added. "Oh, yeah, I know you like people to leave messages that have meaning, so . . . well, a wise man once told me that if you are experiencing a loss, take a moment to at least celebrate being alive. That wise man was you, and I still don't understand it. Please call us back."

Ozzy hung up.

"You're getting better at leaving him messages," Sigi admitted.

"I always feel stupid," Ozzy said looking at the phone in his hand. "I'm just talking into a chunk of glass and metal hoping that someone responds."

"Excuse me," someone interrupted.

Ozzy and Sigi looked up. A man was standing next to their table and he appeared to be talking to them. The man was a couple inches shorter than Ozzy's six feet. His shoulders were skinny and square and he was standing so confidently that he looked fake. He had short, dark red hair that was heavily gray around the ears. He stared at Ozzy with his deep brown eyes that were neither interesting nor comforting—just two pieces of brown ice giving off feelings of cold and discomfort.

The man smiled, and his face became a bit more lifelike.

"Yes," Ozzy said. "Are you a waiter?"

The man laughed.

"No, I'm not qualified for that," he joked.

"Oh," Ozzy said sincerely, "it probably does take a lot of training."

The man bristled slightly. "Let's not talk about waiters. Please, my name's Ray Dench. Do you mind if I have a seat?"

"Yes," Sigi spoke up, "we do mind. We're waiting for someone."

Ray looked around at the restaurant and then back at them. "Actually, I think that the someone you're waiting for is me."

Ozzy and Sigi's empty stomachs suddenly felt full of worry. They had traveled to New York for Rin. Now someone who appeared to lack warmth and humanity was telling them that he was their intended destination. Clark shifted on Ozzy's lap to stay out of sight and not be disturbed with what he was currently doing.

"No, it's not you," Ozzy said to Ray. "We're waiting for someone else."

Without receiving permission, Ray sat at one of the empty chairs at their table. He scooted in closer and then took the cloth napkin in front of him and placed it on his lap. His movements were calculated and annoying—he was like the human version of fingernails on a chalkboard.

"You're mistaken," Ray said. "You are waiting for me. Let me guess, you received a package with a flash drive."

Ozzy and Sigi exchanged worried glances.

"First off, let me commend you for doing what you

should have. It was very wise of you to come, Ozzy," Ray switched his stare from Ozzy to Sigi and attempted to smile sincerely. "However, it was a small, pleasant surprise to see that you brought a guest."

The mood didn't feel pleasant.

"Who are you?" Sigi asked.

"As I mentioned, my name is Ray Dench, and this is my hotel."

Ozzy looked impressed. "The whole thing?"

"Every bit of it," he bragged.

"And you send plane tickets to get people to visit?" Ozzy asked.

Ray laughed and it made him look even faker.

"No," he said. "Just you."

"I don't understand," Ozzy said sincerely.

"You will. You see, I own far more than just this hotel. You might say that most of New York has my fingerprints on it."

"Sorry," Ozzy said.

"Sorry?" Ray looked bothered.

"It must be horrible to have so many possessions to worry about."

Ray wasn't enjoying Ozzy's naïveté and his knitted eyebrows showed it. "I'm not worried, Ozzy. I've achieved great wealth; I'm one of the most powerful people in the world."

"Okay," Ozzy said. "Congratulations?"

There was no bite or snark in Ozzy's words and Ray wasn't sure how to process them.

"Thank you." He dusted off his suit coat sleeve dismissively. "I apologize for getting off topic. This is a happy moment. You see, I'm the bearer of good news."

Ozzy and Sigi looked around as if some great reward was going to reveal itself. But everything looked just the way it already had. The place was still filled with old people and the smell of eggs. And outside, the snow was falling straight down in big flakes.

"Is it the snow?" Ozzy asked. "Is that the surprise?"

"No." Ray took a deep breath. "It's not. Don't you—"

"Does it always snow this early in the year?" Sigi interrupted.

Ray's fake face scrunched up into a much more human expression. He took a moment to exhale. "It's happened before, but I'm not here to deliver the weather, I'm here to deliver good news."

"Then let's hear it," Sigi insisted, "before we call the police and report that someone we don't know is sitting at our table and bragging about how powerful he is."

Ray stared at Sigi. "I can see why he brought you."

"I didn't bring her," Ozzy corrected him. "Sigi has a mind of her own. I was just happy she used it in a way that included me."

"Well, then . . . oh." Ray was momentarily off his game—somehow two teenagers had thrown him off balance. It was not a feeling he enjoyed. He had addressed rooms full of world leaders and powerful people with ease. He had taken over companies and influenced governments without breaking a sweat. But now a couple of kids from Oregon were giving him fits. He sat up as straight as he could and pressed the mental reset button in his mind.

"Listen," he said calmly, "no more talk of snow. I have brought you here because I wanted to speak face to face. You see, Ozzy, I knew your parents."

Ozzy and Sigi both kept quiet and stared at him as if he were speaking a different language than the one they knew.

"They were great friends of mine," he added. "When I heard your story I knew that I needed to meet you."

"How did you hear the news?" Sigi asked with suspicion.

"I am very well-read. There are not many things that escape my attention." The way Ray said *escape* made the inside of Egg Up become as cold as the weather outside.

"You could have just Skyped him," Sigi said.

"I don't like such cold forms of communication," Ray replied briskly. "Look, here we are, face to face." He looked at Ozzy's left hand as it rested on the table. "Charles told me about your birthmark."

Ozzy's neck burned red. "You worked with him?"

Clark heard the name Charles and pulled himself away from the spoon's gaze. He lifted his head in Ozzy's lap to pay better attention.

"Hold on," Ray said. "Before you go accusing me of anything, I want you to know that I am so sorry for what

Charles did. He was a foolish man with a personal agenda. I am not him and I only want to help."

"By tricking me into coming here?"

"Well . . ." Ray stopped to smile cruelly. "I thought you might like to return to the city where you were born. And there are a few things I need to ask you."

Hearing Charles's name made Ozzy uneasy. "I think we should leave."

"I'm sorry to hear you say that," Ray said sympathetically. "And you should know that you can't. At least not yet. Let's not make this ugly. I just need a little information from you."

Ozzy's face burned. Sigi was sitting on the edge of her seat, looking as if she were going to pounce.

The waiter returned to the table with their food. He saw Ray and began to twitch and stutter.

"Mr. D-D-Dench," the waiter said. "I didn't know you were here. Can I get you something?"

"No," Ray said seriously, gazing at Ozzy. "I think I already have everything I need right here."

Ozzy and Sigi stared at the eggs and hash browns that had just been placed in front of them. The food was beautiful, but the mood was not.

"Eat," Ray said.

"No, thank you," Ozzy whispered.

"It's delicious."

Ozzy and Sigi stared at their food.

Sometimes loss of appetite is the least of one's concerns.

CHAPTER TWENTY-ONE

STARING AT THE ENEMY

Ozzy and Sigi sat motionless at their table in Egg Up. Ray's cell phone rang, and he moved across the restaurant so he could talk in private. They watched him standing by the entrance talking into his phone and keeping an eye on them.

"What do we do?" Ozzy whispered.

"I'm not sure, but we need to get away from him."

"What if he has answers?"

"To what?"

Clark stuck his head up over the edge of the table. "For what it's worth, I don't like him at all. He gives me the tweets." The bird shivered in Ozzy's lap. "You should let me work him over."

"Thanks, Clark, but I think it might be wise to find out what he knows."

"What can he tell you? Your parents are gone," Sigi said kindly. "It's horrible, but their deaths can't be changed by something this guy knows. And who does he think he is? Luring you here and wanting us to follow him. We need to call the police."

Ray was done with his call and walking back to the table.

"So," he said as he stood next to Ozzy, "why don't you two come with me to my office? We can talk privately and I can show you the information I have about your parents."

"No, thanks," Ozzy said.

"Yeah." Sigi was disgusted. "What makes you think that we would just follow you anywhere? We're leaving."

"I don't think that's a good idea," Ray said. "You see, there's nowhere for you to go."

Ray waved his hand and six men in blue suits and dark glasses materialized all around the restaurant. It seemed as if they had stepped out of the wallpaper. They stood there looking menacing, their faces turned toward the boy and girl.

"Don't be alarmed," Ray said. "They're just a few of my security detail. They're here to protect me. They're also fast and can quiet a problem in seconds if needed."

Ozzy looked around the room, surprised that the old people eating didn't seem to even notice them. Ozzy was suddenly glad that he hadn't eaten his food—because if he had, he would be vomiting.

"You can't frighten us," Sigi said, even though the quiver in her lips seemed to suggest that he already had. "We can get the police."

"Let me help with that." Ray smiled and waved his hand again.

A tall, thick man in a police uniform walked into the restaurant and up to their table. He had a big face with a wrinkled forehead and a strong chin. His chest was as big as a barrel, and his arms were the size of tree trunks. He stood next to Ray and looked down at Ozzy and Sigi.

"Hello, Sergeant," Ray said. "These children have something they want to say."

Ozzy was speechless, Sigi was not.

"Are you really a cop?"

"I am. My name's Sergeant Windhorst." His voice was strong, but not brutal. "How may I help you?"

"We just want to leave," Sigi said, pointing at Ray. "He's tricked us into coming here, and now we want to go."

"I wouldn't advise that," the sergeant said. "New York is a big place and I never recommend children running around by themselves. There are just too many things that could go wrong. I suggest that you hear Mr. Dench out. He only wants to help."

Ozzy found his voice. "I don't understand. He can tell the police what to do?"

"Well," Sergeant Windhorst said, "it's like this—we do what's best for the city. And helping Mr. Dench is always a benefit to New York. Now why don't you both stand up and follow us? I think you'll be pleased by what he has to say."

"We already aren't pleased," Sigi said. "What if I just start screaming? The people eating here will help."

"You might get a small scream out before we silence you," Ray said. "But even if you screamed all day, these people wouldn't care. They have routines and concerns that don't involve helping you."

"Understand?" Sergeant Windhorst asked. "Now, since we all know the deal, let's have you two follow Mr. Dench to his offices at the back of the courtyard."

"It's a nice, private place to talk," Ray said.

Ozzy glanced around quickly, looking for anything he could use to fight their way out of the restaurant. But all he saw were security guards and old people who didn't seem to care what was happening.

There was only one thing Ozzy could do: It was time to release the Clarken.

Ozzy briefly glanced down into his lap and saw the bird look up and nod. The boy returned his gaze to Ray and tried to appear calm. He felt Clark positioning himself on his lap to launch up.

Ozzy smiled as if he knew something Ray didn't.

Unfortunately, Ray knew something himself, and before Clark could spring up out of Ozzy's lap, a security guard's hand swooped down and grabbed the bird tightly. The movement was so sudden and so fast that neither Ozzy nor Clark saw it coming.

"I've got it," a tall, dark security guard reported.

Ozzy stood up. "Let him go!"

"Right now!" Sigi added as she jumped up from her chair.

Clark squawked loudly.

For the first time, a few diners looked up from their meals to see what was going on. When they realized that they themselves were in no danger, they returned their full attention to their food.

"Inside voices," Ray instructed all of them. "This is no place for yelling."

"What about kidnapping?" Ozzy asked loudly. "Let him go!"

Ray waved at the tall dark bodyguard. "Bring it here."

"Stop calling me an *it*!" Clark chirped as he struggled to break free from the bodyguard's grip. "I have a name."

The bodyguard handed Clark to his boss. Ray held the bird tightly in his right hand and stared at him, nose to beak.

"Amazing," Ray whispered.

"That's better," the bird insisted. "But most people call me Clark."

"Emmitt created you, didn't he?"

"If you mean Ozzy's dad, then yes. Now let me go so I can peck your eyes out."

"Oh, I'm sure you would. I've heard stories."

"Well, they're all true . . . or false, depending on which ones make me look good." Clark struggled. "Now let me go."

"No." Ray's voice was suddenly serious. "There were rumors of your creation years ago. I had heard that Emmitt had invented a sentient bird. And even though I've never known anybody smarter than him, I still didn't believe it was possible."

"Well, soak it in," Clark chirped loudly. "Because here I am. Now let me go."

"No," Ray reiterated. "You're a tremendous bonus."

"You can't keep him!" Ozzy insisted. "You have no right."

"Money buys me rights that others can't afford. Now come," Ray said with a syrupy kindness that made their teeth and hearts hurt. "Let's go talk. I promise you'll be happy we did."

Ozzy and Sigi were frozen, unsure of what to do.

"Come," Sergeant Windhorst said. "You'll be safe."

Neither child believed the sergeant, but they had no other choice. They both stepped away from the table looking miserable and scared.

Outside the windows, the snow continued to fall.

"Follow me." Ray waved his bird-free hand and began to walk.

Ozzy and Sigi reluctantly followed behind him and Sergeant Windhorst. The bodyguards moved in closer as if they were performing a synchronized dance they had rehearsed many times. They formed a circle around Ozzy and Sigi as they traveled through the restaurant and down the wide stairs.

Ray led the way, keeping his eyes directed forward. He didn't look back to see if things were in order, because he knew that thanks to his men, things were. He held Clark tightly in his right hand.

As they crossed the lobby, Margo looked at the children. She saw them being herded by the bodyguards and quickly glanced away. Sigi tried to make eye contact with her, but she wasn't having any part of it. Margo had worked at the Resort in New York for fifteen years and she knew perfectly well that some things were not her business.

The somber group exited the back of the lobby through glass doors that led to a large courtyard behind the hotel.

CHAPTER TWENTY-TWO

RETURN OF THE RIN

Ozzy and Sigi stepped out into the courtyard, following Sergeant Windhorst and Ray. The cold pushed up against them like an annoying little brother. The sky was unusually dark for it being only afternoon, and the heavy clouds were practicing alchemy by turning water into a never-ending cascade of snowflakes.

One of the bodyguards popped open a large umbrella and held it over Ray as they walked.

"You probably should let us go," Clark squawked. "I'm only going to warn you a handful of times."

"Please don't," Ray said. "I might have to remove your beak."

Ray led the small group along an outdoor walkway and beneath a wooden trellis that did an acceptable job of keeping the snow off of them. The fat clouds and inclement weather had chased everyone out of the courtyard and into the hotel. The lack of guests made the scene feel incomplete and ill-fitting.

Looking out from under the trellis, Ozzy could see large trees and gardens that the snow was attempting to hide. The courtyard would have been beautiful in sunlight, but beneath the cinder-colored clouds and heavy snow it seemed forgotten, a place best left alone. The only sound was that of snow crunching beneath their feet.

"Any suggestions?" Sigi whispered as they walked. "We're not really going to follow him somewhere we don't know, are we?"

"Excuse me," Ray interrupted Sigi, "let's save our talking until we are out of the weather and in my office. I can't hear what you're saying, and I'd hate to miss anything important."

"Good luck with that," Clark told Ray. "They're both teenagers. They're going to talk whether you like it or not. We went to a movie last week and during the good part Sigi kept—"

"Quiet," Ray said. "I don't need some hunk of metal telling me what to do."

"Hunk? I have to say for a bad guy you're pretty free with the compliments. I like that. I actually think that all—"

"Quiet!"

Clark shut his beak.

The snow continued to blanket the courtyard. With no

wind, every flake fell straight down and blended into the mounds piling up on the ground.

Ray turned off the walkway and marched directly through the snow across the center of the courtyard. The team of bodyguards continued to ring Ozzy and Sigi. They passed a large swimming pool and a massive fountain in the shape of a lion.

"Why is your office out here?" Sigi asked Ray.

"I have many offices," he answered without stopping or turning around. "This is just the most private. It also has access to the tools and instruments I want."

"*Tools?*" Clark asked.

"Quiet."

"It's a good question," Ozzy spoke up. "Why would you need tools?"

"It's not what you think," Ray explained. "I'm not talking about hammers and needles. You need to open your mind and realize that anything can be a tool."

"I think you prove that point nicely," Clark said.

Ozzy's finger buzzed, and the boy trembled. His shoulders and arms burned and his already unsettled stomach contracted in pain.

Snow fell all around him, making the scene look like a static-filled screen. His head rocked and pictures of his past flashed inside his mind. He saw the cloaked house, his parents sitting on the porch. He heard their screams and relived his terror as he realized that his parents were being taken from him. He felt the loneliness and fear of being abandoned for so many years. His heart was racing and his mind ordered his feet to stop. Ray was connected to his past in some horrible way, which meant that he wouldn't take another step forward.

"Stop, Sigi!" Ozzy said, throwing his words down like a hammer. "We're done, Ray. This is wrong. You have to let us go. We're not going any farther."

Ray stopped and turned around.

Through the falling snow the man's eyes connected with Ozzy's—despite the age and power difference the boy didn't look away. The ring of bodyguards all came to a halt and each one stared directly at the two children. Sergeant Windhorst put his hands on his hips.

"I told you two to do as instructed," the sergeant insisted.

"He can't force us to go somewhere," Ozzy said. "If you're going to hurt us or threaten us with tools, do it here."

The bodyguard holding the umbrella over Ray's head kept it positioned perfectly. Ray was the only one dry. Snow continued to build on everyone else's shoulders and head. Ray had Clark in his hand and even under the dark clouds and white weather, his cruel snarl was visible on his fake face.

Ray laughed softly. "You don't understand. I am not going to hurt you unless I have to. But you should know that you have no choice in the matter. Stop walking, and my men will bind your arms and carry you. Which means you will be joining me and there is nothing you can do to change that. So come." Ray waved with his free hand. "Why make things more uncomfortable than they need to be? Besides, this is all for the best."

The way Ray said *best* made Ozzy and Sigi shiver more than the cold and snow.

"For the best of what?" Ozzy asked.

"Well, for me and my interests."

Ozzy and Sigi were so focused on Ray that they failed to notice the two bodyguards slipping up behind them. The men grabbed them and lifted Ozzy and Sigi as if they were made of nothing but feathers and fill.

"Let me go!" Sigi yelled.

Both fought against the men that held them, but their hold was too strong. Clark shook in Ray's hand trying to escape, but it was no use. The three of them were bound and in trouble.

Ozzy closed his eyes and tried to calm his mind. He felt his body shake. A feeling similar to that he'd felt on the top of the mountain as he fought Charles washed over him. He tried to control what Ray was doing. He willed the man to let Clark go. He focused on Sigi and her being released.

Nothing.

The bodyguards began to walk. Ozzy saw the building they were heading toward. It was five stories tall and made of stone. Tall trees surrounded it. Snow-covered ivy climbed every inch of stone. For those who care about architecture, it was an historic and imposing building, with gargoyles staring down from the top ledge and arched windows that burned brightly. For Ozzy, however, it looked like a prison, a place they were going to be forced to enter.

"No," Ozzy said, struggling to get free.

"Let us go!" Sigi yelled.

The black clouds above them tightened up and a light wind began to blow. The snow that had been falling straight down began to twist around them like thick white ribbons. And the courtyard grew darker as fear raced in from all four corners and filled the space up.

"Please!" Ozzy shouted.

"He said please," Clark tweeted. "What kind of monster are you?"

"Let us go," Ozzy added.

Ray didn't answer, but the wind increased, and with it visibility dropped to near blindness.

A disembodied voice called out.

"What's wrong with your ears?"

Ozzy and Sigi stopped struggling. Everyone swiveled around, looking through the swirling snow to see where the voice had come from.

Ray's breath and his ears steamed.

"Who said that?" he demanded.

The blowing snow grew more violent.

"Let them go!" the voice answered.

"Who are you?" Ray asked angrily. "I don't appreciate others sticking their noses into my affairs."

"Well," the voice said ominously, "appreciation has never been anything I've worried about."

Ozzy's heart began to beat rapidly as his finger buzzed. And Clark began to chirp like a loon as both bird and boy recognized who was speaking.

"*Rin?*" Ozzy whispered excitedly.

"*What?*" Sigi said. "Where?"

The wind picked up, blowing the snow on the ground back up and into the air where new snow was still falling. Ozzy blew the flakes from his face as he tried to spot the wizard.

"The bird warned you," the voice said.

The wind and weather made it sound as if the words were coming from everywhere and all over.

"The boy warned you."

The bodyguards twisted and turned in an effort to spot who was speaking.

"The girl warned you."

Ray was only ten feet away from Ozzy, but the blowing snow was now making him almost invisible. The wind had grown so strong that the building they had been walking to was lost in a veil of white.

Still, the two guards held onto the boy and girl.

"Let them go!" the voice demanded.

"Show yourself!" Ray shouted.

"By the time you see me it will be too late."

"Somebody do something!" Ray yelled.

There was a tremendous crack, followed by the sound of Ray screaming. Both Ozzy and Sigi took the noise as their cue to act. Ozzy lifted his right leg and threw it back into the knee of the man who was holding him. The man's leg buckled and they both fell to the snow-covered ground. Sigi went limp and slipped halfway out of the arms of her attacker. He attempted to squeeze her harder, but her teeth connected with his right forearm and she bit down with a sense of purpose.

As a rule, bodyguards are trained not to scream, but the one holding Sigi bellowed like a pro.

"Ahhhhhhh!"

Sigi fell to the snowy ground and sprang up to run. The bodyguard dove forward and grabbed her right ankle as he came crashing down on his own knees. A bit of black peppered the white air and shot through the snow like a sentient bullet. Clark hit the guard's hand with a forceful impact. The bird's beak tore the bodyguard's skin, causing the large man to cry like a small child.

The snow was now so blinding that it was impossible to see Ray or Sergeant Windhorst or anyone any longer.

Ozzy scrambled to get to his feet and as he did, he found Sigi reaching out to give him her hand. The two of them were so twisted around and confused that they couldn't tell which way to run.

"They're loose!" they heard one of the bodyguards yell. "We've lost the subjects!"

"Find them!" Ray yelled back.

The powerful Mr. Dench sounded angry. His plan that had been running so smoothly was falling apart.

Another bodyguard screamed.

Ozzy and Sigi were snowblind but determined to get away. They ran as if they had some idea of where they were going. Clark landed on Ozzy's shoulder.

"He's here!" the bird tweeted happily.

"I heard," Ozzy replied, his breathing becoming labored. "Where is he now?"

"Who knows," Clark said. "That wizard has a mind of his own. Just keep running straight. When you hit a wall you've gone too far. Feel around for a door."

"Where are you going?"

"I've got enough charge for a couple more strikes. I want these guys to remember me."

"There's no way anyone could ever forget."

"Thanks," Clark tweeted humbly. "You say the nicest things. It's one of the reasons why I'm so fond of you. I think—"

"Go!" Ozzy shouted.

Clark shot off the boy's shoulder and returned to the scene of confusion. Ozzy could hear some yelling and screaming, but he held tight to Sigi's hand.

Together they ran until they hit a wall.

"Feel for a door!" Ozzy hollered.

The snow felt like a plastic bag over their heads, making it hard to see and breathe. Sigi's hands found the door and then the knob. She pushed it open and both children spilled into a hallway and out of the courtyard.

They collapsed on the carpeted floor as the door slammed shut behind them.

Sigi rolled onto her back, trying to capture enough air to appease her lungs. To her left, Ozzy was on his hands and knees choking.

He caught his breath and looked at Sigi.

She was wet and cold and shivering as she lay on the floor. Her curly hair was like a dark sponge that had soaked up gallons of snow and water. A puddle the size of a small tub was forming where her head lay. Ozzy wasn't in much better shape. His body was a popsicle and his face felt like it had been slapped by an angry and out-of-line Mother Nature. They were both a mess, but none of that mattered, because Rin was back.

CHAPTER TWENTY-THREE

RIN

Ozzy and Sigi lay in the empty hallway until they caught their breath. Then they moved as quickly and quietly as they could down the hall and toward the hotel rooms. To the best of their knowledge, nobody aside from Clark knew where they had gone. Now their hope was that they would be able to get out of the hotel before anyone else could detain them.

Reaching a long hallway, they spotted a sign with an arrow that that said *Lobby*.

"Should we go a different way?" Sigi asked. "We might run into more bodyguards."

"I still think it's our best choice," Ozzy replied. "I'm just not sure where any of the other exits go. They might lead us right back to the courtyard. We know the lobby will get us out. We just need to get to the street. Then we can hide until Rin finds us."

"Okay," Sigi agreed.

Ozzy took off running down the hall toward the lobby. An old woman with a small dog came out of her room and blocked the way for a moment. But the two children pushed around her and kept sprinting.

Getting closer, they could hear the piano playing.

"Should we sneak through?" Ozzy asked as they ran. "Or just see what happens if we dash?"

"Let's try the dashing thing!"

The end of the hallway was in sight. They could see into the lobby and felt the hope that came with the possibility of freedom.

Unfortunately, freedom often has a few snags.

Margo stepped into the hallway. She stood still, staring straight at them, blocking their way.

"Should we just knock her down?" Sigi yelled.

There's a good chance that Ozzy was going to say something chivalrous and kind like, "No, I can't run down an innocent person." But no one will ever know, because Margo moved to the side of the hall and motioned for them to hurry past.

"Thanks!" Ozzy yelled as brushed by her.

"The second door from the right pushes out easiest," she yelled.

There wasn't time to stop and figure out what she meant—there was only running. The boy and girl blew into the lobby, past the piano player, around the fountain, and toward the front doors.

"Stop!" someone yelled from the far side of the lobby. "Stop them!"

There were a few elderly patrons milling around the space, but none of them attempted to stop the speeding children, as that would increase the possibility of broken bones. Most shuffled out of the way as quickly as they could while shouting things like, "My word!" and "I never!"

Everything was moving so quickly that it was hard for Ozzy to clearly see what was happening. Old people were stepping away, the piano playing had stopped, and shadowy bodyguards were closing in from all sides, racing toward them. The treasure-chest lobby was chaotic and frightening.

Ozzy eyed the front doors.

There were bellhops near a couple of them and patrons walking through a couple others. But the second door from the right wasn't blocked. Ozzy reached back to grab Sigi's hand, but she was already moving in front of him.

"Second door from the right!" he yelled.

"I heard her," she yelled back.

Sigi slammed up against the glass door and pushed it with such force that Ozzy felt certain it would shatter. But the glass held, and the door swung open violently.

Once again they were face to face with the freaky weather. The snow was blowing down the street like an enormous ghost working its way through a giant maze of buildings. Sigi and Ozzy were swallowed up by the sound of traffic and street life, disguised by the snow.

Without saying a word, they turned right and continued running.

They wove through people on the snowy sidewalk and down half a dozen blocks before turning left and ducking into a drugstore.

Trying to act normal, they walked down one of the aisles toward the back of the store. Once they were near the vitamins and cold remedies, they stopped to get their bearings.

The store's high shelves hid them from the view of any other shoppers and gave them a small sense of security.

"I don't think they followed us," Ozzy said, breathing hard.

"How could they?" Sigi replied. "I could barely see three feet in front of myself."

Ozzy wiped excess snow from his dark hair and dusted off his shirt and trousers. He looked at Sigi and smiled.

"We made it out."

"I can't believe it." The relief in Sigi's dark eyes was evident.

"What about Rin and Clark?"

"I think I'm more worried about us," she replied. "It seems like a wizard and a bird stand a much better chance in this city than we do."

"This is *not* how I saw this trip going," Ozzy admitted.

"Nothing you do ever is," she pointed out. "I should have been mean to you when I first saw you on the beach."

"I can't argue that."

"We should find a way back to the airport," Sigi said softly. "We can wait there until our flight tomorrow morning. Hopefully Rin and Clark will contact us."

"Can you sleep at an airport?"

"It's not comfortable or advised."

"So just like most of the stuff we do," Ozzy said.

"Exactly. They won't kick us out. Especially with weather like this."

"But if Ray has control of the cops, how do we stand a chance of getting out of here? I'm also not leaving this city without Clark and Rin."

"Well, then, how do you propose we find them?"

"Maybe now he'll answer his phone."

Ozzy took Sigi's phone and attempted to call the wizard one more time. When Rin didn't pick up he left another message.

"Rin, this is Ozzy. Please call us. We need to find you. Oh, and I guess I'll say maybe the world would be a better place if people stopped trying to harm other people."

Ozzy handed the phone back to Sigi.

"That was a pretty generic message," she said. "Of course, the world would be better if everyone stopped trying to harm others."

"I was specifically talking about people doing harm to us."

A couple of aisles over, they could hear an old couple arguing.

"Maybe we should get out of here," Sigi suggested. "I'll

feel better when we're as far away from that hotel as possible."

The arguing couple raised their voices.

Sigi unlocked her phone and looked for the Uber app.

"We could get an Uber to the airport and—"

Sigi stopped talking. Ozzy's eyes were wide and his head was tilted as if he were listening for something.

"What?" she asked. "Should I not get an Uber?"

Ozzy ignored her, deciding instead to turn and march down the aisle.

"What are you doing?"

He came to the end of the vitamin row and moved two aisles over.

"What—?" Sigi tried to ask.

Ozzy held his finger to his lips. He then poked his head around the corner of the aisle and gasped.

"I don't believe it," he whispered.

Sigi took a look.

Not more than fifteen feet away in front of the nail polish section the old couple arguing turned out to be a wizard arguing with the metal raven on his shoulder. The sight was like a hundred Christmases and ten Halloweens rolled together—celebratory and sweet.

Rin bent forward, trying to read something on the front of a bottle of nail polish. Even bent he looked tall. In fact, the time they'd been apart made him look larger than life. His long dark hair and beard were speckled with bits of gray that shimmered under the fluorescent lights of the drug store. He was wearing his gray felt hat and his short yellow robe. Beneath the robe he had on a black T-shirt and long trousers that were made out of a colorful tartan fabric. The trousers were a new addition. He had always sported dark jeans, but now his plaid legwear stood out like a fashion statement that didn't instantly make any sense. In his left hand he was holding a long tree branch.

Despite the trousers and the branch, Rin and Clark were a sight for sore and worried eyes.

Ozzy and Sigi both walked awkwardly up to the aisle and stood two feet away from them. Ozzy cleared his throat, but the wizard and the bird were so caught up in their own conversation that they didn't seem to notice.

"It's not right," Clark argued. "Say the name out loud and you'll see."

"Coal," Rin said.

"Do you hear it?" the bird tweeted. "It's just like 'Cole,' and there's a boy named Cole at Ozzy's school who did a report on how birds are a disease trap. *Disease trap?* Please, I clean my talons with metal polish twice a month."

"Okay," Rin said, putting the bottle of coal-colored nail polish back and picking up another. "Dark Night."

"How's it spelled?"

"N-I-G-H-T."

"Nope. Is there a Dark K-N-I-G-H-T?"

Still unnoticed, Ozzy and Sig continued standing at the end of the aisle.

"No," Rin insisted. He picked another bottle. "Black Licorice."

"See if it smells."

"Why? You can't smell things."

"Still, I'd like to know that it smells good."

Sigi took a turn clearing her throat.

Both Rin and Clark turned their heads and made eye contact with her and Ozzy. Rin smiled wide, acting as if a strong grin was the sign of a real wizard. Clark didn't grin, but he tilted his head a couple of times, which meant he was okay with what was happening.

"Hello, Sigi," Rin said. "Hi, Ozzy." He then turned his attention from them and back to the nail polish. "So we're going with Black Licorice?"

"Unbelievable," Sigi complained. "That's all you have to say? *Hello?* We haven't seen you in four months, we almost got kidnapped just now, and for some unknown reason you just happen to show up in New York where we happen to be."

"Nothing just happens," Rin said kindly as he looked at a couple more jars of nail polish. "And the things that do, do so, so that we can master our reactions."

"Ooooh," Clark chirped. "I like how that last sentence sounded—'the things that do, do so, so that . . .' It's fun to tweet."

"Thanks," Rin said humbly.

"*Dad,*" Sigi said with disgust.

The wizard turned from the staring at the wall of nail polish to stare lovingly at his daughter.

"Have you gotten taller?"

"No, it's only been four months."

"In *your* time," Rin reminded her. "It's been much longer for me."

"Well, that still wouldn't change things here." Sigi stopped talking to rub her forehead. "What's with the branch?"

"This?" the wizard questioned as he looked at the long branch in his hand. "This broke off a tree in the courtyard. It may or may not be the thing I used to hit Ray so he'd let go of Clark. I actually need a staff, and this looks just about right."

"None of this looks right," Sigi insisted.

"I agree," Ozzy said. "Is there a reason you're shopping for nail polish?"

"Yes," Clark answered. "Do you remember when we were dealing with those ugly men in the blue suits earlier?"

"You mean a few minutes ago?"

"Yes," Clark said. "Well, while I was putting a couple of them in their place I suffered a few scratches. We figured nail polish would fix things up."

Clark flew from Rin's shoulder to Ozzy's right arm. Holding onto his sleeve with his talons, he spread his wings and showed off the two long scratches on his metal belly and chest.

"Pretty bad-A, right?"

"I don't know what that means," Ozzy admitted.

"Me neither," the bird said, "but I feel tougher."

"And you'll feel even tougher once you get a good coating of Black Licorice nail polish on you," Sigi said sarcastically.

"We should stop talking about nail polish," Ozzy said, exasperated. "This is New York, and none of us belong here. But here we are. In the same shop. This is phenomenal."

Clark looked around. "I've seen bigger stores."

"Not the store, the coincidence."

Rin reached out and put his right hand on Ozzy's left shoulder. "Have you forgotten what magic is?"

"I think what I forgot was how hard it is to get a straight answer from you. I'd just like to know how we all ended up right here right now."

"It's best not to go asking questions when you've already formed the answer in your head," Rin counseled him. "Do you want me to say that I tracked Sigi's phone and knew where you were and what you were doing every step of the way?"

"Is that what happened?" Sigi asked.

"No, but even if that had been the case, there's still wonder in the process. Does it matter how a wizard works, or is the importance in what outcome the work provides?"

"How about you just tell us how you knew we were here," Ozzy said.

"I'm a wizard. You should know that—you were the one who originally answered my ad."

Ozzy's finger buzzed and Rin noticed it.

"Just as I thought," he said confidently.

"What?" Ozzy asked. "My finger?"

"Do you know what's been happening to Ozzy?" Sigi asked.

"I know just what I should know, and I don't care for what I shouldn't."

Sigi looked upset. "What?"

"That plaque there." Rin pointed to a shelf behind Ozzy and Sigi. It was filled with dozens of hand-painted plaques with folksy sayings on them. The biggest plaque had the words Rin had just spoken on it. There were others that had some of the things he had said earlier.

"So you don't know what Ozzy's going through?" Sigi asked.

"That's not true. In fact, I came back because of it."

"You did?"

Rin nodded and said, "There can only be one me so I'll make me my best."

Ozzy and Sigi shook their heads.

"Can we at least have this conversation somewhere without plaques?" Sigi asked.

"Of course," Rin replied. "We should also make our way out of this city. I have a feeling that those men aren't going to just give up."

"I agree," Ozzy said.

Rin looked at his daughter and then at Ozzy. Still holding his branch, he placed his left hand on Sigi's right shoulder and his right hand and staff against Ozzy's left arm as if he were going to push them together. Instead, he smiled and said,

"Love is the soul giggling."

"Stop reading the plaques," Sigi insisted.

"They really are awful," the wizard said. "I've always hated the word *giggling.* Now, I want to tell you two that it is very fortuitous and wonderful that you found me here."

"I agree," Ozzy said.

Sigi looked to make sure that her dad wasn't just quoting another plague.

"It's especially wonderful because I forgot to bring any money and Clark needs that finger paint."

Ozzy purchased the nail polish and the four of them got into an Uber in front of the store that drove them through the fading snowstorm toward the airport.

"These rideshare apps are enchanting," the wizard said. "You need to go somewhere, and *poof*! a way is provided. Such a magical world."

It felt good to have Rin back.

Of course, it felt bad to know that they were in a situation so dire that it required the help of a wizard.

CHAPTER TWENTY-FOUR

IN THE SUBWAY

All four friends and Rin's branch sat in the way-back of the midsized van. Their Uber driver was a man in his late fifties with a small wisp of gray hair on the top of his head, and facial features that looked to have been slowly sliding down his face over the past ten years. He took a moment to stare at Rin's hat, robe, and stick. He followed up his stare with a droopy smile.

"You're headed to the airport?" he asked. "I don't know how they'll feel about that stick."

Sigi opened her mouth to answer, but Rin beat her to the punch.

"We're not going to the airport after all," the wizard said. "We just need you to take us to the nearest E train station. And if you had any imagination, you would be able to see the majestic staff this stick will one day be."

The driver's face got droopier. "I've never had much imagination. Which is why I didn't imagine I'd be taking you to the station just up the street. I thought I'd be taking you to the airport."

"I thought it would be warm today," Rin replied. "Life gives us all kinds of chances to be surprised."

The driver pulled away from the curb and entered the heavy traffic. The snow had stopped falling and blowing which made the evening's visibility considerably better than it had been. Everything was wet with melting snow.

"What are we doing?" Sigi whispered to her dad.

"We're just taking a detour," he whispered in return while looking out the back window. "I think our path needs a few alterations."

"What about the paint?" Clark pleaded as he stuck his head out of Ozzy's pocket. "I feel damaged. Maybe just a quick coat?"

"Not yet," Rin said. "But I promise we'll get to it."

Clark sulked back into his fabric cave, muttering something about wizard promises being worth next to nothing.

"I'll paint his scratch," Sigi offered.

"There isn't time," Rin said. "Can I see your phone?"

"It would only take a second," Sigi said, handing him her phone.

"Too late. We're here."

The van pulled over to the curb and stopped. The driver then turned to look at them. He glanced at Ozzy and Sigi before stopping to stare some more at Rin.

"What are you all dressed up for, anyway? A costume party?"

"I'm a wizard."

"At what?" the driver asked.

"At everything."

Ozzy opened the door and they climbed out. Before closing the door, Rin gave the driver one last piece of advice.

"Remember, a man who questions absurdity must also question the norm."

Rin slammed the door shut before the driver could even dare to question absurdity a second time.

"Come on," the wizard said.

With Clark in his pocket, Ozzy trotted down the stairs into the subway station. Sigi had his right hand, and Rin was on his left. The place was packed with busy people doing busy things.

"We'll need some tickets," Rin informed them. "And since I am once again working to solve your problem, I'll let you pay and subtract it from the final bill."

"I think I still owe you from last time," Ozzy said. "What problem are you going to solve?"

"There's no such thing as a single problem," Rin said. "Everything's connected, which makes all your problems a part of your . . . successuses? Successesses? Successeti? Well. You get the drift."

"Barely," Ozzy said honestly.

Rin helped Ozzy and Sigi figure out the machine to purchase subway passes and then they all went through the turnstiles and got on a train.

"This feels right," Rin said as they took their seats. "Watch for other wizards. These trains are loaded with them moving between Quarfelt and reality. We love to travel the rails."

Sigi looked around.

"What this train is loaded with are feelings that make me think of our last train ride," Sigi said. "That wasn't pleasant."

"Years from now you'll tell that story as if it were one of your fondest memories."

"I think you mean fondest near-death experiences."

The subway began to move and Ozzy spoke up.

"I know you two have a father-daughter thing to work through, and that's great. You abandoned her, and she . . . did nothing wrong. But I'd really love to know what is going on with us being on this subway and not heading to the airport."

"That question is more than fair," Rin replied. "It's because we're being followed."

Ozzy and Sigi glanced around for a brief second before the wizard could warn them to stop doing that and act natural.

"They knew we were in that car," Rin said.

"How?" Sigi asked.

"Probably your phone," he answered.

Sigi frantically felt her empty pockets. "Where *is* my phone?"

"You gave it to me," her father said.

"Good." Sigi reached out her hand.

"And I, in turn, left it in that car."

"*What?* Why?"

"What good's a phone if it keeps whispering your location to the world?"

"That was my *phone*." Sigi's cheeks burned. "All my stuff is on it."

"It's just a thing."

Sigi swore.

Rin looked repulsed. "Did your mom teach you that word?"

"No, you said it earlier when you were fighting with Clark about nail polish."

"I'm sorry," Rin argued, "but it makes no sense to have any other color of black besides *cauldron*. As for your phone, you can always get a new one. Before I left it in the car I did a quick spell to preserve your information."

"So you made sure it was backed up on the cloud?"

"A good wizard never spells and tells."

Ozzy held up his hands to stop them both from talking. "Just tell me if we're still being followed."

"I think so. There are two men at the other end of this section, and both of them are wearing blue suits. They were tailing us in the car and probably saw us come down into the subway."

"How do we lose them?" Ozzy asked. "Won't they know we're going to the airport?"

"No, because this train goes the opposite direction.

Two stops from now we're going to get off this train, acting like we don't have a worry in the world."

"Then what?"

"We'll see," Rin said excitedly.

"You are the worst," Clark chirped from Ozzy's pocket.

Rin looked down. "I forgot what a funny bird you were."

"How about a spell?" Ozzy begged the wizard.

"No, thank you, I'm fine."

"No, how about you *doing* a spell?"

"Still no, and still thank you."

Two stops later they all stood up acting as if they had no idea that anything was wrong or that anyone was following them. They exited the crowded subway onto an even more crowded platform. It was the end of the work day and everyone was moving as one gigantic mass to get home.

"They're still following," Rin reported. "Just keep walking."

The crowd of people moving across the platform and toward the stairs to the street was suffocating. Ozzy couldn't tell one person from the next, and his vision was cut off in most directions because he was pressed up against other people. He held onto Sigi's hand and followed behind Rin.

Looking up, he realized that there was a problem.

"We'll never lose them," Ozzy said loudly. "Your hat and staff stick out like a beacon above the crowd."

"Of course," Rin replied. "Keep your heads low and get ready to pivot."

The wizard pushed through the crowd as if heading toward someone specific.

"Clark," Rin said loudly, "do you think you could make some noisy distraction off to our left without being seen?"

"I don't know," the bird chirped passive-aggressively. "Do you think you can keep a promise?"

"You make some noise and I'll give you three coats of finger paint. Plus something crinkly to chew on."

Clark needed no further persuading.

The bird crawled out of Ozzy's pocket and worked his way down toward everyone's feet. The space near the floor was tight and chaotic, but Clark was agile and quick. He zipped around people's legs like it was a connect-the-dots puzzle and completing the picture was a matter of life or death. When he reached the wall, he instantly began to stir things up.

Staying low against the ground, he forcefully bumped into the ankles of anyone near him. It only took a couple thumps before someone looked down. That same someone thought he was a rat and screamed accordingly. A small group of people near the screeching man joined in, trying to scatter and avoid the small black thing ricocheting off their feet.

Clark's distraction was perfect. The entire crowd of commuters temporarily turned their attention from what they were doing to look toward the commotion.

Rin jumped into action. He lunged forward and, with one impressive twist, pulled off his robe and placed it on the back of a vagrant who was working his way to homeless. Rin flipped his hat onto the man's head with his right hand. Then, executing a quick juke move, he pushed Ozzy and Sigi sharply to the left and through the thick noisy crowd while keeping his branch down.

The three of them kept their heads low until they reached the left wall. From there they turned and headed down a flight of stairs that led to another platform.

Ozzy felt Clark grab onto his leg and work his way back up to his pocket. When they reached the platform, there was another train getting ready to leave.

"*Holdorus forallaofus!*" Rin shouted while holding his branch up.

The three Oregonians and Clark slipped onto the subway a single second before the doors shut.

"That was close," Sigi said in awe.

"Nothing is close or far," Rin said, "just connected."

"Well, I'm glad that connection didn't end with us being slammed in the door, Dad."

Rin looked at his daughter. "Does your mother know you're here?"

"No."

"Good. I'd hate for her to worry."

The train they were on was half-empty, making it easy for Rin to find an open seat.

He sat down and smiled contently.

Rin looked like a different wizard without his hat and robe. He appeared younger and fitter than many of the wizards Ozzy had read about in books. His tree branch was resting against the metal bar in front of him.

"We can ride this train all the way to the airport," Rin announced. "It'll take about an hour."

Ozzy sat down next to him. "That was impressive. It's too bad you lost your robe and your hat."

"I've made a tremendous sacrifice."

"They're just things," Sigi reminded him as she sat on the other side. "And I can't believe that worked. You just put your stuff on someone and they followed him?"

"People love pursuing the things they already know and understand. It's not a good trait."

Rin put his arm around Sigi, and for the first time since Ozzy had known either of them, they looked like father and daughter. Without his hat it was easier to see the similarity of their eyes and how closely the shape of their ears matched. Sigi's skin was dark and nicely highlighted by the lights of the subway, while Rin was tan and fairly well preserved for his age, which he claimed was because of Quarfelt. According to him, things were so perfect there that it caused all wizards to age slowly.

Father and daughter sighed, and the movement and motion of their exhale was identical.

Unfair.

Ozzy heard the word in his head, broadcast throughout his being like a bulletin of envy. It was a strong, selfish emotion that he didn't like being a part of. He would never have what Sigi had, and because of that a suffocating feeling of hopelessness shook him as the train rolled over the tracks. The feeling was not hard to figure out.

Ozzy missed his parents.

The revelations he had had recently were neither satisfying nor comfortable. And no matter how he formulated the problem, the answer was never what he wanted.

His parents were gone.

A small part of him felt resentment. Ray's intentions seemed sinister, but the nagging thought of what he might know or what knowledge he could have given Ozzy made Ozzy wonder if he hadn't missed an opportunity to find out more. He had been afraid for himself and Sigi, but the fear he felt in the courtyard was nothing compared to what he had lived through over the last seven years.

Ozzy sighed in a way that didn't resemble Sigi or Rin at all, and the subway suddenly felt oppressive and lacking enough air to properly breathe.

The heavy moment was broken up by a bird, as Clark cleared his beak.

All three of them looked down at Ozzy's pocket. The bird's head stuck out and he looked up at them.

"I hate to be all self-involved and sparrow-like," he chirped, "but I'm wondering why nobody has brought up the fact that it was my distraction back there that really made our escape possible. It's not like it was easy. I got stepped on twice."

"Sorry," Sigi apologized.

"Me, too," Ozzy said, feeling the mood lighten with

the self-centered concerns of his bird. "Actually, I was just about to bring it up."

"Well, then, go ahead."

So as the train moved on in the direction of the airport, Rin, Sigi, and Ozzy all took turns extoling Clark's virtues and dishing out bird-worthy accolades. It was a nice distraction on a night that had already come with plenty.

And through it all the train rumbled on.

Ozzy and Sigi never looked around for any other wizards that might have been using the train. There was no need. They had Rin, and his presence made it feel like something was happening.

CHAPTER TWENTY-FIVE

REASONS TO WORRY

The subway car cleared out even more as people got off at each stop and no one new joined the journey. The train ran all the way to the airport. It appeared that only Ozzy and his group were among the few planning to take it that far. The three of them sat on the subway seats looking weary and worn. Without his hat and robe, Rin seemed a little less magical. With nobody but them in their part of the train, Clark crawled out of Ozzy's pocket and perched on his left knee.

The bird looked over at the trousers Rin was wearing.

"What's up with your pants?" Clark asked. "They're not as boring as before."

Rin sat up straight and sniffed. "I was given these because I'm now advanced."

"In age?" Clark asked.

"No," the wizard replied, "I have moved from novice to advanced."

"And they give you new trousers for that?" Ozzy questioned.

Rin nodded. "The wizard levels in Quarfelt are indicated by trousers. You should see the ones the grand wizard wears."

"So you advanced?" Sigi asked, sounding more embarrassed than proud.

It wasn't easy for Sigi to talk about Quarfelt. For years, her father had told stories about the place as if it really existed. It was humiliating to her and her mom. It was only recently that she had found the patience to believe in it for his sake. She had seen him work magic four months before, but for Sigi there was still doubt.

"I did," Rin answered her. "When I stepped back into Quarfelt I was immediately greeted with these. It seems that what we accomplished on that mountain helped me considerably."

"And to honor *that* they handed you pants?" Clark was still struggling with the idea. "Why not a trophy . . . or two trophies?"

"Trousers are a much more dignified and traditional reward. You should see the respect that other wizards were forced to give me when I walked by. The spell of envy is one I love to cast."

"Then why'd you come back?" Clark asked. "I would have just stayed there strutting around. Do they make those in size bird?"

"I don't think so," Rin answered. "Birds in Quarfelt

aren't big on modesty. I actually came back because Ozzy called."

Ozzy was shocked. "You got my phone messages?"

"No," Rin said. "Information like that is received differently in Quarfelt. A wizard named Ted poked me and told me there was some kid trying to reach me."

"Really?" Ozzy asked.

"Yes. I've got the bruise on my arm to prove it." Rin pulled up the right sleeve of his black T-shirt to show them a small bruise about the size and shape of a nickel. "Ted is a competitive poker."

"Did he tell you Sigi and I were in New York?"

"No. That wasn't necessary," Rin looked contemplative. "Let me think. . . . What's the best way to explain this?"

"Briefly," Clark suggested.

"No, that's not it," Rin said. "Here's the thing. Quarfelt knows where and when to open up and drop people off. And because time and space are so much different there, we can travel at remarkable clips. One minute I'm standing in a field near the Low-Wizard's summer vacation castle, and the next I'm in a courtyard watching some man who's too lazy to carry his own umbrella boss you two around."

"Amazing," Ozzy said.

"Yeah," Sigi said skeptically. "If that's the case, then it seems like you would have easily been able to attend at least one of my piano recitals over the last ten years."

"Who's to say I didn't?"

"Were you there?" she asked.

"No and yes."

Sigi sighed. "So, no."

"And yes," the wizard said defensively. "As in yes, I wasn't. A wizard's time is not always his own, and I don't make the schedule in Quarfelt. That's for someone with much nicer trousers than I. The important thing is that I'm here now. There's no need to worry about the 'what ifs' and 'how comes' of the past when we're moving forward."

Ozzy raised his hand—it was something he did a lot recently. Having lived alone for so long and having so many things that he still didn't know or understand, it seemed almost magical to be able to raise his hand at school and have someone automatically listen to him.

"You don't have to raise your hand here," Sigi said.

"I like it," Rin replied. "Very professional."

Ozzy put his hand down and spoke. "I'm looking for a way to explain what happened back there, but I can't. You appeared and saved us with magic?"

"I appeared and hit Mr. Too-Good-To-Hold-His-Own-Umbrella with this branch. He dropped Clark, and the two of us, combined with the weather, were able to create a bit of chaos so you and Sigi could get away. If you fail to see the magic in that, then I pity you."

"Are you taking credit for the weather?" Sigi asked.

"What are they teaching you in that school?" Now Rin looked embarrassed by his daughter's lack of knowledge. "Since the dawn of time wizards have used the elements to our advantage. Have you never heard the story of Merlin's Ark?"

"Yes," his daughter replied. "You used to tell it to me as a child, but what does it have to do with weather?"

"Well, for starters, that ark couldn't have flown without those tornadoes. And it illustrates the point that wizards use weather to disguise their gift all the time. Hiding magic in a storm or earthquake helps people with small thoughts cope. It gives them something to blame the phenomenon on."

"Please," Ozzy begged. "That's great, and very plaque-like, but I'm tired, and I just wanted a reasonable answer."

"Okay," Rin conceded. "Ask a question and I'll keep my answers reasonable."

"Almost four months ago you disappeared," Ozzy said seriously. "You left me and Sigi and Clark alone to make our way home and answer thousands of questions from Sheriff Wills, social workers, lawyers, everybody. We didn't know if you were dead, or lost, or ever coming back. Then we got a mysterious envelope with a plane ticket in it and the address to a hotel whose initials spell out your name."

Rin looked confused.

"Resort in New York," Sigi explained.

"My name's not Riny."

"That's what *I* said," Clark chirped.

"Forget that," Ozzy insisted. "Because even though it wasn't you who sent for us, it was you we found. I still can't figure out exactly what's real in this world and what things are just misunderstood ideas that I never figured out growing up alone."

"Alone?" Clark said with disgust.

"Alone with a winged piece of metal that doesn't know much more than I do."

"That's better," Clark said.

"And you," Ozzy said to Rin as he sat right next to him, "you make the space between reality and the unknown even more confusing. *I* think you're a wizard. I mean, after all we've been through, it really seems like a possibility. But there are also signs and science pointing toward the fact that you can't be."

"I'm not sure I heard a question in there," the wizard said kindly.

"I guess . . ." Ozzy paused to find the right sequence of words. "I guess I question everything about you."

Rin turned his head to look directly at Ozzy. His dark eyes reached into the boy's uncertain soul and began to pull out feelings of confusion and wonder.

The wizard stood up.

Even without his robe and hat, his 6'4" stature made him seem otherworldly. He took hold of a silver bar connected to the roof of the subway car and twisted his body to face both his daughter and Ozzy. There was no one else in their section of the train, making the scene feel empty. His beard appeared to wriggle and move even though there was no wind. Holding onto the bar with one hand, he lifted the other and pointed at Ozzy.

"You seem to have gotten better at speaking your mind," Rin observed. "That's going to bode well for us. You are no longer the boy who phoned me, desperate to find your parents. You are something different. I know what has been happening to you, strange forces doing things that you're not in control of. I know that worries you, but it doesn't worry me. A condition such as yours is something to be praised in Quarfelt. And you may find this hard to believe, but I arrived at the hotel because you were there."

Ozzy's finger buzzed and he closed his eyes.

"As you can tell by my trousers," the wizard continued, "I have moved forward with my training, but now I am at an impasse. I have been informed that any progress I make from this point will require the help of someone else. You see, no man is an island—unless you're talking about Karl." Rin looked defensive. "I'm sorry, I can turn someone *into* an enchanted island, but it's not my responsibility to turn them back."

"What?" Ozzy asked.

"Right. The point is that for me to move forward, I need an apprentice."

Ozzy opened his grey eyes.

"And I believe that apprentice is you."

Rin continued pointing at Ozzy.

"Is he talking about me?" Clark asked, standing on the boy's lap.

"I'm not," Rin said with conviction.

"And he's obviously not talking about me." Sigi sounded both disappointed and unsurprised.

"Of course not," Rin told her. "You're my daughter. You don't require apprenticeship. If magic is what you pursue, you will be grandfathered in."

"Because you're so old?" Clark asked Rin.

"No, it's just a term."

"I don't understand," Ozzy said. "You need an apprentice?"

Rin nodded.

"And you think that it's me?"

Rin nodded again.

"I'm not sure what to say," Ozzy admitted. "I know that what I've been through since meeting you is hard to define, but I still don't know if I'm a believer."

"Good," Rin said. "Doubt often brings answers."

"And what does apprenticeship require?" Ozzy asked. "I don't fit in great at school now. If I have to wear a robe and a hat, I think I'll be done for."

"You can wear what you wish."

"This doesn't make sense." Ozzy's finger buzzed and his forehead began to sweat. "I don't feel right. I think I need to be home to make this kind of decision."

"Of course," Rin agreed. "That's why we're headed to the airport."

"We might not be able to just fly out, you know," Sigi told them. "If Ray is as powerful as he said he is, he'll have people waiting at the airport to stop us. He knows what time we fly out—he bought Ozzy's ticket."

"Right," Rin said. "He *did* know. That's why I purchased us all tickets for a new flight leaving from a different airport tonight. It's not a direct flight, but it'll get us to Portland by way of Denver. And by the time Ray realizes you haven't shown up for your flight tomorrow morning we'll all be long gone."

"How'd you get tickets?" Sigi asked. "I thought you didn't have your wallet."

"That's not important," Rin insisted. "What really matters is that this is our stop."

The train began to slow.

Sigi and Ozzy stood up next to Rin, and Clark took his place in the boy's pocket. When the train came to a stop, the doors opened and they exited in silence.

There were numerous things to think about and worry over, but getting back to Oregon undetected was foremost on their minds.

"We're going home," Clark whispered happily.

"We haven't even been gone a day," Sigi reminded him.

"Still, I miss the mailbox."

Everybody has something they long for.

CHAPTER TWENTY-SIX

STOPPED SHORT

Once they were in the airport, Rin checked his branch as luggage.

"Be careful with that," he told the woman at the counter.

"It's just a branch," she said, sounding confused.

"It's funny how little some people see," he said, acting and sounding as if she couldn't understand. "This is much more than a branch."

"Well, then, maybe we shouldn't let you check it in," the woman said, throwing back some attitude. "It could be something dangerous."

"Right," Rin conceded. "It's just a branch."

The woman tagged the branch and printed out their boarding passes. The four of them moved away from the counter and sat down on a small cluster of chairs near the escalators, a bit out of the way, giving them a small amount of privacy. It was the perfect spot to figure out what to do with Clark. They needed to get the bird past security without having him taken away or causing a scene. They also needed to apply the nail polish that Clark had been whining for.

Clark sat on Ozzy's lap as the polish was applied and they all brainstormed.

"I could pretend I was a brooch and hang onto Sigi's shirt," the raven suggested.

Ozzy shook the nail polish.

"Nobody wears brooches anymore," Sigi informed the bird. "Especially one that looks like you."

"Maybe they'll think he's something harmless and just let him through," Ozzy said.

"I doubt that," Clark said. "Obviously I'm intimidating."

Ozzy opened the polish and brushed two streaks of black over the thin scratches Clark had procured during the courtyard fight.

"Much better," the bird said happily.

"What about a spell, then," Ozzy suggested to Rin. "Can't you say a few words and make Clark invisible? At least until we're through security? If you want me to be an apprentice, I probably need to know how to do things like that."

"True," Rin said. "But why make things more difficult than they have to be? Look."

The wizard pointed toward the ceiling. There, in the metal rafters, a real sparrow was flying around.

"It looks like some birds have gotten into the airport,"

he said. "So as much as I'd like to whip up a spell, I suggest that Clark just act like himself and fly though."

Clark looked up at the sparrow in the rafters.

"I'll be honest," he chirped softly. "I've always felt superior to real birds. But I don't mind pretending to be one for a few minutes. I'll just need to get into their heads." Clark rubbed his temples with the tips of his wings. "Okay, okay, I'm flighty and I like seeds. Wow, not much to work with. Maybe I should spend a moment with that real one before I slip into character."

Clark brushed his head feathers back with his wing. He blinked his small eyes and tried to look down at his freshly painted chest. Then, without saying a word, he shot up into the rafters. They watched him land by the real bird and begin squawking.

"That's great," Ozzy said to Rin. "But it's not a spell, and it didn't teach me anything."

"I'll try to not look disappointed," Rin said happily.

The three of them left the small grouping of chairs and walked across the ticketing area to security. The line was long, but it moved quickly. Rin without his wizard wear was just a taller-than-average person whom nobody seemed to stare at or make fun of. The only glitch was when Rin had to show the TSA agent his ID to get though. The agent looked at it a moment before saying,

"Good evening, Brian."

Rin bristled as Ozzy and Sigi smiled.

"I go by Labyrinth, but my friends call me Rin."

"I go by the IDs," the TSA agent informed him. "Are you traveling for work or pleasure, Brian?"

"All travel is pleasure," the wizard replied. "And it's Rin."

"Where are you flying to?"

"I believe it says that on the boarding pass that you're holding."

"Fair enough." The TSA agent stared directly at Rin's eyes. "Still I'd like to hear it from you."

"First off, I prefer 'More than fair,' and second, we're flying to Portland."

The TSA agent looked at the underdressed wizard and decided he didn't have the desire or the time to waste on him any longer.

"Enjoy your flight, Brian."

"It's Rin."

Sigi helped pull her father away from the agent and over to the conveyor belt, where they placed their shoes and bag in a bin. After going through the scanners, putting their shoes back on, and exiting the security area, Rin searched the airport directory on the wall for a place that might serve eggs at this time of day. There wasn't one.

"Reality is so backward," Rin said, frustrated. "Lack of breakfast food is a shame. These are some of the things you might be dealing with someday, Ozzy."

"It feels like I'm dealing with them now."

They settled for eating licorice and almonds from a vending machine.

When they reached their gate, people were already lining up to get on the flight. There was no sign of Ray or any of his security detail. There was also no sign of Clark.

"He'll get here," Sigi said.

They waited to board, hoping that Clark would show up. But eventually the gate agent informed them they needed to get on or the flight would take off without them.

"Don't worry," Sigi said, as she held Ozzy's hand. "I bet he slipped onto the plane before we got to the gate. We'll see him inside."

The wizard's daughter was typically an honest person, but she was wrong about Clark. Because after they got on the plane, they took their seats and the door was closed. Then, following a brief safety message, the aircraft took to the sky without any of them ever seeing Clark.

Rin wasn't concerned.

"Fretting about that bird is a waste of worry. I don't know a more capable thing. Do you think they serve pretzels on this flight?"

"You should have done a spell," Ozzy complained.

"I offered."

"Technically, you didn't," Sigi pointed out. "You only said you would have."

"Some words can have double meanings."

"Not any of those," Sigi insisted.

The flight to Denver was uneventful and a little disappointing because of a certain bird's absence—and a lack of pretzels.

While transferring planes in Denver, Ozzy hoped with renewed effort that Clark would appear.

He didn't.

The second flight, from Denver to Portland, was just as uneventful as the first and just as void of pretzels.

"Peanuts are like a trash snack in Quarfelt."

"Then let me have yours," Ozzy offered.

"That would be less than fair to Sigi."

When they landed in Portland, it was one in the morning and there was still no sign of Clark. They collected Rin's branch at baggage claim and then Ozzy bought three tickets for a shuttle bus that was heading to Otter Rock.

The weary travelers got in the shuttle and took seats in the rear. The only other passengers were the driver, whose name was Rene, and a woman wearing a shawl and shorts. The woman was lying across the first row of seats, doing what most people do at one in the morning—sleeping.

"This isn't good," Ozzy said as they traveled home, his stomach feeling queasy.

"Don't define things you can't clearly see," the wizard insisted. "I can't have an apprentice who lacks the patience to wait for the whole picture to come into focus before describing it."

"I'm not your apprentice."

"Once you realize what it comes with, you won't want to choose anything else."

"What does it come with?" Ozzy asked. "The ability to give vague advice and crave breakfast food?"

"Those are just happy byproducts. Apprenticeship comes with . . . the gift of wonder."

It was dark in the back of the shuttle bus, but Sigi rolled her eyes with such commitment that Ozzy could see it.

"Dad, you're making it sound worse."

"Then I have failed. Because, Ozzy, if you had any idea of what that meant, you would be weeping with joy and anticipation. This is not just a simple position or title. The wizard's apprentice is entitled to a single purchase of wonder."

"Well, then," Ozzy said, "I wonder where Clark is."

"He's right where he should be," the wizard insisted. "You just don't know where that is. In Quarfelt we call that being temporarily blind."

"Here we call it missing," Sigi said.

The woman who was lying across the front row seats began to whistle through her nose as she slept.

"What song is that?" Rin asked.

"It's not a song." Sigi's voice sounded embarrassed. "She's just breathing as she sleeps."

"Well, it's very haunting. Someone should record it."

"I would if I still had my *phone*." Sigi's tone was not happy. "Actually, I probably still wouldn't. You have a phone. Use yours."

"I'm out of space."

The shuttle van traveled west.

Sigi leaned her hair and head against the window and

closed her eyes. As the wheels of the vehicle sailed over the road, the engine hummed in time to the whistling nose.

After a dozen miles, Ozzy spoke to the wizard.

"Do I have to go to Quarfelt to be an apprentice?" he asked quietly.

"No. All five tasks will happen here."

"Five tasks?"

"Yes," Rin said with a hushed excitement. "The Cinco-Wizard Competition."

"Is that anything like the Triwizard Tournament in Harry Potter?"

"No, this one has five things. And it's just for you."

Ozzy groaned. "You know, I want to believe everything you say."

"I sincerely hope you don't."

"Does that mean you're lying about this quest?"

"The Cin-Wiz-Com? No, not at all. Your completing it is essential. What I need to do can't be done on my own, and I am wizard enough to know that I need help. But our first step is to figure out what's going on with you. You walked into the ocean and don't remember anything about the episode?"

"Only a feeling of fear."

"This seems to be tied to what your parents were working on, correct?"

Ozzy nodded.

Rin sighed in a way that seemed to empty the van of oxygen. "Your parents." He shook his head. "Sometimes people work so hard to manufacture magic that they ignore all the ruin they leave in their wake."

"Are you calling me ruin?"

"I'm just pointing out what seems most obvious. Tell me about your finger."

"It buzzes now."

"Is that new?"

"Sort of," Ozzy said quietly. "I first noticed it on the mountain as Charles was trying to kill us. For a moment my mind felt as if it had some control over him."

"And now . . ."

Rrrraaacccck!

Rin's words were cut short by the horrifying noise of something hitting the front window of the shuttle bus. Whatever it was struck with such force and surprise that Rene panicked and pressed on the gas instead of the brakes. His hands flailed as he spun the steering wheel and the bus flew off the edge of the road and down into a field of wet weeds and mud.

Rene shouted loud, fear-filled prayers as he fought to control the vehicle.

Everyone inside was tossed to the right as the shuttle bus came to a sudden and uneven stop in the mud. Sigi was baffled by waking up to such a chaotic scene, and the woman in the shorts and shawl wouldn't stop screaming as she tried to figure out what was happening.

"We hit something," Rene yelled at her. "We're all right!"

Sigi calmed down as Shorts-and-Shawl released a few quick squeals before trying to catch her breath.

Rene let go of the steering wheel and climbed out of the van to assess the damage. From where Ozzy was he could see that the front windshield was completely covered with cracks from the impact.

Ozzy looked at Rin. Rin smiled.

"And you were worried that Clark wouldn't find us," the wizard said happily.

Ozzy leaned forward and threw open the door. He stepped out into the dark and muddy field. The high beams and interior lights of the shuttle bus lit up a small ring of the ground outside the vehicle. Ozzy tried to calculate where Clark might have ended up after hitting the windshield.

"You'd better be okay," he whispered.

Ozzy walked to where the shuttle bus had come off the road. As he stepped through the mud something landed awkwardly on his left shoulder. He stopped walking.

"Wow," Clark said into Ozzy's left ear. "I didn't realize I was capable of getting a headache."

"You hit that windshield really hard," Ozzy said as he reached up and took his friend into his hand. "You're lucky you still have a head to ache. What were you thinking?"

"I missed the first flight in New York," the bird confessed. "I got to talking with that sparrow and lost track of time."

"Sparrows can't talk."

"I know—I had to carry most of the conversation," Clark complained. "After I missed the flight, I flew around the airport a while just to give people some thrills. I heard someone talking about their flight to Portland. So I followed them to their flight and hid out in a large paper bag some man was transporting a cake in. I must have blacked out from lack of charge, because I didn't wake up until the plane landed and the man noticed me in his bag. He made the mistake of holding me where there was light, and I made the mistake of scratching him more than was absolutely necessary to get free. Also—and this is the part where you might think less of me—I noticed there was a pen in the man's shirt pocket. It accidentally got caught up in my talons as I struggled to get away from him."

"You took someone's pen?"

"That's what you might think, but it turns out it wasn't *just* a pen. It was some sort of bendy pen light. Which, if you think about it, makes my taking it more of a fortunate circumstance than it was theft. I wouldn't have been able to fly in the dark without it. I bent it so that I was able to hold one end in my beak and have the other end back behind my head to light up my stripe. I must have dropped it when I hit the van. Can you help me look for it?."

"Not right now. That still doesn't explain why you hit our windshield."

"When I got to the airport I figured your plane had already landed and you were driving home. I just wasn't sure what vehicle you guys were riding in. So I had to fly up to each one I passed and take a look. Let me just say that some people don't react well to glowing birds peeking into their car windows. Anyhoo, long story short, I spent too much time looking into the windows of a Tesla Model 3 that was going much faster than any of the other cars, and when I turned back to investigate the few I'd passed up, I saw you guys through the windshield. I guess I was so excited that I flew into the glass. No harm, some fowl."

"That's not the expression."

"I'm pretty sure it is."

"It doesn't matter," Ozzy said. "I'm glad you're okay."

"I may have dented my beak."

"We can fix that."

Ozzy put Clark in his pocket and trounced through the mud and back to the van. Rin and Sigi were still in the vehicle with Shorts-and-Shawl. Rene was standing in the mud talking on his cellphone to someone who was coming to help.

Five minutes later, two police cars arrived.

Twenty minutes later, a backup shuttle bus with a driver named Stev got there.

And it was just after four in the morning when Ozzy and his crew finally arrived at 1221 Ocean View Drive. The shuttle dropped them off and Ozzy got a receipt from Stev.

"Remember to keep that receipt," Rin said. "I've heard that people use things like that for taxes."

Once they were inside, Rin opted to stay and sleep

on one of the couches in the living room. He wanted to make sure Ozzy didn't do something like jump out another window. There was also the risk of Ray sending someone around to cause more trouble. Things were concerning enough to require both a wizard and a guard-bird.

"Besides," Rin said as he searched the hall closet for a blanket to use, "I'm no stranger to couches. I spent many nights on them before the divorce all those years ago. Slightly fun fact—my place doesn't have an actual bed. It's more like a couch."

"I'm not really interested in couch talk," Sigi said. "So goodnight. Besides, I'm hoping all of this will make more sense in the morning."

"Well," Rin said, "that'll be fun to see."

And with that they all went their separate ways. Ozzy still had a missing window, so he went back to the couch in the study. Rin went to the couch in the living room, and Sigi went to her bed. Clark took a couple of minutes to make a new nest out of a few dish towels in the kitchen and then shut down.

In less than a minute, the house was filled with humming and snoring that would have made Shorts-and-Shawl proud.

CHAPTER TWENTY-SEVEN

BEING PULLED APART

Ozzy woke up before the others and quickly washed up and got dressed. The scratches on his arms and face were fading, but his body felt tired and beat-up from the long trip to New York. He stared at his grey eyes in the bathroom mirror, trying to imagine he saw anything that even remotely resembled a wizard's apprentice. His whole life he had wondered if he possessed any magical gifts or abilities, but he still saw no evidence in the mirror.

He left the bathroom by the kitchen and stopped near the microwave. He tapped Clark on the head in his towel nest and quietly said, "Shh," as Clark clicked and whirred to life.

From where they were, Ozzy could see into the living room. Rin was sound asleep on the couch. His branch was laying on the floor, and his long hair and beard spilled over the edge of the couch as he slept on his side.

"Wanna go for a ride?" Ozzy asked.

Clark jumped up onto Ozzy's shoulder and the boy and bird left the house as quietly as they could. They walked across the breezeway and entered the garage. Ozzy wheeled out the old motorcycle.

"I'm so glad we're doing this," Clark tweeted.

"Me, too."

"That trip was messed up."

"We got Rin."

"Like I said, messed up."

Ozzy put on his headphones and started the bike. With Clark flying next to him, he rode down the driveway and into the forest. It wasn't legal for him to drive the motorcycle on the roads, so he had found a route that took him through fields and forests until he reached Mule Pole Highway. When the highway was clear, he crossed it and traveled through the forest along the same routes he used to walk heading into town. This morning, however, he traveled the path in reverse, heading toward the spot where his heart still resided. With his earbuds in, the music made the experience seem much bigger than just a boy riding a motorcycle among the trees.

Clark raced through the air next to Ozzy.

Using wheels and wings, the journey took considerably less time than it used to on foot. In no time at all, they arrived at the place where Ozzy felt most complete. He turned off the motorcycle and the music.

Clark settled on his shoulder and they looked longingly at their onetime home.

The cloaked house was just that, a small wooden cabin almost completely hidden by the overgrown forest. The front porch was a bed of wildflowers and the windows were decorated with wide fans of branches and ivy. Tall trees circled the home, their leafy appendages covering most of the roof. In some spots, branches had pushed themselves through the walls and roofline.

"I wish we could still live here," Clark said solemnly. "I mean, I like Sigi's place, but where's the charm?"

Ozzy stepped onto the porch. It was the last place he had ever seen his parents. They had been taken from that very spot.

It was his darkest memory, and Ozzy had more than a few dark ones to choose from.

Despite the home being a reminder of sadness, the cloaked house was a piece of the world that Ozzy found worthwhile.

He unlocked the front door.

In the past, there had been no locks on the doors or the windows. But when he moved out, Patti and Sigi had helped him install some so that it would be more secure as it sat alone in the forest.

"I hate that there are locks on the door," Ozzy said.

"Same," Clark agreed, "but I'd be lying if I didn't admit that I like the keys."

Inside, the house was still filled with boxes. There were far fewer than there once had been, but piles of book-filled boxes still dominated the space. They were the same boxes his parents had shipped here when they'd first moved from New York.

"I'm going to go see if that annoying squirrel is still hiding out in that tree near the stream," Clark said.

The bird dashed out the front door and Ozzy took a seat on a small red couch. He put his headphones back on and pressed play. He was a fan of silence, but like the Ben Folds Five cassette that his parents had left, the new CD was more than just lyrics and melody. It was a connection that he desperately needed and a cure for some of the sadness he felt.

And all the world was used to love
And yes, we'd still be happy in another time

Ozzy stood up from the couch and walked between the tall piles of boxes to the stairs with the black stars painted on them. He climbed the starry steps to reach the attic bedroom in which he'd slept and dreamed for so many years. He gazed out the round window at the forest view he knew so well. For a moment the home felt like a weight, a piece of his past that was anchoring him to a sadness he shouldn't hold on to. It was a tombstone, a place he visited to remind himself of all he had lost.

The feeling began to suffocate him, and when he looked down at his hand, he could see that his finger was buzzing.

"No, no, no. Not now."

His eyes became cloudy and his heart raced.

"Clark!"

Ozzy's mind took over.

The boy turned from the window and descended down the starry stairs. He walked swiftly through the boxes, out the front door, and climbed onto the motorcycle. He started it up and tore off into the trees, heading west.

His mind maneuvered the bike through the forest as his speed increased.

Hearing the motorcycle engine start up, Clark stopped arguing with the squirrels and flew off to investigate. By the time he caught up to Ozzy, the boy was racing through the forest at a frightening and dangerous speed.

"What are you doing?" Clark squawked as he flew near Ozzy. The bird dodged two tree branches and a large bush. "This can't be safe!"

Ozzy swerved around a large oak tree and narrowly missed a massive stone jutting out of the ground.

"Seriously! Stop!"

Clark flew onto Ozzy's back and began clawing at his shoulders with his talons. When that got no response, he started pecking him in the ears and on top of his head.

"Snap out of it!" he tweeted loudly. "You're going to kill yourself! And you're not wearing a helmet!"

Ozzy wove around three trees as if he were on an obstacle course.

Clark shot down and grabbed the top of the helmet, hooked onto the back of the motorcycle. He yanked it off and flew up. As he tried to jam the helmet down on Ozzy's head, he hit a small overhead branch and spun sideways. The helmet went down, but it was on backwards. Ozzy was blind.

"Crow!" Clark exclaimed.

Even without his sight, Ozzy swerved and maneuvered perfectly through the trees.

Clark grabbed onto Ozzy's shirt at the back of his neck. "Sorry!"

Ozzy kept racing.

"You can't see!" the bird yelled. "Where are you going, anyway? This is the way to the beach! Wait—are you just trying to recreate the good times we used to have?"

Ozzy didn't answer.

"We had some laughs, but it wasn't worth dying for!"

The motorcycle was running at top speed, and Ozzy was weaving and maneuvering through the forest like a skilled, blindfolded pilot.

Clark clung to Ozzy's shirt and continued to peck and scratch. He looked up and saw that the woods were coming to an end.

"You can't see it, but the trees are ending!" the bird screeched. "You're heading to the stone and sand?"

Clark's warning was too late.

The motorcycle burst out of the forest and flew twenty feet through the air before coming down hard on the stony ground that ran into the sand. The bike bounced and shook as it continued to race forward.

Remarkably, Ozzy held tight and stayed atop the motorcycle.

"Stop!" Clark insisted.

As if listening, the motorcycle obeyed. Ten feet before the water, the front tire hit a patch of sand soft enough to pull the wheel down and stop the motorcycle in its tracks. The back of the bike flipped up and sent Ozzy sailing straight into the ocean.

Clark clung to Ozzy's shirt, chirping, "I'm too interesting to die!"

They splashed down into the water and Ozzy instantly came to—his mind was his own again. It took a moment for him to realize what was happening, but once he did, he stopped thrashing about and pulled the helmet off. He stood up.

The water was only waist high.

"Owww," he hollered, pulling Clark off the back of his shirt. "What are you doing?"

"I didn't want to sink in the ocean, and I couldn't let you go," Clark chirped.

Ozzy felt the back of his neck where Clark had given him a few good scratches. "What happened?"

"You took off and were trying to drive into the ocean."

"Is the motorcycle okay?"

"*That's* what you're worried about?" Clark complained.

Ozzy glanced around and saw the portable CD player lying nearby on the sand. He walked out of the water and picked it up.

"We should get you home," Clark insisted. "This is just the sort of thing a wizard should be dealing with."

Ozzy stood on the shore near the bike and stared out at the sea.

"Do you think it's weird that I've tried to head into the ocean twice?"

"I think there's lots of weird things about you."

Ozzy's finger buzzed.

"What's wrong with me?"

"This is the kind of thing you should ask Rin."

Ozzy lifted the motorcycle and got on. Both he and the bird were relieved when it started up on the first try.

"Do you care if I hitch a ride?" Clark asked. "That last flight took a lot out of me."

The bird grabbed onto Ozzy's shirt and held on tightly as they drove through the trees and back toward 1221 Ocean View.

There was something in the water, and now Ozzy knew it. Something—or someone—was pulling him toward the sea.

His mind raced to find a reason.

CHAPTER TWENTY-EIGHT

I JUST DON'T CARE

Ray was unhappy, and when Ray was unhappy, a whole host of other people felt the discomfort along with him. His men had lost Ozzy in the courtyard, failed to catch him on the subway, and somehow let the boy fly out of New York.

"This is unacceptable!" Ray yelled at the head of his security team. "He's a boy and he slipped your grasp. Pathetic."

"We'll get him back."

"No, you won't," Ray said. "He's in Oregon now. You're no longer involved."

"Yes, sir."

"But stay," Ray ordered.

The guard did as he was told. He'd been through the drill before. Ray was a powerful person who lacked close friends or mentors with whom he could share his thoughts. In the past he had used Charles, but Charles was dead.

Ray was the kind of person who needed to hear his own voice, and he required someone to listen patiently.

"You don't understand," Ray said, seething. "This boy possibly holds the key to something so powerful it could change the course of all history."

The guard stayed put and kept quiet.

"And I want that bird," Ray pouted. "I need that bird. Is it too much to ask that people do what they're told? And the other visitor in the courtyard. Was that the wizard? Just some pathetic actor trying to live out a fantasy? Well, now I have a score to settle with him. Nobody strikes me down."

The guard stared straight ahead without blinking.

"I want that bird," Ray said again. "I want that bird, that wizard, and that boy. The girl is not a concern."

The guard remained expressionless.

Ray picked up a paper from his desk. It was a notice from a source telling him about Ozzy's parents' safety deposit box in Portland and that the contents had been given to the boy. Ray threw the paper down on the desk.

"What a child. Ozzy Toffy. He doesn't understand what he's doing. He's as blind as his parents were."

Ray stood up and walked out from behind his desk. He stared up at the giant bodyguard and poked him in the chest. "That boy doesn't understand! I will sacrifice *everything* I have to get what I want."

Ray looked the guard up and down.

"Go," he finally said.

The guard was happy to leave. As he exited the office,

he questioned his life and wondered how much longer he could put up with the madness and cruelty that was Ray Dench.

At the moment, even one more day seemed too long.

CHAPTER TWENTY-NINE

I STARE AT THE WINDOW

When Ozzy got back to 1221 Ocean View, it was just past noon. Sigi was in her room and Rin was in the kitchen making eggs and bacon. He was wearing a new yellow robe and a new gray felt hat that both looked remarkably similar, though a little less beat-up, to what he had placed on the unsuspecting homeless man in the New York subway.

"Hey," Ozzy said as he saw the wizard. "You got new clothes?"

"I made a quick trip to my house."

"I always forget you have a house," Clark said, settling onto the edge of a sink. "Where is it?"

"Not far." The wizard skillfully flipped the two eggs in the pan.

"What's it shaped like?" the bird asked.

Rin stopped to think. "Hard to say—it has angles and edges. Oh, and there's a moat."

"You have a moat?" Ozzy asked. "Like a castle?"

"I don't like to brag," the wizard said.

"Is that because your castle doesn't have a bed?" Ozzy said.

"Wizards prefer couches," Rin insisted. "They bridge the world between sleeping and sitting much better than a flat mattress."

"I can see that," Clark agreed. "Maybe I should reconfigure my nest to be more couch-like."

"I highly recommend it."

Rin slid the fried eggs out of the pan onto a plate. Then he threw a couple of pieces of bacon into the skillet. As he turned to grab the spatula, he knocked over a glass of orange juice he had poured earlier. The glass fell to the ground and shattered, spilling juice and bits of glass all over the floor. Rin looked at Ozzy as if busted.

"When did you say Patti would be home?"

"In two days, on Tuesday."

"Whew."

Rin cleaned up the mess as his bacon sizzled. Clark offered to help, but then flew off before the wizard said yes.

"Have you thought about what I said yesterday?" Rin asked Ozzy, wiping orange juice off the floor.

"Yes," Ozzy said seriously, "and I don't think I'm the apprentice you're looking for."

"Oh," Rin said, "right. I was actually talking about how I said you should keep your receipts for tax purposes.

But the apprentice thing is the most important. It shows great Rin-telligence that you brought it up."

"*Rin-telligence* is not a word. And I don't think I should be worrying about any of that right now. I have bigger things to concern myself with. Things like Ray. Also, I just drove the motorcycle into the ocean."

Rin stood up. "Interesting. On purpose?"

"No. In fact, I don't remember doing it. One minute, I'm standing in the cloaked house and the next minute I'm in the ocean and Clark's yelling about not wanting to die."

"He does fear drowning."

"So do I," Ozzy said sincerely. "I'm going to wake up dead if I don't figure it out."

Clark flew back into the kitchen squawking at Ozzy. "I know you don't like surprises, but . . . surprise! Someone's here."

"Who?"

"That guy with the mustache?"

Ozzy just stared.

"He's bossy," Clark added. "And he drives that flashy car."

Ozzy and Rin followed the bird into the large living room. Through one of the windows they saw a police car parked in the driveway.

"Oh," Ozzy said, "it's Sheriff Wills." He turned to look at Rin, but Rin was nowhere to be seen.

Clark fluttered in the air looking around.

"Where'd he go?" the bird chirped. "He just disappeared."

"I don't think he wants to talk to the sheriff."

"Neither do I."

The doorbell rang and Clark flew off. Ozzy walked to the door and pulled it open.

Sheriff Wills stood on the front porch looking serious. The tall sheriff's green uniform was a couple sizes too small. His thin mustache was nicely trimmed and his brown hair was in the process of surrendering to the gray creeping up around his neck and ears.

"Hello, Ozzy," he said. "Mind if I come in for a moment?"

"I don't think I do," Ozzy said honestly. "Unless you're planning to tell me something I don't want to hear."

Sheriff Wills didn't smile or respond.

"Oh," Ozzy said nervously. "Am I in trouble?"

There was still no smile. "Is there a place we can sit down?"

Ozzy stepped out of the doorway and the sheriff came in. He walked through the foyer and into the large living room. Ozzy closed the front door and followed him.

"Mind if I sit?" Sheriff Wills asked as he sat down on a large white couch in front of the window.

"No," Ozzy replied needlessly. He then took a seat on a blue wingback chair across the room, facing the sheriff and the window.

"How are you doing, Ozzy?"

Sheriff Wills and Ozzy currently had a civil relationship. Ozzy had caused the sheriff a great deal of stress in the past, but in the last few months Sheriff Wills had attempted to be helpful where he could. He had checked up on Ozzy and assisted his lawyer with some of the things that had needed to be sorted out.

"I'm doing well," Ozzy reported.

"Good to hear. Have you traveled anywhere lately?"

"You mean like to school and back?"

"No. I mean like to New York and back?"

Ozzy gulped mentally, but kept quiet.

"I got a call from their police department this morning," Wills said. "They were asking me questions about you. They also wanted me to question you about some damage that was done to a hotel there."

"I don't understand." Ozzy knew that Rin was somewhere in the house. He also knew that now would be a good time for the wizard to use some magic. "What damage? What hotel?"

"Damage to some trees at a fancy hotel."

"I like trees," Ozzy said defensively, trying very hard not to glance at the branch lying next to the wall.

"I'm sure you do. They also said that Sigi was there, and another man who they described as . . ." Sheriff Wills pulled out a small notepad from his breast pocket and opened it. Reading from the page, he said, "A lunatic wearing a bathrobe and a pointed hat."

Ozzy tried to look shocked.

"Does that sound like anyone you know?" the sheriff asked.

"No. It's been a long time since I lived in New York," Ozzy answered. "But I've heard it's full of strange people."

"Where's Patti?" Wills said looking around.

"She's in Seattle at a conference."

"Does she know you went to New York?"

Before Ozzy could speak, another voice joined the conversation.

"Nice try," Sigi said as she entered the room. "He didn't say he went to New York."

There were many reasons why Ozzy was happy to see Sigi. On a good day she was easily his favorite human in the world. And on a day like today, as she stood in a white printed T-shirt, wearing blue jean shorts and black Doc Martens, Sigi looked too good to be real—like a Disney princess that had burned down the castle and was living by her own rules. Her dark curls surrounded her head and face, creating a halo of hair that made her eyes look as if they could see the past, present, and future.

"Sigi," Sheriff Wills said, acting unfazed by her interruption, "so you weren't in New York with your father?"

"I'm not sure why that's any of your concern." Sigi had a hard time with authority, especially when it came from Sheriff Wills.

The sheriff shifted the subject.

"Where did you get those cuts, Ozzy?"

"I fell out of my window. It was during all that wind two nights ago."

"How does someone fall out of their window?"

"With the help of gravity," Sigi informed him. "Maybe you should come back when my mother's here."

"I'm only trying to help," the sheriff said. "The officer I spoke to in New York insisted that I pick Ozzy up and take him in for questioning. I told them we don't just do that without probable cause."

Both Ozzy and Sigi stared at him.

"He also wanted me to find out if you had received anything from your lawyer."

"What?" Ozzy said, his finger buzzing.

"I guess they were concerned that you might have gotten something that didn't belong to you."

"Like what?" Sigi asked.

"He wouldn't tell me." Sheriff Wills stopped and looked as if he were carefully weighing what he should say next. "I think you know that your lawyer's office was broken into a few days ago."

"That's what Ryan said." Ozzy kept his finger under his leg as he sat.

"I talked to Ryan this morning, and he wouldn't admit it, but I have a feeling that he received something in the mail and gave it to you. The same something that someone broke into his office trying to find."

"I think you're mistaken," Ozzy said. "He only gave me a picture and a music CD."

"Really? I don't suppose you'd let me see them?"

Ozzy walked to the kitchen to retrieve the CD he had been listening to a few minutes earlier. He could hear Sigi telling Sheriff Wills that he was out of line as he pulled the compact disc out of the portable player and slipped it into its case. Returning to the living room, he handed it to Wills.

The sheriff looked closely at the picture and studied the case. He pulled out the CD and examined the small piece of paper with the long number on it.

"What's this number for?"

"We don't know," Ozzy answered. "Ryan tried to figure it out, but he couldn't."

Sheriff Wills handed the CD back and sighed.

"You know, you might not believe this, but I'm worried about you."

"Thanks," Ozzy said sincerely.

"Yeah," Sigi said with less sincerity, "that's nice, but he's fine."

"And what about Brian? . . . I mean Rin," he said. "You haven't seen him?"

"Not for a while." Ozzy was lying on a few levels. For one thing, he had seen Rin in New York. He had also seen him earlier making eggs. And now he was watching the wizard out the front window messing with the sheriff's patrol car. Ozzy tried to not look surprised as he witnessed Rin climb into the police car and release the parking brake.

"How long is a while?" Sheriff Wills asked.

"You know," Ozzy said nervously, "a while."

Sigi could see what Ozzy saw and was trying to remain calm.

"You two are smart kids," the sheriff said. "I'd hate for you to be getting into more trouble. I know that Brian . . . Rin . . . is your father, Sigi, but he has some things I believe he needs help with."

"Um . . . he's just fine," Sigi said unconvincingly, watching her father standing in front of the parked police car waving at them.

Ozzy had to fight the urge to wave back.

Rin began to push the vehicle down the driveway.

"He's not fine," the sheriff insisted kindly. "And he still owes me a few answers about what happened."

Outside, Rin shoved the car until it was rolling, and then he seemed to disappear into the rocks and trees on the other side of the drive.

Sigi's dark eyes couldn't hide her shock.

"Are you okay?" the sheriff asked, turning his head to look out the window. He saw his car rolling backward down the driveway. He hopped up, used a few non-professional words, then dashed out the front door and down the drive, chasing his rolling car which was quickly gaining speed.

Ozzy and Sigi stood up. Through the window they watched the poor man unsuccessfully try to stop his vehicle. He didn't even get to it before it rolled off the driveway and down a small grassy slope. It came to a noisy stop after slamming into a big decorative boulder and wedging itself between two trees.

All Ozzy and Sigi could do was stare out the window in disbelief.

"I hope the engine's okay," Clark tweeted as he fluttered next to them.

"Oh, boy," Rin said as he appeared behind them. "That's only going to make him mad."

Sigi jumped at the sound of her father's voice. "You scared me."

"Wizards can be intimidating," Rin replied.

"You probably shouldn't have done that," Ozzy said.

"My plan was just to turn his car invisible. But then I got to thinking how touchy he can be. If he couldn't see it, he might accuse someone of stealing it." Rin's eyes went wide as he stared out the window. "Uh, oh, here he comes."

The bird and wizard disappeared again.

Through the window Ozzy and Sigi watched the angry sheriff stomp up the drive and back onto the front porch. He knocked aggressively on the door as he pushed it open and stepped inside.

"What happened?" Sigi questioned innocently.

"The brake was released," he answered angrily.

"Didn't you put it on?" Ozzy asked.

They both watched the sheriff count to ten in his head as he tried to calm down.

"I've radioed for help," he finally said. "It's going to take a tow truck to get it out of those trees."

"If we can help, let us know," Ozzy offered.

"You can help by not leaving this house," he insisted. "I don't think you understand what some people will do to get their way. That call from New York made me uneasy. You two are in danger, and I can't help unless you let me."

Neither Ozzy nor Sigi said anything.

"Just please stay put," he begged.

"Tomorrow's Monday—we have school," Sigi informed him.

"Take the bus. We'll make sure you're not followed. Just try not to get in trouble or do anything that draws attention," he growled. "I want to keep you safe."

Sheriff Wills stormed out of the house to the end of the driveway and sat on the boulder next to his errant car.

Clark and Rin were instantly back.

"He seems bothered," Clark observed.

"Some people," the wizard said, shaking his head sadly. "Now my eggs are cold. When I'm done, we need to sit down and discuss what lies ahead."

"'What lies ahead'?" Ozzy asked. "That sounds ominous."

"It is," Rin replied. And with that, the wizard disappeared into the kitchen.

CHAPTER THIRTY

STICKY SITUATION

A couple of hours later, a tow truck finally pulled Sheriff Wills's car out of the trees. In its absence, another police vehicle remained parked on the road at the bottom of the driveway. The officer inside had been told to keep an eye on the house.

Ozzy, Sigi, and Clark all stayed indoors worrying about their new problem. Rin was with them, but he wasn't worried.

"I don't like being watched," Sigi said. "It's like we're under house arrest."

"Don't get me started," Clark chirped. "I'm a bird—any thought of being cooped up or caged makes me sick."

As they complained, they were taping a huge tarp over Ozzy's missing window. Ozzy and Sigi were standing on chairs, positioning the top of the tarp while Rin and Clark handed them pieces of tape.

"Are we supposed to feel safer with a police officer

down the road?" Sigi pulled the tarp up to the left corner of the window frame and stuck it in place with a piece of tape. "Because I don't feel safer. I feel bothered."

"There's no reason to feel bothered," the wizard insisted. "Having someone on the lookout might actually help. Things are happening at a much faster pace than I originally anticipated."

"What things?" Ozzy asked.

"Well, not this." Frustrated, Rin pulled a piece of tape off his hands. "I've never been good with this mischievous stuff."

"I'm great with it," Clark said after delivering a piece to Ozzy. "I like how the sticky part feels in my beak. Which is weird, because you'd think I'd be tape-shy after the airport incident."

"I need some more," Sigi said.

Rin tore a piece of tape off the roll he was holding and lifted it up. Clark swooped in and carried it up to Sigi.

"What things are happening faster?" Ozzy asked again.

"Well, my exit time, for one."

"You're going to leave?" Sigi asked.

"Everyone leaves," the wizard said. "It's just unknown as to where, or how long. A person might go down the hall to the bathroom. Or they might disappear into a completely different realm."

"That's not comforting," Ozzy said. "*Are* you leaving?"

"Someone needs to make sure the quest is progressing," Rin answered, "and it seems as if there are a few loose ends left over from the mission we thought was finished." Rin pulled more tape off his fingers. "New York has reached out to Wills, which means the gap is closing between reality and Quarfelt. But don't worry—I promise we'll find a way to stop whatever Ray is doing."

"You don't need to promise me," Ozzy insisted. "I don't care about Ray or what we might find. I found what I was after months ago. I'm done."

Rin looked at Ozzy with compassion. "Sometimes the finish line moves."

"So I'm *not* done?" Ozzy was exasperated.

"You can live as you lived for so many years in the cloaked house," Rin said supportively. "Alone, just waiting for life to happen. Or you can walk forward and jump on the back of something that might take you farther. Wonder comes along with the solutions, whether they're painful or not."

"My parents are dead," Ozzy said. "How much more painful can it get?"

"You'd be surprised at what a wide shadow sorrow can cast. I can't promise you the answers will be found in the light, because I know very well how prevalent shade can be."

"Why won't this Ray guy just leave me alone?"

Rin looked at Ozzy's finger. "I think you know why."

"My finger?"

"Tell me—were you born with that birthmark?"

Ozzy nodded.

"Are you sure?" Rin turned to look at Clark. "Bird, do

you know that CD case that's in the living room near the window?"

"The one that's as big as me?"

The wizard nodded. "Will you bring it here?"

"I can't fly through doors," Clark said sadly. "Unless you can give me the power to."

"Take Sigi instead."

Sigi stepped down off her chair and opened the bedroom door. She left the room with Clark to get the CD. As soon as they'd left, Rin spoke.

"I saw that CD and picture you showed the sheriff. Where did they come from?"

"My parents had a safety deposit box in Portland. Ryan gave them to me two days ago."

"Of course," Rin said strangely. "Was there anything else?"

"A number and the envelope it all came in."

"What number?"

Sigi and Clark were back, causing the wizard to temporarily stop talking. The bird flew up to Rin and dropped the case in his hands.

"What's on the CD?"

"Music," Ozzy answered. "The Cure."

"I know them," Rin said. "I've always felt bad for the singer, Robert Smith. What a boring name. He should change it to Reef Slaymander."

"I prefer Robert Smith," Ozzy said.

"Is this why you had us get the CD?" Sigi asked. "So you could tell us what your stage name would be?"

"No," Rin said kindly, "I want Ozzy to look at this picture." Rin lifted the case up to Ozzy on the chair.

The boy took a few moments to study the photo he had slipped into the front of the CD case. He looked at his mom and dad sitting on a blanket in a park. He saw himself sitting between them, propped up and smiling. In the picture he was one or two, and his hands were resting on his legs. Ozzy studied his hands.

"My finger," he whispered.

"Let me see." Sigi reached up and took the picture from Ozzy. She focused and then looked up. "There's no birthmark."

From his spot on the chair, Ozzy looked down at Rin.

"This isn't me?" he asked, confused.

"Yes, it is," Rin said.

"I don't understand."

"That's not a birthmark," he explained. "Which means you must have gotten it another way."

"How do you get a birthmark from something besides birth?" Sigi asked.

"Ozzy did, and now he's tagged," Rin said casually.

"Like the stripe on my back?" Clark chirped.

"Not at all," the wizard replied. "Something happened to you, Ozzy, and the result of that something is the mark on your finger."

"How do you know that?" the boy said defensively.

"I came back because of it," Rin admitted. "You're marked, and that means something."

Ozzy stepped down from his chair and stood next to Sigi.

"That makes no sense," she said. "Ozzy's parents aren't connected to your Quarfelt."

Rin's eyes closed and he softly blew as if he were trying to extinguish a shy flame on a birthday candle. He opened his brown eyes and looked at his daughter and Ozzy as they stood side by side.

"I can only say it so many ways, but you must believe me when I tell you that all things are connected. In this world, some have a misguided need to be evil. We must make sure that those who walk such selfish paths don't trample the hope that Ozzy can bring."

"I don't feel hopeful. I feel sick."

"Feelings are the last thing you should trust," the wizard replied. "Now, I must leave you all for a short spell. But when the time is right, I will return."

"Why would you leave now?" Sigi said incredulously. "We could be in real trouble."

"You are," Rin replied. "And the clock's ticking."

Ozzy stared at the wizard.

"You'll be okay until I return. Wills will keep an eye on you. Just make sure you don't tell him I was here. This is an important part of the Cin-Wiz-Com. You must find your first challenge without my help."

"What?" Sigi asked, confused.

"Ozzy understands," Rin said. "So listen closely to my meaningful last words as I leave. Because I will be standing where the answer was found." Rin stopped talking and just stood there.

"Are those your last words?" Ozzy asked confused.

Rin started to say something but stopped as he realized that if he did, it would make the words he had just said his second-to-last words.

The wizard walked out of Ozzy's bedroom without saying another word—or having said anything meaningful, for that matter.

"Is it me or is that wizard flightier than a bird?"

"Did he really just leave?" Ozzy's face burned. "I don't get it. 'I will be standing where the answer was found.' That doesn't help."

"He said he'll be back," the bird reminded them.

"When?" Sigi complained. "And what is Cin-Wiz-Com?"

"It's the Cinco-Wizard Competition," Ozzy said, sounding embarrassed. "Apparently, there are five challenges I have to complete as an apprentice."

Sigi stared at Ozzy feeling more embarrassed. "Sometimes I'm jealous that you grew up with no parents."

"Don't be," Ozzy replied. "I'd take odd over absent any day."

"Well," Clark tweeted, "Sigi's got both."

The bird gathered more tape as the wizard's daughter and the abandoned apprentice finished putting up the tarp, trying to find some hope in what felt like a hopeless situation.

CHAPTER THIRTY-ONE

CONTROLLING OTHERS

Ozzy and Sigi stood at the end of the driveway as the school bus pulled up at 8:14 Monday morning. Ozzy liked knowing that the driver was intentionally stopping just for them. They climbed on and took the short ride to school with a police car following. Clark had decided to stay at the house and act as guard bird in case anyone came around. It felt strange not having the bird in his pocket. Clark had stretched out the right-hand pockets in all of Ozzy's trousers into a custom-sized place for him to be carried around.

When they reached their destination, Ozzy and Sigi got off the bus and parted ways.

Otter Rock High School was a typical high school. There were teachers and students and lockers and halls. It had a cafeteria, a gym, and classrooms set up to teach specific things in a very general way. The outside was boxy and ordinary, with a blue bulldog painted on the front.

Inside, the walls were white, the floors were blue, and the ceiling was a shade of gray that nobody would ever choose as their favorite color.

Ozzy walked down B Hall toward his first class. He was wearing a black shirt with blue jeans and burgundy sneakers. Getting his clothes to match was something he still struggled with. It was a life skill he just couldn't master. Living alone, he had never thought about clothes or worried about things matching. Now that he was a part of society, he did. Sigi was willing to give him advice on the matter, but he wanted to be able to do things on his own, so he rarely asked for help.

This morning he'd done okay, and his burgundy-colored feet helped move him down B Hall. He weaved through other students making their way to places all of them didn't want to be.

For the most part, Ozzy was still ignored at school. There had been stories about what he and Sigi had been through, but they hadn't been told by either Ozzy or Sigi. He was a mystery, just unusual enough for others to stay away for fear that they might be judged for talking to him. He was fortunate to be tall and good looking, but the combination didn't draw people to him, it just helped them whisper kinder things than they might about someone less attractive. Ozzy had an ally in Sigi, but her relationship with the odd boy who now lived above her garage was something that added to the general misunderstanding and mystery of Ozzy Toffy.

Some people might find the feeling of not fitting in too much to bear, but despite being a puzzle piece that had not found its spot, Ozzy liked school. He liked the warm lunches and the conversations he overheard. He liked the huge bathrooms and the drinking fountains. He liked asking questions and hearing answers about everything from Shakespeare to Snapchat. Which is why he smiled slightly as he entered his class and sat in the empty front row.

The teacher, a man named Mr. Hook, had a face that even a mother might struggle to love. His forehead was lumpy and his small mouth did not fit his big head. He began the class by insisting everyone put down their phones and pay attention to him.

Since he didn't own a phone, Ozzy was already ahead of the pack.

"None of you know what it's like to be bored," Mr. Hook said in a huff. "Stare, stare, download, like. This is a geometry class, not a gee-look-at-me class." Mr. Hook paused. It was evident by the quarter-smile on his small lips that he had thought up the bad pun over the weekend and was thrilled to have used it.

Nobody laughed.

"Lame dad joke," a girl two rows behind Ozzy said loudly.

Almost everyone laughed.

"Well, how's this for funny?" a pride-wounded Mr. Hook asked. "If I catch you with your phones out I'll take away ten points from your final test at the end of the semester."

Nobody thought that was funny, but everyone put their phones away.

"Are we all good?" Mr. Hook asked sarcastically.

Ozzy's left hand began to buzz. In a panic, he whispered, "No."

"Excuse me?" his teacher said. "You don't even have a phone."

The class laughed as Ozzy put his hand under his desk to keep it hidden.

"You'd be better off not acting like the rest of this group," Mr. Hook chastised. "Keep your comments to yourself, unless they're constructive or helpful."

Ozzy's hand buzzed again. "Uh, oh."

Mr. Hook's pale round face grew pink. "I think what you meant to say was, 'Yes, sir.'"

Ozzy had no idea what he meant to say, because he was no longer himself. He stood up next to his desk and looked around slowly.

"What are you doing? Take your seat."

Ozzy turned and walked to the door as the other students looked on in joy—class was being disrupted, and they all seemed happy about it.

"Where are you going?" Mr. Hook shouted. He hustled over to cut Ozzy off, but the boy just pushed him aside and exited the room. "Stop!"

Ozzy walked east down the hall as Mr. Hook shouted after him.

"Get back here! Take two more steps and you'll be looking at detention! Mr. Toffy! Mr. Toffy, stop!"

His teacher could have shouted anything he wanted, but it wouldn't have made Ozzy stop what he was doing or turn around. Mr. Hook followed after him.

Ozzy reached the end of B Hall and walked out into the outdoor commons area. Sigi was there with her English class, sitting on a concrete bench listening to her teacher Ms. Neiver. Ms. Neiver had decided that teaching her students outside in the cool morning was a good idea. Of course, she hadn't been planning on Ozzy stomping through, chased by Mr. Hook.

"Ozzy?" Sigi said. She stood up from her spot and ran to grab him. Taking ahold of his left arm, she tugged, but he didn't slow down in the least. "What are you doing?" she asked, even though she had a very good idea of what was happening.

"Stop him," Mr. Hook ordered Sigi.

"I can't," she replied. "He's . . . I think he's sleepwalking."

"You should never wake someone who's sleepwalking," one of Ms. Neiver's students said seriously.

"How can he be sleepwalking?" Mr. Hook said. "He was wide awake just moments ago. And look, his eyes are open."

"It's a condition he has," Sigi lied as Ozzy continued to walk.

Using the word *condition* made both Ms. Neiver and Mr. Hook nervous. A condition was something for a teacher to take care of.

"Oh," Mr. Hook apologized, "I wasn't aware of his condition."

"Nor was I," Ms. Neiver said, sounding apologetic. "What do we do?"

"I'll take care of it," Sigi said.

"No," Ms. Neiver insisted. "We can help."

Both teachers and half of Neiver's class were now following Ozzy and Sigi. Ozzy walked down the sidewalk and past the door to the front office. Mr. Hook waved urgently at one of the school counselors, who was standing outside near the door.

"Mr. Toffy has a condition," Mr. Hook yelled. "You may be needed."

The counselor, Mrs. Sebraski, hurried over and joined Mr. Hook and Ms. Neiver as they marched ten feet behind Ozzy and Sigi.

"Oz," Sigi whispered fiercely as she held onto his left arm, "you might want to snap out of it." Sigi looked back and saw the large group of people walking behind them. "Please," she begged.

Ozzy walked right off campus while the teachers and counselor shouted things that didn't help in the least.

"Is he okay?"

"Should we stop him?"

"Where's he going?"

Sigi looked in front of her and realized they were heading west. "To the ocean," she whispered. "Wake up, Oz," she begged, pinching the back of his right arm.

Ozzy walked across the pedestrian bridge that crossed the highway in front of the school.

Everyone followed.

When he reached the other side, he walked down the middle of the road. Cars began to stop and stare at the small crowd of people following the boy and girl. Some people in nearby houses thought it was a protest of some sort and came out to march with them. There had been a lot of marches and protests in the area lately, and this simply felt like another.

"What are we protesting?" a woman with yellow hair and green eyes asked Sigi.

"Nothing," Sigi told her.

"That's it," the woman cheered angrily. "Fight the nothingness!"

Yellow Hair began to shout as she moved back and marched behind everyone. The woman started to shout things and others in the crowd caught on and chanted along with her.

"One, two, this won't do. Three, four, it's time for more. Five, six, we're tired and sick . . ."

"I love Oregon," Sigi said to Ozzy, "but sometimes we're weirder than we actually need to be."

Having nothing to say about that, Ozzy kept walking. Having too much to worry about, Sigi looked back. The street behind them was filling up with people and slow-moving cars. The growing mass of humanity was chanting, and the vehicles were honking.

"I should never have been nice to you," Sigi said. "I should never have talked to you at all, because this is insane."

Ozzy didn't argue the point.

"Please wake up."

It seemed as if the community of Otter Rock was in the mood to do something outdoors this morning, and now Ozzy was providing them the opportunity to do so. Everyone from the school thought they were just being kind and keeping a sleepwalking boy safe. While the new marchers thought they were there to fight a fight that didn't exist.

"There's a small mob behind you, Ozzy," Sigi yelled. "A small, loud mob."

The boy turned onto First Street and didn't pause—there was no stopping, no looking, and no listening. Sigi tried to pull him back but it was no use. He kept walking as she waved at cars to have them go around.

A couple vehicles honked at her as she yelled.

"He's sleepwalking!"

"That's it!" one of the marchers yelled. "No more sleepwalking—it's time to get woke!"

Sigi looked ahead and saw that they were heading

straight west toward the ocean and a rock formation called the Devil's Punchbowl.

"Please stop," Sigi said as she pulled on his arm and shirt. "I'm not walking into the ocean with you again."

Ozzy didn't stop.

"Okay," she yelled. "I'll walk in with you if it helps, but I don't think it will." Sigi looked back. The crowd was marching and chanting behind. One person even had a protest sign that read, "All for none and none for all."

"Where did they get that?" Sigi complained. "And what does that even mean?"

The marching crowd chanted,

"Hey, ho, we won't go! Hey, hee, let us be!"

The street they were on ended in the parking lot of Devil's Punchbowl State Natural Area. Devil's Punchbowl was a remarkable rock formation on the shore of the Pacific Ocean that had been formed by collapsing caves many years before. It now looked like a ring of stone surrounding a cauldron of water. When the tide was low, a person could safely walk around on the rocks and sand inside the ring. At high tide, anyone with even a dash of common sense was best advised to stay clear. People came from all over the world to view its wonder and beauty. Ozzy and Sigi walked down the road with a good portion of the locals walking behind them.

"This is ridiculous, Ozzy," Sigi pleaded, pulling on his arm even harder. "You have to stop! The road ends."

Behind the small crowd, Sigi heard a police car running its siren.

"Great. Now the cops are here."

The street ended and Ozzy walked into the parking lot. He passed a few parked cars and a small restaurant before coming to the end of the asphalt. Where the parking lot ended, there was a short wooden fence. Sigi moved in front of Ozzy and tried pushing him to make him stop.

"You're going to kill yourself!"

It was a real possibility. The point where the parking lot ended looked down over the large ring of stone. There was a small bit of sand beyond the fence, and then some stone before it opened up into the hole that was the center of the Devil's Punchbowl. The fence was so short that if Ozzy wanted to, he could easily step over it.

"Stop!" Sigi ordered him.

Ozzy stopped two feet from the short fence. He looked out over the Devil's Punchbowl and the ocean. Sigi was thrilled that he had stopped, but she stayed in front of him pushing on his chest just in case he decided to start walking again.

"Don't move," she said through labored breath.

The crowd of school members and spontaneous protestors all shuffled into the parking lot, wondering what the next step would be. They came to halt ten feet away from Ozzy and Sigi.

"Is he all right?" Mr. Hook shouted.

"I think so," Sigi shouted back. "You can all go home."

A few protestors tried to get a new chant going, but it was becoming obvious to everyone that no social change would be happening today. The police car's siren chirped and people parted so that it could roll into the parking lot. It stopped three feet behind Ozzy as he stood staring at the sea. Sheriff Wills got out of the passenger-side door.

"What's going on?" is something someone polite would have asked. Unfortunately, Sheriff Wills's words were nothing like that. He screamed something profane and confusing while hustling up to Ozzy and Sigi. His face was a deep red. The red, combined with his green uniform, made him look festive despite there being no clear reason to celebrate. Officer Greg got out of the driver's side of the police car and began loudly instructing the crowd to break it up and leave the premises.

"I told you two to lay low!" The sheriff ground his teeth as he walked up to Ozzy and Sigi. "It's isn't even nine o'clock yet! This is *not* laying low."

"Thanks," Sigi said. "I needed someone to tell me that. He fell asleep and just kept walking. I couldn't wake him."

The sheriff moved closer and stared Ozzy in the eyes.

The boy blinked.

"Where am I?" he asked as he turned his head slowly.

"You fell asleep," Sigi lied, "and just kept walking."

Ozzy's grey eyes looked cloudy and out of place in the sunlight.

"You're trying to tell me that he fell asleep in school?" Wills asked Sigi. "Then he walked off campus, gathered a crowd of people behind him, walked across the highway, and down here to the ocean before waking up?"

"That's it," Sigi said. "I'll help him get home and get some rest."

"I don't think so. I'm taking you two to the station. I want you in my sight until I talk to Patti. Unless you know where your father is and I can talk to him first."

Sigi shook her head.

The crowd was getting restless. Some were angry that there wasn't a real protest, and those from school were mad that they were going to have to walk all the way back. Officer Greg got into the driver's seat of the police car and answered a radio call.

"You two are more trouble than any two people should be," the sheriff lamented. "I don't understand what's going on with you."

Ozzy's eyes were clearing even further. "Sorry," he apologized. "I don't know what came over me."

The sheriff was softened a bit by the boy's sincerity. "Well, we should have you looked at by a doctor."

"I'm fine," Ozzy insisted. "Just tired."

"From your trip to New York?" the sheriff asked.

"Nice try," Sigi said before Ozzy could speak. "We didn't go to New York."

Sheriff Wills looked at Ozzy for his answer.

"What she said."

Officer Greg was growing more animated sitting in the car talking on the radio. Sigi couldn't understand much of what he was saying, but she heard the word *fire* a couple of times, and when Officer Greg looked up at Sheriff Wills, he looked more concerned than cops usually like to let on. He got out of the car and walked up to the sheriff.

"There's a fire in the forest on the other side of Mule Pole Highway," he reported.

Every one of their heads turned to look toward the northeast. It was faint, but in the far distance they could see a thin string of black smoke twisting up into the empty sky. It was miles and miles away, but it was also coming from a direction and area that Ozzy and Sigi knew well.

The sheriff swore some more.

"That's got to be close to the cloaked house," Sigi said in a panic.

"No," Ozzy insisted as he shook off the last bits of fog in his mind and eyes.

"I'm sure it's not," the sheriff said. "It's probably just some trees. Now, let's get you two to the station and I'll check it out."

"I'm not going to the station." Ozzy felt like a cartoon character who'd just run off a cliff—the ground had disappeared beneath his feet and he was waiting for gravity to kick in. "I don't need help."

"Let me be the judge of that," Wills said. "You need to come with us."

Ozzy's finger buzzed, but the sensation wasn't an indication that he would soon be walking toward the ocean.

This time as his finger vibrated, his mind cleared, and electricity shot up through his legs and into his mind.

Ozzy reached out and pointed toward Officer Greg, who was sitting in the police car's driver's seat with the door open. The officer's body went rigid and he threw the vehicle into drive. Then, without a moment of hesitation, he slammed his right foot onto the gas pedal.

The powerful engine shot the car forward, just missing Ozzy and plowing right through the small fence. It raced down the short, sandy slope, heading directly toward the center of the Devil's Punchbowl. Seconds before it reached the stone ring, Officer Greg leaped out of the open door and rolled along the sand as the car flew over the stone and down into the center of the Punchbowl. A terrific crash rang out. It all happened so fast that nobody had time to react or do anything other than scream.

On the sandy slope below, a shaky Officer Greg stood up and dusted himself off.

"I don't believe it," Sheriff Wills hissed as he stared at the Punchbowl. "That's the second car wrecked in two days. I don't know how you two are—" He turned to scream at Ozzy and Sigi, but he couldn't, because Ozzy was gone.

Sigi appeared to be as surprised at his absence as the sheriff.

"Ozzy—?" she yelled, glancing around quickly.

"Unbelievable," Wills said to Sigi. "Don't you move."

The sheriff pulled out his cell phone and began to call

for help as Officer Greg sheepishly climbed back up the sandy slope.

Sigi stood right where she was. It seemed to be the only option she had. She was worried about the fire, worried about the cloaked house, and angry that Ozzy had left her.

A couple protestors had taken the act of the police car dropping into the Devil's Punchbowl as a solid protest against authority. They continued to chant something about the police being the problem while other tourists moved down the sandy slope to get a look at the car that had fallen in.

The sheriff got off the phone and turned to lecture Sigi some more. His face became an uncomfortable shade of reddish-purple as a look of surprise washed over him.

Sigi was gone too.

CHAPTER THIRTY-TWO

F-I-R-E

Ozzy didn't know how to feel as he ran through the trees. Part of him wanted to stop and revel in the feeling he'd just experienced as he controlled Officer Greg. It was a feeling like the one he'd had on the mountain, but at least a hundred times stronger. Another part of him wanted to stop and worry about his own mind taking him on walks whenever it pleased. But the biggest part of him was filled with fear at the possibility of the cloaked house being on fire. It was the closest connection he still had to his parents and more important to him than just about anything.

His hope was that the fire burning was nowhere near the house. His fear was that no matter how fast he ran, it was already too late.

Ozzy's lungs were in full protest mode as he reached 1221 Ocean View. His legs had reached their limit. Running to the garage, he pulled out the motorcycle and started it up.

The motor roared.

"Please don't be the cloaked house burning," he moaned as he threw on a helmet and tore out of the garage.

He flew across streets and through neighborhoods, not caring if anyone spotted him.

Just past Main Street he turned onto Mule Pole Highway. Normally he rode through the trees, but there wasn't time. He raced along the side of the highway, begging the bike to go faster.

"Come on!"

In the far distance he saw the black plume of smoke growing bigger. The spot it was coming from didn't comfort him at all.

A fire engine roared past him on the road, but Ozzy knew that if the fire was anywhere near the cloaked house, they were out of luck. There were no firebreaks or access roads that could allow vehicles to get near—no way for anyone with any training or skills to reach the hidden and isolated spot in time to do any good.

"Please be okay, please be okay," he said over and over as he flew down the side of the road.

When he reached the train tracks that crossed the highway, another emergency vehicle sped by. Ozzy took a sharp right, away from the road and into the trees. He darted through the forest he knew so well with a sense of urgency that was stealing his breath and causing his blood to simmer.

His heartbeat drowned out the sound of the motorcycle.

Ozzy smelled the smoke and heard the fire before he could see it. His senses protested what was happening. Unlike the protest in the street, there was no chanting with this one, but his chest was heaving and his heart was turning to ash.

Through the trees he saw a blinding flash of orange against the green. It was clear to see what was burning. He raced closer, and then stopped the bike and got off screaming.

"No!"

The cloaked house was completely engulfed in flames.

Ozzy sobbed like he was seven and someone had just taken his parents and left him all alone in the world.

Gone was any peace he had ever felt. Gone was a hope for the world to correct what it had once done. Gone was his faith in anything but sorrow.

The cloaked house was finished.

CHAPTER THIRTY-THREE

Ashes, Ashes, We All Burn Down

The fire devoured the cloaked house. It took what once was and turned it into what now wasn't. It was no longer a house, no longer a hidden home in the dense forest; it was just a smoldering pile of burnt beams, black ash, and wispy smoke.

A few firemen had made it to the spot on foot and had cleared some of the brush away and shoveled dirt on the hot spots. They were sorry about the loss, but relieved and amazed that only the cloaked house had burned.

Ozzy felt just the opposite. As he stood there looking at the charred ruins of his home, he felt betrayed by life, as if he had been kicked one time too many. He wished the entire forest had burned instead of his home.

Sheriff Wills finally made it out with a few of his officers. He saw Ozzy in the trees looking on—and for once, the sheriff had the wisdom to not say anything.

Ozzy whispered the list of what he needed as he stared at what was left of a large piece of his soul.

"I need Clark."

"I need Sigi."

"I need my parents."

He stood there like the kind of statue a very depressed and gloomy sculptor might have made.

Eventually, as some of the firefighters began to leave, Sheriff Wills approached the boy and stood next to him. Together they stared at the burnt remains of the home's wooden body.

"I'm so sorry," the sheriff tried.

"I know," Ozzy replied. "Everyone always is."

"Listen," Wills said compassionately, "there will be an investigation, but according to the fire chief, it looks pretty clear that someone set this fire."

"What?" the idea had never even entered Ozzy's mind. "Why? Why would—?"

Ozzy paused and the sheriff took it upon himself to fill the silence. "We've had more than our usual amount of rain this season. Everything is wet—too wet to burn easily. But it looks as if someone used some sort of accelerant on this place. It was probably gasoline. That's why nothing else around the house burned. Do you have any idea who would do this?"

"You know my life." Ozzy's words were sharp. "You know what happened out here, what happened to my parents. Who knows who would do this? It seems like a normal part of a life where everything is always taken from me."

"You deserve to be upset," the sheriff said.

"Do I?" Ozzy was mad. "What does that even mean? Did I *deserve* to have my parents taken? Did I *deserve* to have my house burned down? Who determines what someone deserves? Because I think I'd rather not deserve anything anymore."

"We'll do all we can to find out who did this."

Ozzy wanted to scream, but instead he whispered. "Good, I hope you do."

"It would help if you were honest to me about everything."

"Like what?"

"For starters, are you ready to tell me about New York yet?"

Ozzy looked around for Sigi. This was normally the point where she would jump in and tell the sheriff to mind his own business.

"Is Sigi at the station?" Ozzy asked, knowing that he had left her with the sheriff.

"No, she took off soon after you did."

Ozzy looked at the sheriff with the tight shirt and skinny mustache. He and Ozzy were about the same height, and he could see in Wills's eyes that he was truly sorry for what Ozzy had lost. But as he talked about Sigi,

Ozzy suddenly realized that there was something far more important than the cloaked house that he could lose.

"Where'd she go?" The boy's voice was unsteady.

"I figured she went to find you." The sheriff's voice was suddenly equally uncertain.

"Even if she walked she would have been here by now."

"I'm sure she's fine," Sheriff Wills insisted. "I'll have one of my staff get ahold of her. She probably just went home."

Ozzy didn't stand around to speculate. He ran to his motorcycle and flew to one of the few things that meant more to him than the cloaked house.

CHAPTER THIRTY-FOUR

DIFFERENT LEVELS OF FEAR

Ozzy rode to 1221 Ocean View with more urgency in his veins than he had had while racing to the fire. In his mind, Sigi had simply slipped away from the sheriff and was now back home with Clark. The problem with that scenario, however, was that if Sigi *had* gone home, she would have told Clark about the fire. And if Clark knew about the fire, he never would have stayed home and not flown out to the cloaked house to see what was happening.

Making record time, Ozzy reached home and leaned the motorcycle against the fountain near the driveway. He ran to the front door and found that it was locked. He pounded on it for a few moments before running back around the house and entering through the door in the kitchen.

"Sigi! Clark!"

There was no answer.

Ozzy ran to Sigi's room but she wasn't there. He checked the library and the master bedroom.

Everything looked empty.

He finished checking the rooms on the bottom floor and then climbed the stairs three at a time and up to the second floor.

"Sigi! Clark! Where are you?"

Ozzy went through all the bedrooms upstairs but there was no sign of anybody or anybird. The last spot he looked in was the bathroom near the upstairs landing.

Ozzy opened the door and gasped.

Clark was in the bathtub with the flash drive, a set of keys, and Ozzy's portable CD player. Music was coming out of the headphones and Clark was chatting up the keys.

"Clark!"

The bird jumped a good six feet. Then he fluttered back down and landed on the edge of the tub. Holding his right wing to his chest, he tried to catch the breath he didn't actually have. As he composed himself, he asked,

"Have you never heard of *knocking*?"

"I don't know what this is," Ozzy said, sounding confused and motioning to the bathtub and office products. "But I'm looking for Sigi."

"The tub has great acoustics," Clark explained. "You see, the flash drive and the keys fell in by accident. I was worried about everything and thought it might be good to just unwind. I've been under a lot of—"

"Clark," Ozzy interrupted, "have you seen Sigi?"

"You mean like have I *ever* seen her?" the bird asked. "Because—"

"No—like have you seen her in the last few hours?" Ozzy turned around and left the bathroom without waiting for an answer. He jogged down the stairs as Clark flew next to him.

"I thought Sigi was with you at school."

"She was," Ozzy said. "But I freaked out first hour and almost walked into the ocean again. Then I left her when the cloaked house burned down. Now I don't know where she is."

"*Excuse me?*" Clark squawked. "The cloaked house burned down?"

Ozzy stopped at the bottom of the stairs and turned to look at his bird. The sadness in his eyes was enough to let Clark know that he had not misunderstood. Clark drifted over and onto Ozzy's right shoulder. He tried his best to wrap his left wing around Ozzy's neck, but one of the metal edges scratched him.

Ozzy let his legs give out and he fell butt-first onto the bottom stair. He sat quietly trying to make sense of what was going on.

Clark wanted to make sense in a less-quiet way. "What happened?" he tweeted.

"I think it was Ray," Ozzy said. "Somehow he burned down the one place that meant the most to me."

"But where's Sigi?" the bird chirped nervously. "I sort of promised Patti that nothing would go wrong while she was away."

"It's too late for that," Ozzy said. "Something has gone wrong, and I have no idea where Sigi is."

"Then where's that wizard you hired?"

Ozzy shrugged.

"No offense," the bird sang, "but if this is how that wizard thinks people help people, then he can look forward to some stinging reviews online. Did you know you can review people?"

"That's horrible."

"I suppose if he'd shape-shift for me, I might give him higher marks. I'd like to see him change into a 1984 Trans-Am."

Ozzy ignored the bird and stood up. He walked across the foyer and threw open the front door.

"What are you doing?" Clark asked.

"Maybe it's time to start acting like an apprentice."

"To be honest, I have no idea what that would look like," the bird admitted.

"What was the last thing Rin said?"

Clark tilted his head and thought. "Watch out for rocks?"

"No, that was that sign you like," Ozzy told him. "The last thing Rin said was, 'I'll be standing where the answer was found.'"

"Is that supposed to clarify anything?"

"It does for me."

"All right," Clark said. "You're the orthodontist."

"Apprentice."

"Like I know the difference."

Taking the motorcycle, the two of them sped away from the house as quickly as possible.

CHAPTER THIRTY-FIVE

STARE AT NOTHING

The sky was the color of faded denim and the air felt warm, like a shirt right out of the dryer. The weather over Otter Rock at the moment could easily have been described as unusually sunny and beautiful if it weren't for the ugly things that had gone on beneath it.

On the shore of the ocean, a boy on a motorcycle raced north. Ozzy was headed toward a spot that the apprentice in him thought might be a good place to look for Rin. As he flew along, the ocean rolled up against the sand and then dragged its wet body back out, only to do it all over again and again.

This had not been the worst day of Ozzy's life, but it ranked near the top, and it still wasn't close to being over.

Clark darted through the blue sky and around the bike as he challenged himself to not only keep up, but to beat the large hunk of metal.

"Where are we going?" the bird squawked loudly.

"How can I beat you there if I don't know where I'm going?"

"You'll see."

In the distance, Ozzy spotted the picnic tables and restroom he was looking for. It was the same spot where he and Rin and Sigi had finally heard the tape that had the formula for the Discipline Serum on it. It had been months ago, but they had brought Patti's stereo out there and plugged it into the outlet on the bathrooms. The tables nearby were empty, but as they reached the area, Ozzy could see someone standing near the bathroom.

"Is that Rin?" Clark asked excitedly.

The person stepped out of the shadows. Not only was it not Rin, it was a woman wearing a sun hat and a yellow dress.

"He looks different," Clark tweeted.

"That's because it's not him."

The woman walked off down a sandy path and out of sight. Ozzy stopped the motorcycle and parked it next to one of the tables. He checked the bathroom, but it was empty.

"This is where we listened to that tape," Clark said.

Ozzy nodded.

"There's no wizard, and no Sigi."

"I can see that."

"Is this what apprentices do?" Clark asked. "They guess at things?"

Ozzy looked around at the two picnic tables and small

restroom building. He could see the outlet that they had used to plug in Patti's stereo. It had been nighttime then, but listening to that last tape had been as magical as anything that had happened with Rin. Hearing new words from his father and his mother, as well as hearing the formula for the very thing that had caused all his problems to begin with.

"Maybe," Clark suggested, "Sigi's not missing, and she just went back to school."

"That doesn't seem like something she would do."

"Yeah, that's more your thing. Maybe she took some time to reconsider hanging out with you. I mean you're handsome, but you come with some heavy baggage."

Ozzy walked onto the sand from the cement pad where the tables and bathroom were. In the not-so-far distance, he could see the waves marching in and storming the beach.

His finger buzzed.

Clark was sitting on his shoulder, but he still felt the vibration.

"Oh, no," the bird chirped. "Are you going to walk into the ocean again?"

"I don't think so," Ozzy replied. But as he said the words, he turned and began walking toward the water.

"You said you didn't think so."

"I'm doing this on my own," the boy replied. "If something keeps pulling me toward the water, then maybe I should get a little closer."

Ozzy walked across the sand. The naked sky mixed with the Pacific Ocean and made everything in front of them look blue. The color fit his mood, but as he stared out at the ocean and sky, something caught his eye.

He walked closer to the water as the bird on his shoulder talked.

"Listen, about that whole bathtub thing back there, it really isn't what you think. It's just that when you play your headphones in there, the little bit of sound that comes out of the earphones bounces off the tub walls and makes it louder. I think the keys like that."

"You're very thoughtful," Ozzy said as he kept walking. There was something on the horizon that seemed worth looking at. It was barely noticeable, but since the view was like a solid blue puzzle, the small imperfection stood out. "Something's flashing."

"What?" Clark asked indignantly. "There was none of that. Just talking and listening to music. Yes, the stapler kept sort of glimmering at me, but there wasn't any flashing. Your dad didn't build me to be *that* kind of bird."

"No," Ozzy said, "something out on the water."

Clark took to the air as Ozzy reached the waves and stood on the wet sand. The bird flew out a good distance and then circled back.

"It looks like an old boat heading out to sea," Clark reported. "I couldn't get close enough to see what was flashing. You already lost the cloaked house today. I'd hate to see what you'd be like if you lost me."

"I'd be devastated," Ozzy said honestly.

"Good."

Ozzy kept staring at the water as his finger buzzed.

"What's the big deal?" the bird asked. "There's always boats out there."

"I need you to fly closer."

"I'm metal, remember? If I run out of energy or get struck down by something, I'll sink to the bottom and never be found. Besides, it's just a boat."

"There are no clouds in the sky," Ozzy said. "So you won't run out of power. And it's the perfect time to see how far you can fly over the water."

Clark shivered on Ozzy's head.

Ozzy stayed silent, staring at the sea.

"Are you trying to control me with your brain?" the bird finally asked. "Because I sort of feel motivated to fly out now."

"I'm not."

"Maybe you should," Clark said. "Then I'd have no choice."

"It's not a thing I can just turn on and off."

"Some super power," Clark sighed. Then he counted to four and flew off. Thirty seconds later, he was back, hovering in front of Ozzy's face. "If I do turn up missing, promise me you'll drag the ocean until I'm found."

"I promise."

The bird shot out over the water and toward the

flashing boat. He quickly became so small that he disappeared into the blue.

Ozzy waited, watching the waves flop onto the sand around him, worrying about Sigi.

"This is stupid," he said to himself.

As time stretched on, he began to pace along the shore, keeping his eyes toward the water. The ocean was immense and all-encompassing and hurt his eyes. As he gazed out, it felt like the world consisted of nothing but water. The boat in the distance had stopped flashing and grown smaller, and still Clark had not returned.

"Seriously, Clark, don't be messing around."

He doubted his eyes for a moment, but the boat appeared to no longer be getting smaller. In fact, it was growing larger, moving in the direction of the shore.

Ozzy stopped pacing and concentrated on watching the boat.

It grew bigger and bigger as it came closer and then began to move south. It was still far away, but Ozzy could see that it was an old wooden boat with a single mast. There were some black markings on it, but the black markings didn't interest him as much as the small black dot he now saw flying toward him.

Clark came in hot and slammed into Ozzy's right shoulder, trying to make a quick perch. He bounced off and then flew back up to stand on Ozzy's head. The bird was excited to the point of being tweetless.

"What?" Ozzy asked. "Is it just a boat?"

"No," Clark finally got out. "It's a . . . boat . . . with a . . . wizard on it."

"You're kidding. Rin?"

"Do you know another wizard?"

"In books."

"Well, *this* wizard said that you have all but solidified your spot as his apprentice by standing in the right spot at the right time."

"That's Rin."

"He's going to the marina just south of here to park the boat," Clark said. "Is that the correct verbiage? Park the boat? Corral the bobber? Plant the floaty?"

"Was Sigi there?"

"No, and he doesn't know where she is."

Ozzy ran back to his motorcycle and headed south.

One found, one to go.

CHAPTER THIRTY-SIX

AND I'M WONDERING WHERE SHE'S BEEN

Marina del Damp was a big marina that at full capacity could accommodate seventy-four boats. It had six worn wooden docks and a small office at the entrance. The marina was filled close to capacity. One of the vessels it was holding was an old wooden boat that didn't seem to match any of the other ones. Written in black paint on the back of the boat were the words

Spell Boat

The bobber was corralled in spot number twenty-four. Ozzy climbed onto the boat and saw a wizard in a yellow robe, pointed felt hat, and red high-tops standing near the steering wheel. Ozzy expected Rin to say something about how it had been magic that brought them back together. Instead, he looked at Ozzy with worried eyes and asked, "Where's Sigi?"

"I don't know," the boy answered. "I was hoping she was with you."

"Where would she have gone?" Rin asked.

"I don't know that either. Can't you use your new crystal ball?"

"Actually, I was trying to juggle with it earlier," Rin confessed. "I may have accidently dropped it in the water. Tell me everything that's happened."

Ozzy filled the wizard in on what had happened, right up until the point where Clark had flown out to the boat.

"When did you get a boat?" Ozzy asked.

"I didn't," Rin said, acting stranger than usual. "I just rented this for a few days. I wanted to check something out."

"But it's called *Spell Boat*."

"I think it belonged to someone who won some big spelling bee."

"Still, that's incredibly fitting," Ozzy said.

"Not really," Rin replied. "I'm a horrible speller. And—oh, wait, I get it. Just another sign that the universe knows full well I'm a wizard."

"How did you know to flash us?" Ozzy asked.

"I didn't," Rin said. "While driving out to sea, I took a few minutes to practice with my staff. The sun must have been bouncing off the end." Rin held up his staff. "Recognize this?"

"Is that your stick?"

"Yes." The branch had been carved and polished and

there was a round silver orb attached to the top. "A famous staff maker made it for me last night. It's an original Gene Payton." Rin pointed to some initials near the orb.

Clark was impressed. Ozzy was impatient.

"What about Sigi?"

"We'll find her," Rin promised. "But we're going to need some help. Can your bicycle hold two people?"

"It's a motorcycle—and no."

"Then I shall provide a way."

Rin pushed back both sleeves on his robe and stood tall. Ozzy and Clark moved back to watch the wizard do his thing. He reached into the pocket on his robe and pulled out . . . his phone. Then he ordered an Uber.

"Are you as disappointed as I am?" Clark asked Ozzy.

"Probably more so," the boy replied.

"You two have such a narrow definition of magic," the wizard said. "How can I expect you to understand the wonders you're soon going to witness if you can't even see the miracles you're already experiencing?"

Rin jumped off the *Spell Boat* and onto the dock. "Leave your bicycle behind the marina office. You can retrieve it later."

Ozzy corrected him again. "It's a motorcycle."

"Right. In Quarfelt, motor-cycles are something cursed motors have to go through before they can be used by wompins again."

"And wompins are like muggles?" Ozzy asked.

"Yes, just with a worse name."

Rin walked with purpose to the entrance of the marina, while Ozzy wheeled the motorcycle back behind the small office and parked it next to a dumpster.

Then the apprentice caught up with the wizard and Clark retreated to his customized pocket.

"Our ride will be here in seven minutes," Rin reported.

All three of them waited impatiently, feeling worried and incomplete due to the important part of their group who was missing.

"By the way," Rin said. "I want to congratulate you on passing the first test of the Cin-Wiz-Con."

"What did I do?" Ozzy asked, surprised.

"You found me."

"I just followed your clue about 'Standing where the answer was found.'"

"Then I'm even more impressed. That clue was for you to meet up with me at Jack in the Box. That's where I solved that riddle."

"You mean that maze on the children's placemat?" Ozzy asked, feeling ill.

Rin nodded.

"Remind him that it took him two tries," Clark tweeted quietly from the pocket.

"I'm not telling him that," Ozzy whispered.

"Wait," the wizard said, "apprentices don't withhold information."

"Trust me," Ozzy said. "You'll be glad I did."

Small, thin clouds began to slide in from the edges of the sky as they stood there waiting for their ride.

"You know, Harry Potter has a broom to ride on," Ozzy complained. "We could get where we're going much quicker if you had some brooms."

"*Brooms*," Rin scoffed. "Any real wizard knows how uncomfortable those things are. And the splinters? I couldn't walk for a week after a particularly long trip I took to deliver some Enzips in Quarfelt."

Ozzy didn't bite, so Rin added, "Don't you want to know what Enzips are?"

"No. Let's just have it be your turn to withhold information."

"Deal."

After a few more clouds, and a few more minutes, their ride arrived on time. It was a 2011 Subaru Outback. It had no splinters in it, but there were more than a few crumbs and dog hairs.

CHAPTER THIRTY-SEVEN

MORE FRIGHTENED

Sigi sat alone in the small room, trying desperately to suppress the fear she felt and figure out a way to save herself. One moment she had been standing in the parking lot of the Devil's Punchbowl and the next she had been picked up and whisked away into the trees. She had kicked and fought as hard as she could, but the man holding her was strong, and something on a cloth near her nose had knocked her out. When she came to, she was in a room with one window, one door, and four gray walls. The window had bars over it and didn't open. There were two wooden chairs in the room and an old black sofa against one of the walls.

The door was locked.

Sigi could see nothing but forest and fields out the window. She tried the door for the fiftieth time and then sat down dejectedly on the couch. Looking around, she began to think of things she could do to escape. As she was thinking, she heard a car pull up outside. It idled for a moment before the engine was shut off. A car door slammed, followed by footsteps on gravel.

A key turned in the lock and the door began to open.

Sigi positioned herself and sprang forward into the person coming through the door. The man grabbed her and spun her around like she was nothing. He gently shoved her backwards onto the couch.

"Just sit," Jon said. "I have no reason to hurt you unless you force me to."

"You—" Sigi said angrily. "You're the one who delivered the flash drive."

"Yes. My name is Jon," he offered, taking a seat on one of the wooden chairs.

"Why am I here?"

"I never said I'd answer any questions."

"You never said you wouldn't," Sigi argued. "Do you work for Ray?"

Jon didn't respond.

"Where are we?"

Jon sighed. "How about this—you answer a few questions for me and then I'll return the favor."

It was Sigi's turn not to reply.

"Okay, I know you're important to Ozzy," Jon forged on. "In fact, that's why you're here. My boss believes that Ozzy won't do anything as long as we have you to barter with."

"How flattering."

"It's just a fact."

"Is your boss Ray?" Sigi asked again.

"Yes," Jon replied. "It seems as if Ozzy might unknowingly have something that belongs to Ray."

"What?"

"Something very valuable."

"Really?" Sigi said. "The mind control formula? Ozzy doesn't have it. Why can't you and your boss just leave him alone?"

"My job is not to rationalize or speculate or guess. I get information and put out fires."

"You mean start fires," Sigi said. "Is it the cloaked house that's burning? Did you do that?"

"No," Jon said, "I'm not sure what you're talking about."

"Right."

"What did Ozzy receive from his lawyer?"

"A picture and a CD," Sigi answered. "Is that worth kidnapping someone for?"

"What's on the CD?"

"Music."

"That's it?" Jon asked. "A picture and a CD? What's the picture of?"

"Ozzy and his parents—who your boss murdered."

"I don't think that's right."

"Well, I don't think someone who kidnaps people has any real idea of what's right."

"Fair enough."

"If that," Sigi said. "Because it's not more than fair."

"Listen," Jon said calmly, "I don't want to hurt you. I

don't even like having to keep you here. Hostages aren't my thing. But I can tell you this—if you give me some answers about what my boss is interested in, things will go much smoother. We don't want to disrupt your life any more than we want to disrupt Ozzy's. But there are things at play here that are bigger than you can understand. What does it hurt to help us find the answers so that you can move on?"

"I don't know anything," Sigi insisted.

"What about your dad?"

"What's *he* got to do with this?"

"Well, if he hadn't interrupted what was going on in New York, none of this would be happening."

"There's nothing to tell you," Sigi said coldly. "I've barely seen my dad in the last ten years. He's what people call a delinquent father."

"It seems like he's been showing up a lot in your life lately."

"If you know that, then why are you asking me questions?"

Jon whistled. "You're stubborn."

"If we're trading insults, you're human garbage."

"Listen," Jon said, "you can't insult me."

"Is that a condition of your low IQ?"

Jon massaged his forehead. "Like I said, you're welcome to throw any words at me. It won't affect how I do my job. Tell me about this bird Ozzy has."

"No, thank you."

"You're going to get hungry," Jon said trying a new

approach. "How about I bring you something to eat and you give me a few answers?"

Sigi suggested something much more insulting and not fit for print.

"All right," Jon said. "I think you need a little more time to cool down."

"You're going to be sorry," she said. "Think about it. If my father is a wizard, and if Ozzy can control minds, and if by some chance we have that sentient bird, then you're going to be in trouble."

Jon stood up and opened the door.

"Actually," he said, "I'm not sure that my boss shouldn't be most worried about you."

It wasn't meant to be a compliment, but Sigi felt stronger because of it.

The door closed and she heard the key in the lock again. A moment later, the car pulled away outside.

Sigi wasn't going to sit this out any longer. She jumped off the short couch and grabbed hold of its bottom. She flipped the whole thing over so that she was staring at its underside. There was black felt covering the bottom, stapled in place along all four sides.

She wiggled a couple fingers under the edge of the felt and ripped the fabric back so that she could see into the bottom of the couch, which was full of wood and springs attached together in various spots. Sigi pulled on the metal springs that made up the seat supports, but they were all screwed tightly into place.

"This is ridiculous. I should be in English class right now."

Sigi picked up one of the wooden chairs and, without pausing, lifted it and smashed it against the concrete floor. Two of the legs bent inward. With the chair lying on its side, she placed her left foot on one of the bent legs and used all her weight to snap it off.

She took the chair leg and jammed it into the bottom of the couch between a long, thin board that was part of the back support and the springs that were part of the bottom support. Using leverage, she pulled back until the wire spring broke loose.

Bending the broken part back and forth with her hands, she worked on it until it popped free. The loose piece of thick wire took some muscle to straighten out. Luckily, Sigi had just enough adrenaline and will to live in her veins to do so.

"Perfect," she said, sweating.

Sigi grabbed the chair leg and held the wire up below the top hinge on the door. She used the leg to pound the wire up into the hinge, popping out the hinge pin.

"They should *definitely* be most frightened about me."

She popped out the other two hinge pins and then jiggled the hinges with the wire until the door fell backward into the small room.

There was nothing but forest in front of her.

Fortunately, Sigi was no stranger to running through the trees.

CHAPTER THIRTY-EIGHT

CAN YOU HELP ME?

The Uber driver who picked them up at Marina del Damp was named Ted. And Ted, in Ozzy's opinion, was driving much slower than he believed the moment called for.

"Do something," Ozzy told Rin.

"Excuse me, Ted," the wizard said, "could you go faster?"

"Sorry," Ted replied. "I obey all the posted signs."

"Very commendable."

"That's it?" Ozzy asked. "You're just asking politely?"

"Sometimes civility is the most powerful potion available."

"Not this sometime," Ozzy said. "Do you have your wand?"

"What kind of wizard would I be if I didn't?"

"I'm not sure what kind of wizard you actually are."

"Well, I'm one that wouldn't be caught wandless for anything."

"Good," Ozzy whispered, "use it to help us get wherever we're going faster."

"Write this down," Rin said. "Don't look for excuses to use magic. Instead, look for ways to see the miracles already in process."

"I'm not writing that down." Ozzy was exasperated. "Where are we going, anyway?"

"Ted knows," Rin said confidently.

"Well, that's great, do you think *you* could tell me?"

"You need to master the acceptance of surprise," Rin said. "Every apprentice should be constantly excited about the uncertainty that comes next."

"If that's supposed to entice me, you're wrong. I'm not sure I want any surprises, unless it's Sigi showing up."

"She's a remarkable person," Rin said.

"I know that," Ozzy said defensively.

"He actually likes her," Clark whispered from the pocket.

Rin smiled. "We all do."

"No, he *likes*, like—"

"Tell me, Ozzy," Rin interrupted Clark. Whispering, he asked, "What did you feel before Officer Greg drove his car into the ocean?"

"Powerful," Ozzy answered.

"Yeah, the gift of influencing the minds of others must be an amazing trick."

"It's indescribable."

"I hope you find the words to describe it someday," Rin whispered. "I also hope you use it wisely."

Ted drove back into the center of town. He turned on Elm Street and drove directly into the parking lot of the police station.

"What are we doing?" Ozzy said, looking around frantically.

"We're doing what we need to," Rin said. "Sigi's well-being is nothing to mess around with. Write this down—sometimes a wizard uses the mortals around him to lift his heavy load."

"This is a load, all right," Clark chirped quietly.

"Come on," Rin said.

The wizard climbed out of the blue car with black leather seats. Ozzy opened his door and did the same. Rin leaned back in to say one last thing to Ted:

"If you only pay attention to the road, you might miss what grows in the surrounding forest."

"Thanks," Ted said, "but I have to pay attention to the road."

Rin shut his door and Ted drove off.

"Some people are so shortsighted."

"We're really going to walk in?" Ozzy asked. "Sheriff Wills might never let us go."

"Let's see if that's true."

Rin pushed open the door and they entered the police station. Wilma was behind the counter as usual. She looked up, recognized Ozzy, and saw the wizard. She knew that Sheriff Wills had been looking for Rin for months, and now here he was walking up to the counter.

"Hello," Rin said. "Is the sheriff in?"

"Oh, yeah," she replied with gusto. "He's been looking for you."

"The whole world longs for a wizard."

"Right," Wilma said. "Wills!"

Down the hall a door opened and Sheriff Wills stepped out. He looked angry and at the end of his rope, but when he spotted Rin and Ozzy, his entire demeanor changed. He didn't smile, but a thick smugness settled over him.

"I'll be . . ."

"Don't say it," Rin interrupted. "I know this is an important moment for you. But I'm not here to wow you with magic or give you a real role model to look up to—I'm here because we're looking for my daughter."

Sheriff Wills walked down the hallway and up to the counter. He looked Ozzy in the eyes and then looked back at Rin.

"Magic can't wow me," the sheriff said. "And the only man I ever looked up to was my father. Which means you must be confused about a few things. But I've been looking for you for a while, Brian."

"It's Labyrinth, but you can call me Rin."

"I should lock you both up right now," Wills said. "But I want to know about Sigi."

"She's disappeared," Ozzy said.

"When was the last time you saw her?"

"Right before Officer Greg drove into the ocean."

"You said you'd keep an eye on her," the wizard reminded him.

"I don't know how you know that."

"It's not important."

"Well, I'm sorry to say that I have no idea where Sigi is," the sheriff said. "She was standing in the parking lot of the Devil's Punchbowl one second and the next she was gone. She seemed to disappear."

"She does have a lot of her father in her."

"Not in a puff of smoke," Wills said.

"Is it possible for you to radio out and let your men know to look for her?" Rin asked.

"I thought you were a wizard. Can't you just poof her back?"

"First of all, I don't poof lightly," Rin insisted, "and second, magic is not something a real wizard tosses out at the first sign of trouble. Discretion is often a wizard's most powerful potion. That and a clear mind."

"Right," Wills said. "Well, then, you're in trouble. Your mind's not right, Brian. You don't know where your daughter is and now your only hope is to come running to someone who can do something."

"Your interpretation of the facts has holes in it," Rin said. "You remind me of Alan the Lacking. He's been trying to graduate to better trousers in Quarfelt for years."

"Do you hear yourself?" the sheriff asked.

"I hear everything," Rin argued. "Wizards are endowed with the gift of second-hearing."

"You're not a wizard," Wills insisted. "I'll get the word out to look for Sigi because I care about her as a citizen. But just remember—you couldn't even save your own daughter."

"Actually," Rin said, adjusting his hat, "we won't be needing your help after all."

"What?" Ozzy asked.

"I wanted to give the sheriff a chance to feel like he could contribute," he explained to the boy. "But as usual, my charity has gone unappreciated."

"Hold on, Bri— . . . Rin," the sheriff insisted. "We will help you find Sigi."

"No, thank you. I'll take care of it myself."

"Don't be ridiculous. It's my—"

The sheriff stopped talking as he stared behind Rin and Ozzy at the person who had just come through the door.

Ozzy turned to see Sigi standing there. Her hair was loose and her dark eyes looked wiser than they had just hours before. Under the police station's lights, her skin glistened with sweat. She smiled at Ozzy and there was weariness in the curl of her lip.

"Um . . ." Sigi said.

Ozzy turned and wrapped his arms around her.

Rin watched the boy hug the girl and then turned back to look at the sheriff.

"I told you I'd take care of it," he said.

"No," Sheriff Wills argued, "no way. There's no way you're taking credit for this. I don't know if she was even missing. Is this a trick?"

The wizard wasn't listening, because he was hugging his daughter. Sheriff Wills came out from behind the counter and positioned himself between the wizard and the door leading out.

"I'm happy you're all right, Sigi," he said.

Sigi stopped hugging her father and looked at the sheriff.

"Well," Rin said, "we'll be on our way."

"No. You won't. There are a few questions I'd like to ask all of you."

"You know I could just conjure something up and we'd all be out of here despite what you want?"

The sheriff looked like he wanted to scream, but he swallowed his anger and said, "At this point I truly don't know what you're capable of, Rin. But there's something going on, and I need some answers."

"Everyone wants answers," Rin said. "The wiser person looks for questions."

"Well, if you're as wise as you say you are, I have a few questions you might like."

"Do you have a comfortable place to sit?" the wizard asked.

"Let's try my office."

Wilma held open the short door on the counter and the sheriff motioned for them all to head to his office.

"Is this a good idea?" Ozzy whispered to Rin.

"How could it be bad?"

As an apprentice, Ozzy didn't yet possess the blind optimism of a full-fledged wizard like Rin. He could think of a dozen reasons why going to Sheriff Wills's office wasn't a good idea. But he kept his mouth closed and followed the wizard and his daughter behind the counter and down the hall.

Clark wriggled in his pocket to remind him that he was still there, and Ozzy felt thirty-two percent less nervous.

Sometimes it takes the wriggling of a bird to make an apprentice feel better.

CHAPTER THIRTY-NINE

YOU ASK ME QUESTIONS

When they walked into the office, Rin complained about his back hurting. The sheriff reluctantly rolled his large leather chair out from behind his desk and let the wizard sit in it. Sheriff Wills opened a folding chair and sat on it behind his desk. Ozzy and Sigi took the two chairs that were in front of the desk. Rin rolled his chair closer to Sigi and near the door. He adjusted the chair's height up, then down, then up, then down just a bit.

"Comfortable?" the sheriff asked.

"Wizards are always comfortable," he replied. "When you know what comes next there's little reason to worry."

"Right," Wills said dismissively. "First off, I'd like to know if all three of you will now admit to being in New York."

Rin frowned. "If we're listing the things we'd like to know, then I'd like to know if you ever caught those boys who were giving me grief at Walmart all those months ago?"

"And I'd like to know if you got your car out of the Devil's Punchbowl?" Sigi asked.

Not wanting to be left out, Ozzy said. "I'd like to know where Sigi was."

"Stop this!" Sheriff Wills rubbed the thumb and pointer finger of his left hand on his thin mustache. "You three are the most exasperating people I have ever met. Can't you see that I'm only trying to help? It's obvious that something dangerous is going on. I got another call this morning from New York asking if I had you three in custody. Ozzy's house was burned down on purpose. There are serious things happening here. I don't care about you *and* those boys at Walmart, or where Sigi might have been hanging out. I care about getting some answers."

"I wasn't hanging out," Sigi said calmly. "I was kidnapped."

Everyone looked appropriately shocked.

"*What?*" the sheriff asked.

"I was kidnapped by a man named Jon."

"Are you serious?" Wills asked.

Sigi nodded and Sheriff Wills opened his notebook and began to write things down.

"He said he works for someone named Ray," she added.

Sigi glanced at Ozzy and her dad, still not ready to admit to the sheriff that Jon had delivered the flash drive that had sent them to New York, and that she knew very well who Ray was.

"Jon grabbed me from the parking lot of the Punchbowl," she continued. "He knocked me out with something, and when I came to, I was in a small building in the woods."

Sigi told them everything that transpired as Rin continued to adjust his seat in an effort to get maximum comfort. She described her escape and how she had easily found the highway and gotten back into town. She had come into the police station because she was exhausted and didn't want to walk all the way home.

"Plus," she added, "I know this Ray guy is serious. I didn't want to go home and find someone waiting for me."

Sheriff Wills smirked. "So, it wasn't a spell or magic that brought you here to the station?"

"I didn't say that," the wizard's daughter insisted.

"Right." Sheriff Wills sighed until it became a moan. "Listen, I don't know what you three are involved in, I still have questions about what happened four months ago, and now here you are mixed up in something that seems much more nefarious. What if I assist you in some way? I could give you some helpful information. Then would you be willing to help me with some answers?"

"That's the same deal Jon offered me," Sigi pointed out. "And he's a kidnapper."

"Okay," Wills said, "I think you should realize that my

offer is different. There are some people in the world you can trust."

"Is that the helpful bit of information you have?" Rin asked. "Seems like something most people already know."

"No," Wills said. He pulled a slip of paper out of his desk and slid it across the top so that they could all see it. Written on the paper was a series of numbers. "Do you recognize this number?"

"Yes," Ozzy said. "It's the one that was in my parent's safety deposit box. You took that from me."

"You let me look at it and forgot to ask for it back," Wills said.

"So that's how the police work around here?" Sigi asked.

Rin picked up the piece of paper and studied it carefully.

"We ran it through a number of databases," the sheriff said. "It took some searching, but we finally got a hit. It turns out that it matches the registration number of a car in Sweden. We're trying to find the owners of the vehicle so we can talk to them. It could be a lead—or it could just be a coincidence."

"That information's not much more helpful than the quip about there being people in the world you can trust," Rin complained, handing the slip of paper back to the sheriff.

Wills growled. "It would help us if you three would tell me what happened in New York. I am at my wits' end with this and I don't even know what I'm hoping to find. Maybe Patti will help."

"What?" Rin asked.

"Patti," Wills said again. "We finally got ahold of her in Seattle. She's on her way back as we speak."

"Is that true?" the wizard asked nervously.

"Yeah," the sheriff said, "we told her about the fire and she was sick about it. She was going to try to call the house before her flight. You probably have a dozen messages from her."

Rin seemed rattled. "When is she supposed to be here?"

"She caught a flight to Portland that should have landed at least an hour ago."

"That means she could be here soon," Rin said, tapping his fingers on the arm of the chair. "We've got to go."

The sheriff laughed as if Rin had told the perfect cop joke.

"Seriously," the wizard said, standing up. "Thanks for letting me use your chair, but we have to leave."

"Nobody's going anywhere. I still have a whole pile of unanswered questions," Sheriff Wills insisted. "So sit back down in the chair I kindly let you borrow, and let's start being honest with each other."

Rin remained standing.

"Honesty is a dangerous substance," the wizard warned. "I've seen you handle a little truth in the past and it wasn't pretty. I don't think you're ready for a full dose. It takes some wizards years to understand the power of an honest answer. And you are no wizard. How about you let us go so that I don't have to honestly show you what I'm capable of?"

"Oh," the sheriff said with a smile, "I'd love to see what you believe you're capable of."

Without thinking, Rin quickly reached his hand into the front pocket of his robe. Unfortunately, it was not the kind of move someone should make when arguing with a sheriff.

CHAPTER FORTY

SLEIGHT OF HAND AND TALON

Sheriff Wills saw Rin reach into his pocket and shot up out of his chair—or at least that was his intention. But the folding chair he was sitting on threw him off, and as he sprang up, the chair moved backward, his feet slipped, and he crashed down on his desk. His head smacked the top of the desk hard, and he slid to the floor looking like a limp pile of law enforcement.

Ozzy and Sigi jumped to their feet.

They'd been shocked by the sheriff leaping up and even more shocked when he did a reverse leap down to the ground. Clark poked his head out of his pocket to see what all the commotion was about.

"Wow," the bird warbled. "Did you do that?"

"I was just going for my wand," Rin said proudly. "I don't know why he's so jumpy."

"Is he okay?" Ozzy asked.

Rin stepped over and felt Wills's pulse.

"He's very much alive," the wizard said. "Well, this makes it easy. I was going to turn him into something he'd regret, but I guess this works. Come on."

Rin waved for Ozzy and Sigi to follow.

"We can't just *leave* him," Ozzy whispered loudly. "He could be hurt."

"I've been knocked out many times," Rin said. "When he wakes up he'll have a better understanding of magic. He'll also have a headache. But don't worry, we'll get him help. Clark, you think you can cause a little chaos?"

"I don't know," the bird bartered. "You think you can grab me a hole punch on the way out?"

"I'm not stealing from the police," Rin said piously.

"Right," Clark said. "You just knock them out."

"Please," the wizard said, "we don't have any time to waste."

"Fine," Clark grumbled.

Rin pulled open the office door and the bird shot straight out. He flew directly over Wilma and intentionally slammed into the glass front door.

Wilma screamed like she was in a contest and was hoping to win "Best Screech." Clark bounced off the glass and dropped to the ground in front of the door.

"What the—?" she hollered.

Wilma stepped out from behind the counter to see what had just hit the glass. As she bent over to get a better look at Clark, the bird sprang up into her hair.

In comparison, the scream she had let out before

seemed more like a whisper, a warmup at best. Clark rooted around in her hair as she batted and smacked at him. She stumbled through the front door and ran into the parking lot. Clark twisted his talons into her hair like a fork spooling spaghetti. He flapped his wings wildly.

Wilma spun in a circle while screaming and grabbing at the bird. But Clark was too crafty and she was too disoriented to get ahold of him. As she ran in a circle screaming, three people slipped out of the front door of the police station and got away without being seen.

Clark flapped around for a few more moments, but his heart was no longer in it. He tried to work his talons free, but as he struggled, Wilma's hair came loose from her head. The bird had been unaware of the fact that Wilma wore a wig. But now, the fact was perfectly clear. Clark flapped away, Wilma's wig attached to his feet. He tried to shake the hair free from his talons, but it was too tangled. The bird had no other choice than to rise higher and fly away from the premises.

Wilma sank down and then abruptly sat in the middle of the parking lot, holding her hands over her head and muttering about stupid birds.

Eventually Wilma went back inside and found her police hat. She put it on and took her place behind the counter. She was glad the station was short-staffed, because it meant that no one else was around to laugh at her or cause her further embarrassment.

The phone rang and she picked it up. From the sound

of her voice anyone could have told that she was pretending like nothing had happened and that everything was fine. In reality, however, things were unreliably off, and unbeknownst to her, her boss was lying on the floor of his office, knocked out.

Wilma finished the phone call and went to the break room to find something to take her mind off of what had happened.

CHAPTER FORTY-ONE

HORRIBLE PEOPLE

Ray was dressed to the nines. He was wearing one of his best suits and a tie that was knotted perfectly. His trousers had front creases so tight they looked razor-sharp and his shoes shone like polished burgundy stones. There wasn't a red hair out of place on his head. His face was clean shaved and moisturized with a lotion that few people in the world could afford. As he sat in the study of his New York apartment talking on the phone, he looked the picture of perfection. But looks can be deceiving, because the truth was Ray was torn up inside.

"What do you mean she got away?" he growled. Then he repeated the question but this time with a period between every word: "What. Do. You. Mean. She. Got. Away?"

"She escaped," Jon replied into the phone. "She broke apart a couch and used a wire to pop out the door hinges."

"She's a child."

"She's clever."

"Not more than I am," Ray said. "But obviously more than you. I'm not happy about this."

"I didn't expect you to be," Jon said. "I'll find them."

"Really? You have none of them in your custody," Ray reminded him. "You've given the girl information she shouldn't have. You haven't gotten your hands on the boy or taken care of the wizard. And where's my bird?"

"I'll make this right."

"You've helped make it wrong."

Ray's disappointment and anger seeped through the phone and covered Jon's ear like a sour syrup.

"I *will* make it right," Jon affirmed.

"You have today," Ray said. "If we don't get this sorted out I might have to make plans to go in a whole different direction. Understand?"

"Yes," Jon replied.

The phone went dead.

CHAPTER FORTY-TWO

A LIT FUSE

Jon rarely failed to accomplish the tasks he was asked to do. He was not used to being spoken to in the way Ray just had and he didn't like the feeling. His reputation was on the line, and a couple of kids and a delusional wizard were making him look bad.

"A wizard!"

As a child, Jon had been forbidden to read any books or watch any movies that involved magic. His parents thought the very idea was harmful. They were against pretending, opposed to imagination, and anti–make-believe. Their house had been one of rules and discipline and work. His father had said hundreds of times that life was not a game and there was no room for foolish timewasters like fantasy.

He screamed angrily at the walls of the small room. As the scream faded, he looked at the busted couch and chair.

He would have been impressed with what Sigi had done if he wasn't so humiliated by how it made him look.

His father had died many years before from a straightforward heart attack. He hadn't lived to see the solider that Jon had become, or the things he had accomplished by living a life with no magic.

Jon screamed once more before getting in his car and driving away.

CHAPTER FORTY-THREE

ROADSIDE ATTRACTION

A wizard, a sophomore, an apprentice, and a metal raven stood in the trees on the side of the highway. Their description, while it sounded like the beginning of a joke, was also accurate. The four were just a few feet away from a small dirt pullout that had a stone marker with a plaque on it. The spot was a roadside attraction that those driving by were encouraged to pull over and read about.

Few people ever did.

The plaque contained information about a famous fur trapper who had once fought off a group of bears at that very spot. Now, four infamous Oregonians were hiding in the trees near it and trying to figure out what to do next.

Rin was on the phone, arguing with Wilma at the police station. He didn't like to admit it, but he was a tiny bit worried about having left Sheriff Wills unconscious. So he had put forth a tiny bit of effort by calling Wilma to tell her to check on Wills.

"Naw, this is noot a crink call," Rin said using the fake accent he had tried out in New Mexico. "Yaw sheriff needs to bees looked in on."

"Who is this?" Wilma insisted. Her voice was still shaky from the encounter she had recently had with her hair and Clark. "The sheriff's in his office," she said for the fourth time. "He's meeting with someone. I'll take a message if you'd like."

"Perfect," the wizard said. "If you find yourself looking for more, don't discount how much more less is."

"Wait a second," Wilma said. "What happened to your accent?"

Rin hung up.

Ozzy and Sigi looked at him waiting for information.

"Well," he said with a sniff, "I tried. Some people are just so resistant to help."

"Is *that* what that was?" Sigi asked. "I doubt she could understand you. Like I told you before, that's the worst accent."

"Oh," Rin said proudly. "That's not the same one I used before. That was more North Hills. If you listened, you could hear that I was now placing a subtle emphasis on the bowels. It's the dialect of the grassy-slope people of Quarfelt."

"I always want to believe you're a wizard," Sigi said sadly. "But when you say things like that, it's pretty hard. Bowels? Don't you mean vowels?"

"No," he said defensively. "Bowels. It's a very guttural

language—probably due to all the jostling and rolling they experience while living on those grassy slopes."

More cars whizzed by on the highway.

"Take a note," Rin instructed Ozzy. "A true wizard always says what they mean. It's not the responsibility of the wise to please the ears of the uneducated."

Ozzy had no pen, no paper, and he was running out of patience.

"How about instead of me taking notes, you tell us what we're doing? When the sheriff finds us, he's going to be mad. He's not going to just sit around wondering where we went." Ozzy took a deep breath. "I'm surprised he hasn't already tracked us down."

"He'll try," Rin said. "Although they're running out of cars."

Rin looked at his three travelers and smiled.

"Nothing?" he said, disappointed that they didn't like his little joke. "Okay, you're right in the fact that we need to get moving. The urgency *has* increased."

"I noticed," Sigi said. "It seems like the urgency increased the second the sheriff told you mom was on her way back."

"It's not easy for wizards to have ex-wives," Rin said defensively. "It has something to do with the chemical properties of resentment and regret. But Patti returning is not the reason for the urgent nature, it's this." Rin held out the small piece of paper with the long number on it. "Why didn't you tell me this was in the stuff found in your parent's safety deposit box?"

"I thought I did," Ozzy said. "It's not my fault you're always distracted. You were probably too busy complaining about something like the disloyalty of parrots to notice."

"He's right about parrots," Clark chirped in. "I don't trust them. All that blinding color and exotic beaks. And say something original for once, why don't you?"

More cars drove by.

"Dad," Sigi complained. "What's so urgent about the number?"

"I'm good with digits," Rin told them as he held the small slip of paper. "In Quarfelt so much of what is communicated is done with numbers. They're comforting to wizards because they're honest and straightforward. Not like some words I know. I should have seen the answer the second Wills showed me this. But I was temporarily thrown off, because the alphabet in Quarfelt has thirty-two letters and no vowels." Rin took a moment to look at Sigi and make sure she had heard him correctly. "That's why it didn't hit me the moment I saw it. But using your alphabet—"

"It's yours too," Sigi said.

"Thanks for sharing it with me," Rin said. "Because using your alphabet, this number was simple to figure out. Just assign a numeric value to every letter but the first four and do a little word scrambling, and 1189–1922914–229523–121145 is translated to 1189 Alvin's View Lane."

"Really?" Ozzy asked.

"I wasn't surprised by the address," Rin said. "It's the same one that flashed across my crystal ball seconds before it fell into the sea."

Clark ratted the wizard out. "It's also the same one you were looking up in the bushes just now."

"Oh. I thought I was alone."

"Your hat blocks a lot of your peripheral vision," the bird explained.

Rin folded the brim of his felt hat up and back.

"Well, I was just checking on my phone," he said. "I like to have confirmation, and Google is remarkable. Reality is stuffed with evidence of magic that's already in motion and just waiting to be accessed."

"Okay," Ozzy said. "It's an address, but where's it located?"

"There's only one listed address in the world that matches it. 1189 Alvin's View Lane, Corvallis, Oregon."

The cars speeding by covered the audible gasps from both Ozzy and Sigi.

"That's not that far away," Sigi said.

"Right," the wizard continued, "I figured it would be best for us to take a short trip there to investigate. It's about an hour away and I've already summoned a ride."

Rin raised his staff and as he said the word *ride*, a blue 2010 Dodge Caravan pulled off the highway and into the dirt space where the marker was located. The timing was perfect.

"Don't even try to tell me that rideshares aren't magic," Rin challenged them.

No one debated the wizard as they all climbed into the van.

"Are you sure you're up for discovering more about your family?" Rin asked, maneuvering his staff into the back and then buckling up.

"No," Ozzy answered.

"Ten points to Toffy," Rin replied. "Admitting you have doubts is an important step to finding answers."

"Wait," Sigi said. "You're giving out points? I escaped being kidnapped."

"Twenty points to Sigi."

"My last name's South."

"I'm not giving your mother's name any points."

"What about me?" Clark asked. "I had to hang out in that woman's hair. I still have product on my talons."

"Fifteen points to Steel. Plus, you earned yourself a wig."

Clark looked at the wig he was holding with his left wing. "It's been a pretty good day."

Ozzy and Sigi stared at the bird.

"Well, aside from Sigi getting kidnapped, the cloaked house burning down, and the sheriff being knocked out."

Ozzy rubbed the bird on the top of his head, letting him know that it was okay to celebrate small victories like getting a wig.

The blue 2010 Dodge Caravan pulled onto the highway and headed west toward what felt like a very solid clue.

CHAPTER FORTY-FOUR

AFTERNOON JAUNT

"Is there any chance you could go faster?" Rin asked the driver. "We don't have much time."

The driver's name was Yona and like their last Uber driver, he was not about to go any faster than he should.

"I know that safety is important," Rin said. "Trust me, as a wizard, I am trained for all manner of tragedies and personal security."

"You're a wizard?" Yona asked as he looked at them in the rearview mirror.

"I am," Rin said.

"It's a pretty good costume. Are you heading to a renaissance fair or something? I read online that there's one going on in Corvallis."

"No," Rin said with disgust, "I don't dabble in pretending, and this is not a *costume*."

"Okay, okay," Yona said, playing along, "I get it. I've

heard that you nerd types like to act as if dressing up is real. So, please, no offense and all."

"None taken and all." Rin rolled his eyes at Sigi and Ozzy as he leaned back into his seat.

"Okay," Ozzy said, "now might be a good time to talk about what we're doing."

Rin smiled. "That attitude is very apprentice-like."

"Seriously," the boy continued, "if that number really does coordinate with this address, then what are we driving toward?"

The wizard closed his eyes.

After thirty seconds of silence, he whispered, "I can see it all. It's a green house with two tall trees out front and a blue front door. The roof is covered with wooden shingles."

"So it's a home?" Sigi asked.

"It takes a family to make a home," the wizard said. "I don't know if there's a family inside."

"Well, then, whose house is it?" Sigi said.

"Sometimes the magic is in not knowing."

Ozzy wasn't feeling well. His pale face and solemn expression showed it. The last few days had felt toxic and draining. Now the van felt stuffy.

"Are you okay?" Sigi asked.

"I don't know," he admitted. "I think I'm just tired of all of this. Isn't there something misguided and pointless with us going to a green house with two tall trees and expecting an answer?"

"Or answer*s*," Rin said. "There is power in plurals."

"Someone almost kidnapped Sigi," Ozzy said.

"Not almost," she corrected.

"That's what I mean. What do we think we're going to find at this address?" Ozzy asked. "I don't know what to expect from any part of reality anymore. I feel like I'm going mad. What happens if we find a way to take care of this Ray guy? Is there someone else, someone I don't know about, waiting in my mind to walk me into the ocean?"

Ozzy shook with a sickness that was building rapidly inside of him.

"The cloaked house is gone. And it seems like they, whoever *they* are, want to harm other things that are important to me."

Sigi patted his right knee and leaned into him.

"I made Officer Greg drive into the ocean."

"Yes," Rin said, "we should probably talk about that."

"I have a metal bird that can strike down whoever I choose."

"It's *whom*ever," Rin corrected, "but point taken."

"I travel with someone who's either a wizard or a lunatic, and a girl who makes even the ocean look bland."

"Not nice of you to call Yona a lunatic," Rin said quietly, "but I get what you're saying. You just need to—"

"There is a good possibility that at any moment my left hand will begin to buzz," Ozzy interrupted. "My finger, that was transformed by something I still don't know about, is purple and, like a rogue wand, it commands me to do its will."

"Oh, *rogue wand*," Rin said. "I like how that sounds. Someone should write that down."

"I've lost my parents, lost my home, and now I feel as if I'm losing my mind."

"Mondays," Rin said, letting out a sigh. "Not the best day of the week."

"My mood isn't the result of the calendar," Ozzy insisted. "Every book I've ever read, every song I've ever listened to, is swirling around in my head fighting to make sense of what's happening."

"Hold on," Rin said forcefully. "Stop this. I've come back for you. And all those books you've read and songs you've heard testify in one way or another that eventually—when all the dust settles and the secrets have been exposed—good wins. Not great, *good*. Great dies trying to climb the highest or gain the most. Good achieves what is right and all reality expands because of it. You were born into something. Now it's up to you to put the picture together so that you can see things clearly. I would understand your pity if it weren't for the fact that you have a wizard on your side."

"I'm not sure that helps," Ozzy said.

"Ouch," Clark chirped from inside the boy's pocket.

"I'm sorry, Ozzy," Rin whispered softly. "I wish I could tell you how little that hurts, but it would be a lie. And as you know, we wizards prefer the truth."

"Wow," Yona said from the driver's seat, "you guys take this pretending stuff seriously."

Nobody replied.

Yona's passengers remained quiet and contemplative for the rest of the ride. Something was wrong with Ozzy—and the wizard, his daughter, and the bird knew it. Actually, Ozzy knew it too, and it wasn't resting well on his troubled mind.

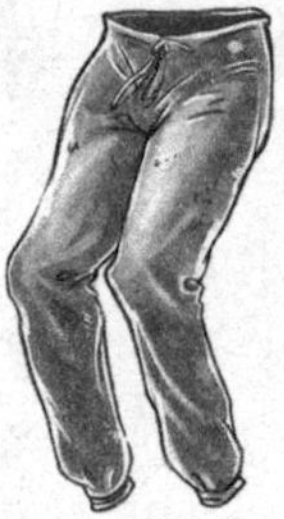

CHAPTER FORTY-FIVE

CYCLOPS

Yona came to a stop in front of 1189 Alvin's View Lane and his passengers got out. Before shutting the van door, Rin gave Yona some advice: "Never sit where you know you should stand."

Yona looked confused so the wizard added, "And only stand in spots worth sitting."

"You even give pretend advice," Yona said with a smile.

Rin closed the door and the van drove away, leaving three humans and a bit of fancy metal to stand at the curb and look up at a blue house with no trees.

"This doesn't look like the place you described," Ozzy said needlessly.

Sigi sighed disappointedly. "That's because he probably looked at it on Google Street View. Those were photos from a while ago. Obviously, the house has since been repainted and the trees removed."

"I often see things as they truly are," Rin said, unfazed. "Those trees live on, and this house knows perfectly well that it looked better in green."

"We know nothing about this place," Ozzy said quietly as they stared at the blue house.

"You want me to fly around and do some reconnaissance?" Clark offered.

"How do you know the word *reconnaissance*, but not orthodontist?" Ozzy asked.

"I've never had teeth."

Clark jumped out of Ozzy's pocket and flew around the house twice before darting back down onto the boy's shoulder. He hunched to make it look less like he was a bird and more like he was just a lump of black metal and wires.

"It seems like the kind of place you humans like to live," Clark reported. "They also have a really small empty moat in the back."

"That's a pool," Rin said.

"Whatever it's called, it would be super easy for anyone storming the castle to get around it. And I have to say," Clark twisted his head to look around, "Alvin's view is nothing great."

All of them took a moment to glance around and wonder what Alvin had been thinking. There were no other houses in sight and no view other than forest.

"Why would my parents care enough about this address to hide it in a code and lock it away in a safety deposit box?"

"Why do most people do most things?" Sigi said. "But we have a much better chance of finding an answer by knocking on the door instead of just standing here."

"I agree," Rin cheered. "Ozzy didn't hire me to stand around."

"I didn't hire you this time," Ozzy reminded him.

"I like your commitment to telling that joke until it gets funny," the wizard replied. "Just follow my lead and let me do the talking."

Rin walked up the front sidewalk with everyone else trailing him. Clark hid in Sigi's hair so that he would be better able to see what was happening.

The sidewalk leading to the house was mostly cracks and missing chips. The front lawn was green and shaggy with five large boulders placed randomly. The sidewalk led to a small porch with a single, black rocking chair. The front door was a shade of orangish-yellow that clashed with the blue the house was wearing.

Rin knocked.

It took less than three seconds before the door opened about six inches. Through the opening they saw a six-inch slice of what looked to be an extremely old man with white frosting hair at the top of the slice. Below the hair was a gray, speckled face with eyes the color of weak coffee, a nose bulbous and wide from age, and a chin that drooped into an indistinct neck of skin and wrinkles. The man was dressed in a purple velvet smoking jacket, though there was no sign of his smoking. His trousers were a pale blue and the bits of his shoes that were visible looked to be more comfortable than stylish.

The man looked at them all with a worn right eye. He showed no sign of excitement, or worry, or humanity.

"I wasn't expecting *you*," he said in a voice that sounded as old as his face looked.

"We are often unexpected," Rin informed him. "But life is best when we realize that the only thing a person can count on is uncertainty."

"You use more words than you need to," the old man scolded.

"Well, allow me to use a few more," Rin replied. "My name is Winch and these are my young students, Till and Grunge. We are currently working on a project that requires us to gather information about Oregonians in this area. Would it be okay if we asked you a few questions?"

"It would not."

"Oh." Rin looked more surprised than a decent wizard should let on. "Well, it would just take a second, and it would help these children achieve their goal of being able to attend the governor's ball at the end of the school year."

"I don't care for the governor or his politics."

The old man's answers were gruff, but he didn't try to close the door to end the conversation.

"I don't care for any politics," Rin said. "But these children have so little."

"They do appear lacking."

"Hey," Sigi complained.

"Look," Rin put his hands on his hips, "you've gone and hurt Grunge's feelings."

"*I'm* Grunge?" Sigi whispered angrily.

"Excuse her whispering," Rin apologized. "She wears her emotions on her sleeve, and as you can see, she really wants to go to that governor's ball."

"I have lived a long time," the old man said. "Ninety-five years, and I don't buy any of this. At the same time, you three look too much like dolts to be a threat. Your eyes aren't the eyes of someone trying to scam the elderly. I'm baffled by you being here on my doorstep at this time—so baffled that I will hear one question."

"More than fair," Rin said. "Go ahead, Till."

Rin had told them he would take the lead, but now he was passing the task of asking a question off to Ozzy.

"Okay," Ozzy said, still feeling ill. "Do you know Emmitt or Mia Toffy?"

The six-inch slice of old man didn't blink or breathe. He kept his right eye with the bushy gray eyebrow over it on Ozzy. After ten seconds of silence he spoke.

"I've never heard of them."

"Do—" Sigi started to ask a question of her own, but the man cut her off.

"—I said I'd hear one question and I did."

The door shut, leaving three humans standing on the old man's porch confused and wondering what they could have done to have handled that better.

"For starters," Sigi said to her dad, "you should have just used our real names."

"Where's the mystery in that?" the wizard replied defensively. "And I don't enjoy pointing at others, but I believe the problem was Ozzy asking him such a strong question." Rin pointed. "If you're going to be my apprentice, I'd like to see you work on your approach. Subtlety is one of the three essential wizard ghost herbs."

"The what?" Ozzy asked, mad that he was being chastised for something Rin had made him do. "You didn't tell me I'd be asking questions. And what are ghost herbs?"

"Now, see, that's an example of a *good* question," Rin said. "Ghost herbs are the three invisible things we wizards sprinkle on everything we do—Subtlety, Substance, and Awe."

"They *must* be invisible," Clark said from the back of Sigi's hair. "I've never seen you sprinkle anything on anything."

"Maybe we should get off the porch and argue about this somewhere else," Sigi suggested.

"No," Rin said. "We're not leaving, which means we must try again."

The wizard turned from Ozzy and his daughter and knocked loudly on the door.

"That's not subtle," Clark tweeted.

The door opened six inches again and the old man's right eye twitched.

"Excuse me," the wizard said while trying to act humble

and graceful. "I'm afraid my young student read the question wrong. What he wanted to ask was how long have you lived in Oregon?"

"I don't know why I opened the door up again," the wrinkled mouth muttered.

"I can be quite charming," Rin replied.

"That's not it," the old man said. "Now, what are your real names?"

Rin looked at Ozzy and Sigi acting as if he didn't understand the question.

"If you are going to pull this ruse off you might consider using names that don't sound moronic," the man insisted.

Rin sighed. "Okay, you caught us. My name is Rin."

"Not you."

Rin looked at his daughter.

"I'm Sigi," she said.

"Not you either." The man's tone wasn't mean, it was matter-of-fact.

His old eye rested on the tall boy with the concerned expression.

"Me? I'm Ozzy."

Once again the man was quiet to the point of it feeling uncomfortable. When he finally spoke he said, "I think you're lying."

"Okay." Rin exhaled loudly. "Rin isn't my given name."

"Still not you."

Rin tried hard not to look hurt.

"I'm not lying," Ozzy told the six-inch slice of old man. "My name is Ozzy Toffy."

The man was quiet again.

After twenty seconds of him just staring at them, Clark couldn't take it and moaned softly. "Come on, already."

The old man flinched. "What was that?"

"It was just me," Sigi lied.

"No it wasn't—what's in your hair?"

"A bird," she answered. "It just repeats what it hears—like a parrot."

They glanced at the man through the six inches of open door and tried to look innocent, needy, and trustworthy all at once.

"Where did you get my address?" he asked.

Ozzy's finger buzzed—his body shook as words quickly formed in his brain and slipped out of his mouth with a punch.

"I think you know."

For the first time since they had met him, the six inches of man looked sad.

"I don't own anything of value," he said. "There's nothing in here to steal or take. No medicines, no coins, not even a TV or a stereo."

"I already have a TV," Rin said, feeling as if that was something the man wanted to know. "Well, my ex-wife does."

"My point is," the man continued, "despite my better

judgment, you can come in. Just know that there's nothing to take and nothing of value."

"You'd be surprised at what we consider worthwhile," Rin said kindly.

The door closed and a chain rattled, then it opened all the way and the four visitors were given passage into the home.

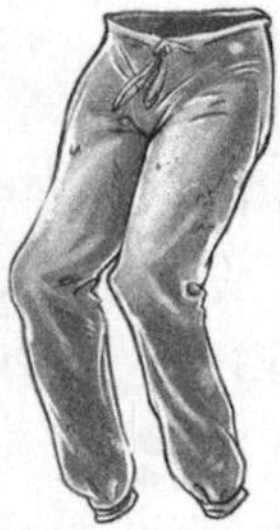

CHAPTER FORTY-SIX

BIBLIOPHILE OF CORVALLIS

Stepping inside the old man's house it was immediately clear why he had no TV, no stereo, no coins or medicine—there was no room for anything else because the place was stuffed with books. They filled every shelf, tabletop, and chair. There were piles stacked neatly everywhere. Books rose from the ground to the ceiling like stalagmites of words and paper.

Ozzy gasped.

The books made the home feel closed in and tight. They also gave Ozzy hope. It felt good to know there were places in the world as interesting as the one he was now standing in.

"Impressive," Rin said. "You might not have a TV, but you certainly have valuables here."

The old man took a seat on a single soft chair near a fireplace that was filled with books.

"I'd ask you to sit," the man said. "But every seat is occupied."

"I could hover," Rin bragged, "but I don't want to make Ozzy and Sigi feel bad."

"Thanks," Sigi said as she took a seat on the floor.

"I'd be fine with you hovering," Ozzy told the wizard.

"It wouldn't be modest. So—when in home . . ." Rin sat down on the floor with crossed legs and placed his staff across his lap.

Ozzy dropped down next to Sigi.

The three of them looked up at the old man sitting in his chair. He wasn't much wider than the six-inch slice they had seen through the door. He was very thin and lacked fat of any kind. His sinewy body was all elbows, knees, and shoulders, sharp points that could easily burst out of the clothes he was wearing. His ears were large, like his nose and lips. He sat with his shoulders hunched forward, holding his arm in front of him as if he were positioned to read a book.

"I doubt there's a library with this many titles within a couple of hundred miles," Rin said as he looked around.

"I wouldn't know."

Rin attempted to make conversation. "I actually like to use the computers at—"

"Tell me about the bird," the man interrupted.

"Well, I think—" Rin tried.

"Not you."

Ozzy shifted uncomfortably as the old man stared at

him. "My father invented him years ago. He's made of metal and wire and powered by light."

Clark heard the conversation and figured the old man would want to see him. So the bird wriggled around in Sigi's hair, getting ready to step out and make an entrance.

The old man changed the subject.

"I never answer my door." He moaned as if auditioning to play a wounded ghost. "Once a week my groceries are delivered. I open the garage and they put them in the refrigerator and freezer."

"Sounds convenient," the wizard said.

Still hidden in Sigi's hair, bothered by no one talking about him, Clark let out a small passive-aggressive sigh.

"I spend all of my time in books," the old man continued. "I order them by phone, and most days three or so new ones are delivered by UPS. I wait by the door until there is a knock. Then I open it up and I take the package."

"Everyone's shopping habits are different." Rin was trying to be supportive of what the man was saying, but he was having a difficult time continuing to feign his interest in how and why this man answered his door.

"Today I waited," the old man went on, "and at three o'clock there was a knock. I should have looked through the peephole, but routine had me feeling certain that it was UPS. It was not. It was you. Had you stepped on my porch at any other moment I would never have opened the door. Tell me who you are."

"I think you know," Ozzy said again, surprised by the strength of his own words.

The old man was quiet.

Clark cleared his throat and Ozzy finally got the hint.

"Would you like to see the bird?"

"No," the man said.

Clark grumbled.

"There's only one person I know who would give you this address," the man said. "I have gone to great lengths to make my life as quiet and out of the way as it is."

"It seems like a jail." Sigi wasn't intending to be mean, but the words sounded less than complimentary.

"This is not jail," the man insisted. "Do any of you know how many poisonous spiders there are in Madagascar? Or the average life span of an Iranian who smokes? Do you remember the lessons of the Zanzibar War, or the poetry of Philip White?"

"Obvious your mind travels freely around the globe," Rin said calmly. "Of course, as a wizard my knowledge goes well beyond the books and reasonings of reality."

"Ah, a wizard," the man said with an uneven smile. "There have been many who have claimed to walk this earth. Do you know the wizard Gazan in India? Or Flees in Argentina?"

"They sound familiar," Rin answered. "Did Gazan have one of those neckbeards with no mustache? Because if he's who I'm thinking, I don't really care for him."

"According to the book I read," the man said, "he did not have a beard."

"All right," Clark squawked as he came out from beneath Sigi's hair and flew onto Ozzy's right knee, "that's enough. Here I am."

The old man looked at Clark for a moment.

"Yes, yes, I see you. Now let me stay on track."

"*Really?*" Clark asked, sounding as if he were disappointed in the whole of humanity.

The man ignored the bird and continued to talk to the others. "As I said, I have gone to great lengths to live just as I am living. I am a recluse, a hermit, and I have not given my real name out in many, many, years."

"Why are you telling us this?" Ozzy asked.

"Because I find it more unbelievable than most fiction that at three o'clock someone knocked on my door and mentioned the name of Toffy. And I suppose as I step closer and closer to my own death, the worry of being discovered has dulled."

"You do look really old," Clark said, still hurt about not being fawned over.

"I like birds better in books," the man said.

Clark's metal head heated up.

"So you *did* know my parents?" Ozzy asked while tapping the bird affectionately on his back.

"I knew one of them better than the other."

"Which one?"

"My daughter, of course—Mia."

Rin, Ozzy, and Sigi all gasped.

"See," Clark said, acting like a bird baby, "that's the kind of reaction I wanted."

Ozzy was incredulous. "You're my *grandfather*?"

"On paper, and in all honesty, but not in action."

The insides of Ozzy felt like a jumble sale of weather—there was a storm, a lull, a depression, and a typhoon. He sat still, surrounded by books, a wizard, a girl, a bird, and now the first real family he had seen since the age of seven.

"Process your emotions," Ozzy's grandfather said. "Then, when you've got ahold of them correctly, you can speak."

It's hard to get ahold of something as big as the information Ozzy had just been handed.

Almost impossible.

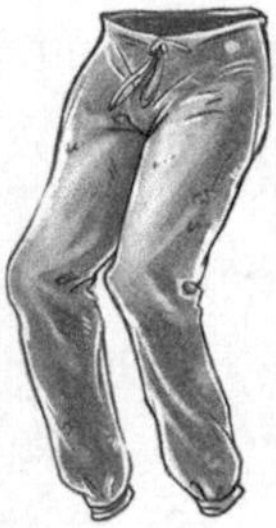

CHAPTER FORTY-SEVEN

A PIECE OF KNOWLEDGE

Ozzy didn't know how to feel—the old man sitting in front of him had just made the claim that he was his grandfather. In a perfect world, hearing information like that would make most people happy and warm. For Ozzy, however, it made him mad. His grandfather had lived less than a couple of hours away from him for all these years and he had never known. Ozzy had been lost and hidden and alone when there was someone so close who could have helped.

The boy's grey eyes were clear.

"I know what you might be thinking," his grandfather said. "Why haven't I ever reached out to find you? Well, I didn't know you were alive. I assumed you disappeared with your parents."

"You knew they came to Oregon?" Rin asked.

"Many years ago I helped them buy all of that land.

They contacted me once after they moved out here. Since then there's been nothing."

"They're dead," Ozzy said coldly.

"I figured as much," his grandfather said. "Your parents were involved in something very dangerous."

"And that's it?" Ozzy was angry. "You knew they were doing something dangerous and just figured we were all dead?"

"Yes."

"That's madness," Sigi argued.

"I'm not sure I care," the old man said.

An intense redness crept up Ozzy's neck like a crimson shadow. It covered his face and colored his eyes.

"Excuse me," Rin spoke up, "I think you should choose your words with better care. I am no stranger to eccentricity, but you're using your selfish lifestyle to justify hurting the one person on earth who deserves compassion from you. And if you choose to sit there handing out nothing but heartless soundbites, then you are choosing to offend not only your grandchild, but a powerful wizard as well. And there are few things more dangerous than ticking off someone who has the magic to make your life miserable."

"Yeah!" Clark added enthusiastically.

"How would you like to live book-free and in a house filled with people?" Rin threatened. "Because I can make that happen."

Ozzy's grandfather shivered. "Book-free? And filled with people? What a horrible thought. And while I appreciate your candor, my position remains the same. Ozzy's mother, Mia, was my only child. Her mother died when she was born, and she was raised by her live-in nanny, Stella. I was around, but I just couldn't be bothered with the day-to-day."

"You're quite the father," Sigi said with disgust.

Rin looked hurt for a moment, thinking his daughter was talking about him. "Oh, right, him. Yeah, you're certainly not a candidate for Father of the Year."

"Is that something people care about?" the old man asked.

Rin stood up. His height and hat made him look like a giant surrounded by a landscape of books. His robe was untied so that everyone could see his high-ranking trousers. He looked imposing and powerful as he held his staff in hand.

"You may throw your words around callously," the wizard said, "but they leave impressions on all who are struck. There must be some part of you that cares. Why else would you invite us inside?"

"Curiosity," the old man said. "You all had a look of determination. I knew that if I shut the door you wouldn't give up. I needed to make it clear that I have no obligation to Ozzy."

"Okay," Rin said calmly, "then let me make a few things clear to you. You are going to answer some questions and pretend to be human. If you need me to write it down and get it published in a book so that you'll actually pay attention to it, then I'll make that happen. But it would be much easier for you to just speak up now. Then we can leave you to your life of bindings and chapters and little else."

"I'm not threatened by you," Ozzy's grandfather said. "But I am old and every breath I continue to take is a surprise to me. So I'll try to match your definition of civility and answer a few more questions."

"Good," Rin said. "Why would your daughter have your address written in code in her safety deposit box?"

"Sentimentality?" he guessed.

"I doubt that," the wizard said. "I've met you and you're not something to get sentimental about."

"Well," the old man mused, "Mia was a genius. Others thought that Emmitt was the smart one. But while he was brilliant, his ability was dwarfed by Mia's. The Discipline Serum was her discovery. Emmitt only did things like build model birds."

"Thank you," Clark said, thinking he was being called a model.

"Together they were unspeakably intelligent. Of course, that intelligence has killed them."

"So you know about the serum?" Sigi asked.

"It was going to change the world." The old man coughed softly into a handkerchief he pulled out of his non-smoking jacket. "Giving the serum to Ozzy was the mistake."

"They gave it to me?"

"Yes, and too much of it. They left New York to save your life."

"I don't understand," Ozzy said sadly.

"If those who were funding the study had discovered that you had the serum inside you, they would have taken you away from them and . . . well, who knows what they would have done."

"Something worse than taking his parents and leaving him for dead in the woods?" Sigi asked angrily.

"I guess that's a matter of opinion," the old man said. "If they had stayed in New York there's a good chance Ozzy would already be dead. Ray would have stopped at nothing to get that formula."

"You know Ray?" Ozzy asked.

"Unfortunately. He believes I'm dead and I sincerely hope you don't tell him differently."

"Do you know the formula?" Ozzy said seriously.

The old man coughed a small cough and took a shallow breath. Ozzy, Sigi, Rin, and Clark all leaned forward anticipating his answer.

"I *do* know the formula," he finally admitted.

Rin looked around nervously.

"Don't worry," the old man said. "It isn't written down or tucked away. It's simply something in my brain that I will never forget."

"It's something I wish had never existed," Ozzy said passionately.

"Wait," Sigi spoke up. "Do you think it could help Ozzy?"

The old man blinked slowly. "Help him how?"

"So that whoever is taking over his mind can be stopped," Sigi answered.

For the first time the old man looked genuinely surprised.

"Someone is controlling your mind?" Ozzy's grandfather began to shake. "I don't believe it."

"It's true," Sigi insisted. "Would the formula help him? Could it cure the effect?"

Ozzy's grandfather panicked. He started to get up from out of his chair and then fell back into it. His eyes closed, and his shoulders fell.

"That means—"

The old man stopped speaking and blinked twice while looking at Ozzy. He coughed and shook for a moment before becoming still. They all stared at him wondering what was happening.

Rin stepped over and tapped his shoulder with the end of his staff. He was hoping to get some response, but it appeared that life had left the old man's body. And just like that, Ozzy had no living relatives once again.

Rin looked at the boy. "I'm sorry, Ozzy."

"Should you bring him back to life?" Clark asked. "Don't we need that formula?"

"Wizards don't bring people back to life just for fun."

"It wouldn't be *fun*," Clark insisted. "I mean, he wasn't exactly pleasant."

"I'm sorry, Ozzy," Sigi said sadly.

"I am too," the boy replied. "All these years, he was just sitting here alone—like me in the cloaked house." Ozzy stood up and walked over to his grandfather. He touched the top of his right hand. "I know my parents were brilliant, but I'm not sure I see the value in what their genius has done to all of us."

"If you look hard enough, you will find the value in everything," Rin said kindly.

Ozzy was only an apprentice and he didn't have quite the vision Rin did.

"This might help," the wizard said. "You've passed the second challenge. It seems like you asked just the right question to get us in here."

"I don't feel good," was Ozzy's only reply.

"Sometimes the results that answers bring can make even the strongest apprentice sick."

CHAPTER FORTY-EIGHT

ACCURACY

"What do we do now?" Sigi asked, looking at the old man. "Should we call the police?"

Rin waved his staff around Ozzy's grandfather as he sat there in his chair. "*Preserva olda humanio*," he said sincerely.

"What does that do?" Ozzy asked.

"Nothing, really, but sometimes just doing something makes people feel better."

"It didn't," Ozzy said.

Rin tried something else. "*Rissupo omano*."

"I don't even know his name," Ozzy said, staring at him.

"He looks like an Edgar," Clark guessed as he jumped up on the old man's shoulder. "Although he acted like an Orson."

As they looked at the lifeless old man they were all so caught up in the loss and sadness that had befallen the room that they failed to notice what was happening behind them.

Someone had entered the house seconds before and was silently standing nearby.

"Well," a strong voice said, "what do we have here?"

Everyone turned to find Jon holding a gun in his left hand, pointed directly at Ozzy.

"You," Ozzy said, "you're the one who delivered the flash drive."

Rin stamped his staff against the ground. "Which means *you're* the one who tried to harm my daughter?"

"She was never in any danger," Jon insisted. "She was more trouble than she was worth. She even broke some furniture making her escape."

"So sorry about your couch," Sigi said sarcastically.

"Wait." The wizard turned to look at his daughter. "Nobody told me about any problem with a couch."

"Quiet," Jon insisted.

"I rarely do what people tell me," Rin informed him. "And I certainly don't take orders from someone like you. Now put that gun away."

"You and I are a lot alike," Jon said. "I don't like taking orders either. But seeing how I'm the one holding the gun, you might want to do as I say."

"You take orders from Ray," Sigi said.

"That's true," Jon admitted. "Well, I suppose if you offered me the kind of money that Ray does, I'd put this gun down and be on my way."

"All right," Rin said. "We'll double what he's paying."

"I'd need to see the money first."

"So sad," Rin shook his head sadly. "Your lack of trust just lost you a lot of money." The wizard pulled out his phone and tapped the screen.

"What are you doing?" Jon asked.

"Ordering an Uber. It will be here in six minutes."

"What? You won't be going anywhere," Jon said sounding frustrated. "You're a bigger fool than I thought. You three really have a knack for stepping in it."

"You mean *you four*!" Clark shot off the dead man's shoulder and flew directly at Jon, squawking. "Don't discount the bird!"

Jon didn't—he was prepared for Clark. He pulled a small net from his back pocket and swiped it at the bird as he came toward him. The net caught everyone, including Clark, off guard and worked perfectly to capture the flying metal object.

Jon held the net closed with his right hand and kept the gun pointed at the others with his left. Clark thrashed and squawked as he tried to fight his way out.

"Nobody move," Jon insisted. His voice had shifted to a more sinister tone. "I'm serious." He swung the small bird-filled net around and then slammed it against the wall.

"No!" Ozzy screamed as he lunged closer.

"Don't do anything stupid," Jon shouted while still holding the gun. The net in his right hand hung motionless.

"He'd better be okay," Ozzy threatened.

"You all have other things to worry about."

Rin growled, "If that bird is hurt, you're in for a world of trouble."

"Let's not focus on the bird," Jon insisted. "There are more pressing things we need to take care of."

"Agreed," the wizard said while lifting his staff. "For starters, we need to talk about you setting that bird down and leaving before it's too late. You only have five minutes before our ride's here."

"I could care less about your ride. And I won't be told what to do from someone who belongs in an asylum." Jon's forehead was growing red. "I've been watching you . . . Brian Mortley," he said with a sneer. "You need immediate help. I don't know who you think you're fooling. You are no more a wizard than I am an angel. Now, I'll take Ozzy."

"I know a few angels," Rin said, "and they would be bothered by you even joking about them."

"This is no joke." Jon waved the gun for emphasis.

Rin was not scared. "Four and a half minutes."

"You're touched in the head." Jon was done wasting time. "Come on, Ozzy. If you want your friends to be safe, let's go. There's no bounty on their heads. They can be comforted by the fact that nobody wants them anymore."

"I beg to differ," Rin said, upset. "I know of at least six bounties on my head. I made a few enemies in Quarfelt my first few years there. Is it my fault I didn't understand the exchange rate on spells?"

"Are you even speaking English?" Jon asked. "Be quiet! Now, Ozzy, do I need to hurt one of your friends before you realize I'm serious?"

"Four minutes," Rin said coolly.

"I said be quiet."

"Do you know how they say *get down* in Quarfelt?" the wizard asked.

Jon's eyes were dark and filled with hate. He had run out of patience for the man in the felt hat and short robe.

"It's *feldart*," Rin informed Jon as he took a quick glance at his daughter and Ozzy. "*Feldart!*" he ordered.

Ozzy and Sigi dropped to the floor as Rin spun around, swinging his staff. He hit a book on the top of a stack and the volume sailed across the room and hit a surprised Jon directly in the face.

Jon shot his gun into the ceiling as he fell backwards.

The wizard kept the assault going—he spun like he was possessed, sending book after book flying with incredible accuracy. Jon's gun hand was nailed by the *M* volume of an encyclopedia and the weapon went flying across the room and up against the wall.

Rin kept spinning.

Book after book thwacked Jon as he struggled to fend them off and stay standing.

Tolstoy to the face.

James to the gut.

Shakespeare to the groin.

The air was filled with flying books—the room seemed

to spin with the motion of the whirling wizard and his staff. Ozzy and Sigi stayed on the floor as histories, biographies, and mysteries flew over them.

"*Sintablio balcatium!*"

Rin sent a collegiate dictionary across the room and it made full contact with Jon's face. The man dropped onto his stomach and then blacked out. The wizard summoned a whirlwind of books that tumbled from shelves and buried Jon on the floor.

Ozzy stood up and grabbed the gun near the wall as Rin stopped spinning and glanced down at Jon. The wizard looked powerful, strong, and a bit dizzy from all the turning.

"That was impressive," Ozzy said.

"I'm glad I practiced my staff work." Rin tipped to the right and looked at his phone. "One minute, thirty seconds."

"Is Jon okay?" Sigi asked.

"Yes." Rin tipped a bit to his left and steadied himself. "He'll come to soon, so we should hurry—one minute," he reported.

"What about my grandfather?" Ozzy said. "We can't just leave him."

"Why not?" Ozzy's grandfather said. "It's what I want."

Ozzy and Sigi both jumped.

"You're not dead!" Ozzy said excitedly.

"Not yet. Now would you please leave me?"

"You should play dead until Jon wakes up and leaves," Rin suggested. "Or hide."

"I'll do what I please. But leave me the gun just in case."

Ozzy handed him the gun and his grandfather hid it under some books.

"Now go," he ordered.

"Thirty seconds," Rin said.

Ozzy grabbed the small net that was holding Clark. The bird wasn't moving and seemed as lifeless as his grandfather had been moments before. He looked at the old man, still sitting in his chair surrounded by books, telling them to go. Ozzy wanted to feel something sad, or moving, but all he felt was anger toward him and all those in his life who had been too selfish or misguided to be of help.

"Fifteen seconds," Rin said with urgency.

They dashed out the door, down the sidewalk, and to the curb just as a red 2016 Toyota 4Runner pulled up.

"Magical," Rin cheered as they all climbed in.

Jon burst out of the house yelling. He had come to, and he sounded upset.

Ozzy closed the car door and Sigi yelled at the driver, "Go!"

The 4Runner drove away from Alvin's View as Jon ran to his car.

CHAPTER FORTY-NINE

EVERYTHING'S COMING TO A GRINDING HALT

The red SUV traveled at three miles over the speed limit down the highway heading east. Rin was in the passenger seat up front, the bottom of his staff wedged down by his feet and the top half sticking into the back, where Ozzy and Sigi and a net-covered Clark, tucked away in Ozzy's pocket, sat. Rin was giving the driver more grief than the poor man deserved or wanted.

"Go faster, Terrance!" he told the driver.

"I'm not going to speed, and I told you my name's Jeff."

Jeff was in his thirties, balding, and missing a neck. He was also wearing sandals, shorts, and a T-shirt that said *Mr. Wonderful.*

"Jeff is a common nickname for Terrance," the wizard tried.

"No, it's not," Sigi said from the back seat.

"She's right, and what's with your stick and getup?" Jeff asked. "Are you a wizard or something?"

"I'm a wizard *and* something," Rin said proudly. "This is how we dress. And as a wizard I am asking you to drive faster."

"Uber's rules are very clear," Jeff said seriously. "I can't jeopardize my job."

Sigi turned her head and looked out the back window. "Jon's not chasing us."

"He will," Rin said. "Now go faster, Jeff."

"Where are we going?" Ozzy asked.

"To the marina," Rin said. "If we ever get there."

"I'm not going to speed," Jeff insisted.

"Where I come from there are no speed limits," the wizard bragged.

"Where's that?"

"Quarfelt."

"Is that in California?"

"It's everywhere."

"Jon's still not chasing us," Sigi reported.

"Is there really someone after you?" Jeff's question sounded anxious. "I thought you were joking."

"Being chased is no joke," Rin said. "Unless you're playing tarot tag at Dumbledore Days in Quarfelt. That competition is a joke. Steven P. got extra points for giving me paper cuts when he flicked his cards. What's that about? Know the rules, Card Master."

Jeff turned to look at Rin. "Are you okay?"

"I already told you I'm a wizard, so yes. But I'd be even better if you drove faster."

"Not going to happen." Jeff growled lightly. "I can call the police, if that helps. I mean, if you're in trouble, they might be able to assist you."

"Really?" Rin asked. "Have *you* ever called the police for help? It's not an easy thing to do. We've tried, but the results have been less than stellar. You see, Jade—"

"It's Jeff."

"You should consider changing that," Rin said. "Jade is much more *now*. But that's beside the point. You see, Jeff, I am a wizard, but Ozzy back there is my apprentice. And I don't think you'd want to live in a world where a wizard, apprentice, and the wizard's daughter required the help of the police. Now go faster."

"If you ask me to break the law one more time, I'm going to have to stop and let you out."

"Then I'll wait to ask at the right time."

Ozzy had pulled Clark out of the small net and was fiddling with the bird. He held him down low so that Jeff couldn't see him.

"Is he okay?" Sigi whispered.

Clark had been in worse shape before. His head was out of line with his body and his right wing was bent. Using his thumbs, Ozzy popped the bird's head back into alignment. As he tightened the neck, he could hear a soft click followed by a short hum.

Clark's eye's opened and closed.

Both the boy and the girl smiled. The wizard was too

busy arguing with the driver to notice what was going on just behind him.

Ozzy held his finger to his lips to let Clark know that him being quiet was a good idea. He then bent the twisted wing back into its regular shape.

"Easy!" Clark squawked.

Thinking the words were directed to him from Ozzy, the driver slowed down to where he was going only one mile over the speed limit. And Clark crawled into his pocket to sulk about being bent into shape.

They rode in silence for twenty minutes, Sigi looking out the back window every thirty seconds to see if Jon's car was there.

"I don't understand," she said. "Why isn't he following us?"

"I don't like this," Jeff said loudly. "So someone's chasing you?"

"No," Rin insisted. "Have you not been listening? There's no one behind us. This is just a little driving game that we play. It's called 'Someone's After Us.' It helps pass the time on road trips."

"Oh." Jeff sounded unconvinced. "Well, you're going to need to pass a little more time because there's construction up ahead."

Rin, Ozzy, and Sigi could see a line of brake lights in front of them. The vehicles were waiting to be waved through by a man wearing a yellow hard hat and safety vest standing on the side of the road. The man was holding a tall wooden pole with a stop sign on top of it.

"Great," Ozzy said, frustrated.

"Great, indeed," Rin said happily.

The SUV slowed down and came to a stop behind a green truck loaded with old mattresses. Cars began to stop behind them as the line of waiting vehicles grew longer.

"This construction is the worst," Jeff said. "They've been working on this part of the road for months. A few days ago, I waited here for over twenty minutes."

"He's back there," Sigi reported.

They all turned to see that the sixth car behind them was a beige compact with Jon sitting behind the wheel. It was hard to see his expression, but his eyes were focused on their vehicle and he clearly wasn't smiling.

"He must have been tailing us from far away," Ozzy guessed. "Now all he has to do is wait."

"That's good," Rin said. "He can't do anything while we're in line with all these cars."

"Are you guys for real?" Jeff asked. "There's actually someone back there?"

"Just part of the game," Rin insisted. "Don't take us out of the fantasy with your logical questions."

"Okay," Sigi said, "he can't do anything now, but eventually we'll start moving and he's only six cars away."

"This feels like a super lame car chase," Clark said from the pocket. "No one's even moving."

"Who said that?" Jeff asked, having heard a voice he hadn't yet associated with any of his passengers.

Ozzy looked at Rin, who looked at Sigi, who looked at Jeff.

"Sometimes we use funny voices while playing 'Someone's After Us,'" Sigi said sheepishly. "It makes it more interesting."

Jeff just shook his head. "I don't know about you three. Maybe you should order another Uber while we're here in line. Actually . . . too late. I think we're about to get moving again."

The man in the yellow hard hat and stop sign twisted the pole he was holding to reveal the other side of the sign that read *Slow.*

All the cars that had been waiting obeyed and began to move forward slowly. Yellow Hat waved his arm to motion for people to drive past him and on down the road.

"If he stops the line before we get through, I think you three should call another Uber," Jeff insisted as he followed the car directly ahead of him. "There's something about you guys that isn't normal."

"Thanks," Rin said sincerely.

The SUV was now twelve vehicles away from passing Mr. Yellow Hat.

"Do you mind if I roll my window down?" Rin asked Jeff. "It's a little stuffy."

"Maybe you shouldn't wear a bathrobe."

Rin rolled his window down.

The sign up ahead still read *Slow*. But now, instead of waving people through, Yellow Hat was talking to someone on the two-way radio he was holding in his non-sign hand.

Ozzy and Sigi kept their eyes glued on the beige vehicle, still six cars behind them.

"If we get lucky, they'll stop the line after we go through but before Jon does," Sigi said quietly.

"Luck is blinding," Rin loudly. "It hides all the mechanics and miracles that magic makes possible."

They were now four cars away from the slow sign. Yellow Hat was still talking on his two-way radio as he held the pole.

Three cars.

Two cars.

One car.

Rin cleared his throat. "Is that a March birch tree?" he asked Jeff while pointing out the windshield to the left.

Jeff turned his head for a split second to look left.

In that same split-second, Rin thrust his staff out the open window, hitting the closest edge of the slow sign. The sign spun and the edge grazed Yellow Hat's chin as he held the pole.

Rin retracted his staff back into the car and tried to look casual.

Ozzy and Sigi glanced back and saw that the sign was now instructing all the cars behind them to stop, while they continued to drive on. Yellow Hat was feeling his chin, trying to figure out what happened, and why his chin was scraped.

Ozzy could see that the beige car was once again sitting still, pinned in by the vehicles in front and behind it.

Jeff had been distracted from the two-second event looking for a made-up March birch tree, which is why he had no clue or concern about what had just happened.

"What are you talking about?" Jeff complained to Rin. "There's no such thing as a 'March birch' tree. My aunt's an arborist."

"I'm sorry to hear that," Rin sympathetically. "Ignorance is an ugly thing. But I wasn't talking about a tree. I thought I saw Midge Birch. He's a guy I used to know in Quarfelt."

Jeff shook his head and continued driving.

Once they were past the construction, the SUV picked up speed until it was going one mile over the speed limit again. Jon had been temporarily tricked into being left behind, but eventually Yellow Hat would spin the sign and let another long string of cars through.

Rin turned and looked at Ozzy in the backseat.

"How much money do you have on you?"

Ozzy pulled some bills out of his non-bird pocket and counted them. "Sixty-seven dollars."

"Perfect," Rin said, reaching back for it. "Consider it a business expense."

Ozzy handed him the money. "Then should I be getting a receipt from you?"

"No," the wizard replied, "but if I had one it would also say that you have just successfully passed the third challenge."

"Lending you money is one of the challenges?" Sigi asked, disgusted.

"Charity is one of the things a wizard needs most."

"Of course," Sigi said sarcastically. "Why do you need sixty-seven dollars?"

"Don't worry about it."

"I'm going to," she insisted.

"Hey, Jeff?" Rin asked. "Do you think you could go faster?"

"No, and I warned you—if you ask me to break the law one more time, I'm leaving you all on the side of the road."

"Well, as a wizard-slash-customer I demand that you drive at least twenty miles an hour faster than you are." Rin was trying to sound serious. "You have to do what the customer-slash-wizard asks."

Jeff applied the brakes and quickly moved the 4Runner off the road onto the dirt shoulder. He brought the car to a sudden and grinding stop. Everyone rocked back and forth in their seatbelts as the vehicle settled on the side of the road.

"That's it," he said. "I don't care if you leave a bad review. I'm not driving you three around anymore. Get out."

Rin handed Jeff the sixty-seven dollars he had gotten from Ozzy.

"Take this," the wizard said quickly. "We will also

accept your charge for the full ride if you just continue to drive to Otter Rock. When you get there, stop at the doughnut shop on Main Street called DoughJo. Buy yourself one of their twice-dipped, twice-dripped, better-than-sleep doughnuts. They are tastier than two-thirds of the food in Quarfelt."

Jeff took the money. "Get out."

Rin and his posse climbed out of the SUV and shut the doors. Jeff drove off going much faster than the speed limit and without saying goodbye. The road was silent and empty, since all the cars behind them were still stopped at the construction site.

"Why'd you do that, Dad?"

"That boring looking guy would have caught up to us," Rin said. "We'll give him the slip. Plus, I believe I know a shortcut."

The wizard held up his staff and dashed across the open road. Sigi, Ozzy, and Clark followed him. They stood on the shoulder of the road looking down into the forest. The trees below were growing on a steep slope of the mountain that appeared to descend forever.

"Are we climbing down that?" Sigi asked.

"Climbing or tumbling," Rin said. "Whatever gets us to the bottom."

Ozzy was feeling sicker. "Shouldn't we walk farther down the road to find a safer way through the forest?"

"We shouldn't," Rin said.

"Maybe we should call and see if Mom's home," Sigi suggested. "She could pick us up."

"We *definitely* shouldn't do that," the wizard insisted. "Now come on, this will only be scary for—"

"Uh, oh," Clark squawked.

The sound of a high-revving car engine suddenly filled the air. They all swiveled their heads to see a very beige and very rapidly approaching vehicle.

"Jon got past the construction!" Sigi yelled.

"Into the trees!" Rin yelled louder.

The three humans jumped down off the shoulder of the road and into the trees—their hearts, heads, and bodies bracing for a tumble. Between the trees, the light grew darker and safety seemed like a destination they would never arrive at. And in the rush and fear of what was happening, none of them noticed that they were minus one bird.

CHAPTER FIFTY

THE ENEMY WITHIN

Jon was beside himself. He sat in the stolen beige car fuming, pinned between a red van and a blue sedan.

Somehow the boy and his companions had gotten away. He had lost a gun, but he had more. He was also out of sorts because he'd passed out. It had happened a few times in the past while performing much more difficult and dangerous jobs, but now some books had worked him over—and the people who had done it were getting away.

Well, Jon wasn't having it.

He tried to pull out onto the shoulder and around the van in front of him, but the vehicle was too close. He tried to back up, but the sedan was only inches away. It honked, letting Jon know that it couldn't back up if it wanted to because of the cars behind it.

Jon swore.

He was most angry at himself. To get tricked by a

couple of kids and a loon was an embarrassing blow to his devious pride.

Jon swore again.

He threw the car into drive and pushed on the gas. His bumper hit the van and he accelerated even more. The van moved a couple of inches, honking its horn to let him know that what he was doing was extremely unacceptable stuck-in-traffic behavior.

He jammed the gears into reverse and flew backward into the sedan. The airbag in the red car went off as Jon gave his vehicle gas and pushed the red car back a foot or so. There was more honking from a number of cars as he put his into drive again and rammed the van with force.

He backed up into the red car again and turned hard to the right.

His inconsiderate driving had created just enough room for him to weave around the van and race up the shoulder toward the man with the yellow hat. The road-worker waved his hand and lifted his sign in a frantic gesture. If he thought his sign would stop Jon, he was dead wrong. Which is why he jumped off the shoulder and into the bushes in an effort to not be dead *dead*.

Jon scraped up against two of the vehicles in front of him as he flew up the shoulder. Passing the first car in line, he swerved back onto the road and raced with purpose in the direction that Ozzy had just gone. The road was absent of any other cars, leaving Jon free to floor it. He took four turns faster than the signs suggested he should. Screeching around another corner, he could see something in the distance. Up ahead on the side of the road was Ozzy with his wizard and Sigi.

Jon's eyes burned with anger as he tried to push the gas down even harder. He focused on Ozzy and saw him jump off the road into the trees with the others. What he didn't see was the black bird who had just flown up under his car.

Using the knowledge he had recently acquired from YouTube videos and books, Clark grabbed onto an engine mount and then twisted up on top of the engine and began biting at wires and hoses. He wasn't impressed with the engine of Jon's car. He also wasn't sure where the fuel line was on an early 2000s beige Corolla, so he just kept biting and tearing.

He missed the fuel line but did a bang-up job of cutting the brakes and three of the four spark plug wires. The already-underpowered engine began sputtering, firing on only one cylinder.

Inside the car, Jon realized that now might be a good time to stomp on the brakes and slow down. Unfortunately, the brakes were no longer working. He tried to turn, but the steering wheel was locked. The beige Corolla kept flying straight toward where Ozzy and the others had entered the trees.

Jon screamed as the car launched off the side of the road into the forest.

CHAPTER FIFTY-ONE

THROUGH THE BUSHES AND INTO THE DARK

Running frightened down the tree-packed slope, Ozzy and the others could hear trees cracking and screaming as momentum, inertia, and gravity hurled the beige car down toward them. They scrambled madly out of the way in hopes of not being hit.

Trees snapped and flew forward, barely missing Sigi and the wizard. The car hit a tree big enough to stand its ground, and the front of the vehicle compacted like a tin can, leaving it wedged between a least a dozen smaller trees.

Ozzy and the others were only a few feet away from where it had come to a stop.

"That was too close," Sigi said, shaking and on the verge of tears.

Through the cracked windows, they could see Jon in the front seat. The air bag had gone off and he was angrily trying to get out of his seatbelt. But his restraint was jammed and he was stuck tightly in place.

"You'll pay for this!" Jon yelled.

"You should quit while you're ahead," Rin said.

Clark crawled out from under the bottom of the car near Sigi.

"I accidently cut the brakes," Clark explained. "And the steering. And some sparky wires."

Rin smiled. "I'm glad we're friends and not enemies."

Up above them all, where the car had flown off the road, they saw people looking down at Jon's vehicle.

"Are you okay?" a man yelled.

"That's our cue," Rin whispered.

They turned from the car and ran away from any attention, farther down the tree-covered slope. The ground was so steep that their descent was more of a controlled fall than a run. They bounced and spun between trees, letting gravity move them. Rin led the way, Ozzy right behind him, and Sigi in the back, Clark zooming all around them.

"Keep going!" the bird yelled, sounding like an uncaring coach.

After what felt like just shy of forever, they slowed their pace to a lumbering jog and tried to catch their breath. Rin snagged his robe on a low-hanging branch for the tenth time, causing him to almost lose his footing. He pulled his robe free from the branch and it flew back, hitting Clark squarely in the beak. The bird flew backward a few feet and then zipped forward, nipping the wizard on the fingers that were holding his staff.

"That's my conjuring hand," Rin complained.

"How would I know?" the bird squawked back. "I've never seen you conjure. And what would it kill you to change shape every once and a while?"

"Who said I don't?"

"If you do, it's probably into something lame like a broom."

"Hey," Rin said defensively as he ran, "have *you* ever tried to sweep an entire castle without one?"

The wizard continued to move through some tight trees, Ozzy and Sigi right behind him.

"Can you tell us where this shortcut is?" Ozzy asked.

"No."

"Is that because you don't know?" Sigi said.

There was a long pause as they all stepped carefully through a wide patch of scrub brush and tall bushes.

"I know," Rin finally answered, "and it's not far."

Clark wanted to change the subject. "Do you think that bland guy will stop following us now?"

"He doesn't seem like the kind of guy that just lets things go," Ozzy observed. "Even if he's been taken down by a bird."

Rin's robe got caught again and he jerked back and fell to the ground. His hat came off and his staff smacked him on the head. Ozzy and Sigi stopped to help him up.

"Thanks. Trees have always been an ally," he said,

confused. "It seems now as if they're conspiring to take me down."

Clark chastised the wizard. "I don't think you're wearing the best running-through-the-woods-frantically clothes."

They all took a moment to stand still and further catch their breath. The trees around them were an avocado green, filled with birds complaining about them traipsing through their private and secluded woods. The air smelled like pine, and sweat, and uncertainty.

"Would you please knock it off!" Clark yelled at the birds.

They didn't listen.

"Well, I tried," Clark said. "I'm not Ozzy's parents. I mean, it's not like I have the ability to control the minds of other birds."

Everyone stared at him as he sat perched on a branch.

"What?" he asked. "Too soon?"

"Come on," Rin said beginning to run again. "It's not much farther."

Ozzy lost his footing and took a turn tumbling onto his back before Rin stopped him.

"Do we really have to be running?" Sigi asked. "I don't think anyone's following us."

"We're not running to escape something," her father said. "We're running because time is perishable. Come on."

Everything began to close in as the tops of the trees prevented more and more light from reaching them.

The slope ended abruptly, and then they were standing in a stone-filled ravine. A small trickle of water ran through the stones and gave the quiet forest a background gurgle.

Ozzy was used to all the forest running, but for the rest, it was taking a toll. Rin tried in vain to appear in control and wizardly as he hacked up a lung.

"Where are we?" Ozzy asked.

"Lost," Clark suggested.

"Not lost." Rin coughed. "This way."

The wizard walked west down the rocky ravine. Ozzy and Sigi followed, stepping carefully along the trickling stream of water and wet stones. Overhead, long branches blocked most of the sky from view.

"Here." Rin turned and walked directly into a wall of bushes that were growing on the stone wall of the ravine. The growth parted and swallowed the wizard whole.

"What the shrub?" Clark chirped.

Ozzy pushed into the bushes, following Rin. Sigi clung to the back of his shirt with Clark in her hair. Everything was dark for a few moments before Rin turned on his phone's flashlight.

In awe, Ozzy looked around.

Sigi did the same as her father moved his phone to light up more of the space.

"It's a little dark for my taste," Clark complained.

The space they were standing in was a large cave, filled with a cool dampness. It had a high ceiling and a dirt floor peppered with small stones. To the left they could see the mouths of three dark tunnels. To the right was a big rectangular space with a thin pool of water on the far side.

"What is this place?" Clark flew up and hovered in front of the phone's flashlight. "Is this where you live?"

"No," Rin insisted.

"How'd you know it was here?" Sigi asked.

"Let's just say some heavy things happened here years ago."

"What things?" Ozzy asked, wishing he were in bed, or lying down.

"I don't know," the wizard said, sounding curious himself. "But I'm sure something did. Follow me."

Rin walked over to where the thin pool of water was and sat down on a flat rock near the water's edge. Ozzy and Sigi picked their own rocks and took a seat.

"What now?" Sigi said. "Are those tunnels the shortcut?"

"I've always thought caves were the perfect place to talk," the wizard said without answering his daughter. "In Quarfelt, we hold most of our important conversations in caves."

"Dad," Sigi said, "could we not talk about Quarfelt now? We're in trouble, and I don't believe speeches about Quarfelt are going to help. You think it does, but all the magic things you claim to show us are just things that can be written off as luck."

"You're encouraged to doubt," Rin said kindly. "Just don't let the questioning end before the right answer arrives. And you're always welcome to just borrow some of my and Ozzy's understanding until the time comes that it makes sense to you."

"Don't borrow mine," Ozzy said softly. "I think I feel the same way as Sigi."

Rin looked wounded.

"Sorry, I've read and re-read all the books I can about wizards, and they still seem more fictional than factual. Nobody else buys into them as something real."

"Are we going with what everyone else knows?"

"No," Ozzy insisted, his stomach twisting in knots, "but one of my teachers at school said that wizards are just a lazy writing device."

"I do like to relax."

"And why do you refuse to ever cast a real spell?" Ozzy asked. "Or work the kind of magic that we need?"

"I—"

"You're about to say something that makes more sense on a plaque than in reality." Ozzy's head hurt and his words weren't what he wanted them to be.

"Reality is not something I aspire to please," Rin reminded them.

"Obviously," Ozzy said.

Clark moved from the glow of the flashlight over to Ozzy's right knee. "Listen, I find him infuriating as well, but he did make that car fly on and off that train."

"Did he? Or was it just bad driving?"

"I get it," Rin said. "You're nervous about becoming

an apprentice. You've passed three tests and now, as the fourth one looms, you're getting cold feet, or as we say in Quarfelt, ice nubbins."

"You don't get it," Ozzy insisted. "I'm saying that I can't be your apprentice because I can't accept that everything you say is true."

"Don't discredit the impossible because you don't believe me," Rin said seriously. "Magic happens despite what we do or don't believe. There is good—and there is evil. In life, some good wins and some evil is victorious. What you or I believe doesn't change that—it just changes *us*."

"Is that supposed to make me feel good?" Ozzy argued.

"No," Rin replied.

Ozzy stood up and walked away from Rin and Sigi and back toward the three tunnels. After only two steps away, the darkness swallowed him. Sigi got up, but Rin motioned for her to stay seated.

"He needs to be alone." Rin closed his eyes. When he opened them ten seconds later, he looked serious and like someone who was about to tell a scary story. "Sometimes walking into the dark helps a person to see how valuable the light is."

"Dad, this isn't a game."

"I agree with you."

"And you should know that Ozzy's not saying anything that I haven't thought in ways that are even stronger. Magic took you away from me and Mom."

"That's not true," the wizard insisted. "Your mother and I didn't see eye to eye on too many things to make it work."

"Yeah. Things like this wizard stuff." Sigi was upset. Even in the cool cave her face burned. "I've had no dad for most of the last ten years. Except for when you showed up to embarrass me. Do you know how horrible it is to have your father show up on career day to tell your class he's a *wizard*?"

"You're strong enough to put up with anyone who doesn't understand."

"Don't," Sigi insisted. "One of the best times of my life was the time in New Mexico. I was scared, confused, and overwhelmed, but what you did for Ozzy made me proud to be your daughter. Now I can't help but think you just love using rideshare apps and hiding in caves. I'm one of those people you just mentioned. One who doesn't understand."

Rin moved over to a stone right next to Sigi. His phone was still glowing, but the dark hid both their eyes and their expressions.

"I can't force you to believe what I'm saying is true," he said softly. "I can only say that I'm sorry you feel the way you do. And even though those last two lines rhymed, I mean them as sincerely as the driest poem you've ever read."

"You're still sticking with Quarfelt being real?" she asked.

There was a long silence before Sigi spoke again.

"If you're nodding, I can't see it."

"I *was* nodding," Rin told her. "Quarfelt is real whether you want to believe it or not. I would be a poor excuse for a wizard if I lied about its existence."

"I've never heard anyone else mention it," she argued.

"Do you know other wizards?"

"No, but it seems like something like that would come up when people talk about myths, or legends, or aliens, or Bigfoot, or conspiracy theories about nuts."

The words were meant to sting, but Rin didn't sound stung.

"Yeah," he said, "I do think Quarfelt could have a better marketing and advertising campaign. The banner that hangs off the capital castle reads 'Quarfelt: Quar-feel the Magic.' Not a great slogan."

"Is telling me that supposed to help me believe?" Sigi groaned. "People think you're crazy, Dad."

"Well, I suppose we're all crazy in some way," Rin admitted. "If I was an accountant, or a salesman, they might still feel the same. As a wizard, I make it easy for them to point and laugh. But people don't point and laugh at you, Sigourney."

Sigi softened at the sound of her father using her full first name.

"They might pity you because of what I am," her dad continued, "but there will come a time when they will realize just how much this world needs a wizard."

"I don't see that ever happening."

Rin stood up. "Do you know what I call this cave?"

"No. Up until a few minutes ago I didn't know it even existed."

"I call it the Multiple-Choice Cave."

"Why?"

"Because of the three tunnels that lead off this room. They all lead to three very different spots. One of them is safe, one is dangerous, and one . . ."

"One is dangerous?" Sigi said standing up.

"Yes, yes," Rin said defensively, "but the other one leads—"

"Ozzy!" Sigi called out. "Oz!"

There was no answer other than the echo of her own voice.

"Ozzy!" she tried again.

"He might be exploring the tunnels."

"What if he went down the dangerous one?"

Sigi yanked her father's phone out of his hands and ran toward the tunnels, yelling, "Ozzy! Clark!"

Rin came running up behind her.

"Which one's the safe tunnel?" she asked, shining the light at the three entrances.

"It's multiple choice," Rin said excitedly. "You have to choose. That's why I named it—"

"Dad! Ozzy could be in trouble, and there's no light in those tunnels to charge Clark. So stop with the multiple choice and tell me which tunnel to take."

"Well, it's cheating, but that's the safe one." Rin pointed

to the middle tunnel. "Wait. It might be that one. No—we should take the middle one. Ozzy makes pretty good choices and I'm sure the middle one is the one he took."

Sigi looked at the battery life on her father's phone. "Your phone's down to 19 percent."

"Some see the battery as 81 percent empty," the wizard told her. "I see it as 19 percent full."

"Unbelievable. I don't understand you. Mom said that when I was little, you used to worry about everything. Now you act like nothing is wrong even when everything's falling apart."

"I wasn't a wizard back then," Rin told her. "Now, should we stand here and worry? Or run into the dark?"

Sigi took off into the tunnel of her choice.

CHAPTER FIFTY-TWO

THERE ARE RIGHT TIMES TO SCREAM

Sigi led the way into the thin, dark tunnel, hunched over because of the low ceiling. Sigi could feel air coming from somewhere. The air was comforting, but everything else she felt was quite the opposite. Holding the phone in front of her, she moved as quickly as she could without slipping on rocks or banging her head on the ceiling.

"You might want to slow down," her father told her from behind.

"Why?"

"Because in a moment there's a large hole in the floor. You'll need to stick to the right and scoot forward against the wall."

Sigi didn't slow, she stopped. "A hole?"

"Yes." Rin confiscated his phone and took a turn as leader. He walked slowly, scanning the ground in front of him with the light. His six-foot-four height required him to be almost completely bent over as he moved. His hat brushed a stalactite and was knocked off, flying back at Sigi.

"Dad."

"Just hold onto it," he instructed. "There."

The flashlight exposed a hole on the tunnel floor in front of them. They both moved as far as they could to the right and inched forward, their backs to the wall. Their feet scooted along a lip of dirt no wider than six inches.

"I can't see the bottom of the hole," Sigi said nervously as she scooched forward.

"It's deep," Rin replied. "I don't think either one of us should find out just how far down it goes."

As Rin moved, a chunk of dirt broke free from the lip they were scooting on, creating a ten-inch gap between him and Sigi.

"I don't like this." Sigi whispered harshly. "I'm too scared to move."

"Look at me," her dad said.

In the dim light, Sigi tried her best to see her dad. She could see his robe, his staff, and his beard.

"Wait," she said breathlessly, "if you're a wizard, we should have nothing to worry about, right?"

"Right."

"Then why am I worried?" she argued softly.

"Because you refuse to see the purpose of uncertainty."

They had their backs against the tunnel wall, their arms pressed to the stone. Rin held his phone in one hand and his staff in the other.

"Do you see where you are?" Rin asked.

"I can barely see anything," Sigi said. Her breath was shallow from the fear an open hole in a dark tunnel can cause. "I can barely see anything, and I bet your phone's down to 15 percent."

"Twelve," Rin informed her.

"I'm scared," Sigi said bravely. "It would be stupid for me to say otherwise. I'm not going to cry, or scream, but this isn't right. I'm scared, and I don't think my father is the right person to help me."

"Hold onto this," Rin said, extending his staff back slowly. "And don't worry," he said kindly. "This is such a little thing. That small gap you're going to step over is insignificant. It's a single breath, a blink of an eye, or the wag of a finger. There's nothing to it. After you've moved forward, you're going to wonder why you ever paused at all."

"I hate you," Sigi said, almost involuntarily.

"That sounds about right for a fifteen-year-old."

"I'm sixteen."

"Where does the time go?" Rin sighed contently. "Now, just close your eyes and move forward."

Sigi shut her brown eyes and lifted her right foot to step over the missing ground in front of her. As she moved, the dirt beneath her still-planted foot cracked and gave way.

Sigi screamed appropriately and yelled out a few things that most daughters never get to tell their dads.

CHAPTER FIFTY-THREE

FINDING A SPOT OF INK IN A TUBE OF TAR

As his daughter screamed, Rin yelled, "Grab the staff!"

The tunnel turned darker, but she caught the end of the stick and held on for dear—and near-death—life. Rin swung her up and forward over the rest of the hole and onto solid ground. She landed on her butt near the spot Rin had flung his phone to better hold the staff.

The wizard scooted the rest of the way past the hole and kneeled down next to his daughter.

"And you thought I should have left this in New York," he said, holding his staff tightly.

Sigi was stunned. She sat on the tunnel floor trying to shake off the fear she had just felt.

"Are you okay?"

"No." Sigi held her right hand to her chest. "And this is the *safe* tunnel?"

"That's not what I said," Rin told her as he helped her back onto her feet. "I said this is the one Ozzy probably chose. The safe tunnel just leads right back out into the ravine."

"What?" Sigi was beside herself. "Where's the third tunnel go?"

"It goes back for about fifty feet and then dead-ends."

"If we get out of this alive, I want Mom to have full custody."

"She's always been the more responsible adult."

"So, the multiple choice was a tunnel with a quick dead-end, one with a short turn back outside, and one that leads to death? How do we know Ozzy even went this way?"

"He told me once that he was good at tests," the wizard said. "And since this one takes us where we need to go, I figured it would be his choice."

"Where does it go?"

"The ocean."

Sigi moaned and the sad sound filled the tunnel. "What's the battery life now?"

"Nine percent."

Sigi had no choice but to follow her dad farther into the tunnel.

There were no more open holes beneath them, but there were plenty of stones to duck under or crawl over. There was also some spongy ground near a trickle of water that ran from one wall of the tunnel and under the other.

They stopped near the wet ground and Rin showed Sigi the phone.

"Three percent," she said sadly. "When it dies, will we have to start crawling to feel our way forward?"

Rin lifted the phone and shone it down the tunnel in front of them. He swept the light around as if showing Sigi what the last place they might ever see looked like.

"I hate caves," Sigi admitted.

"We should keep moving," Rin said. "This last two percent of battery might be all we need to—"

"What's that?" Sigi asked excitedly. "Hold the light forward!"

She looked up ahead and saw the glint of something sliver flashing under the light. Sigi ran down the tunnel as her father jogged behind her. She fell on her knees and smiled as she looked down at the ground.

"Clark."

The bird's head was jammed into the soil as if he had taken a hard nosedive, and he wasn't moving. Sigi reached up and her father handed her the phone. She lowered it down so that the last bit of flashlight shone directly into the silver strip that had caught her eye seconds before.

"Two . . . one percent," she reported as she kept the light over Clark. "I don't know if it's enough to shock him back to life."

"Maybe the battery life is like a gas gauge on a car," Rin suggested. "When it gets to zero you still have fifty miles left."

The phone died and the tunnel was perfectly dark.

The choice they had made to even enter the cave in the

first place now seemed grave. Rin reached down and put his hand on Sigi's left shoulder to let her know he was still there.

"I'm not going to last long in this dark," Clark chirped weakly. He had come back to life under the last bit of light.

"Clark!" Sigi yelled as brought him closer to her face. "Where's Ozzy?"

"I don't know. What direction is back?" The bird was whispering to conserve energy. "He was out of his mind and walking deeper into the tunnel."

"Out of his mind?" Rin asked.

"You know, under some other control," the bird cheeped. "He wouldn't snap out of it. I bit him multiple times." Clark coughed to remind Sigi and Rin just how weak he was. "I was trying to fly back to you when this darkness . . . Oh, no, I'm fading."

Sigi held the bird gently in her hand.

"Ooooh," he hissed. "There's something else. He's in—"

Clark was out.

The situation felt so dark, so heavy, and so hopeless that Sigi began to cry. It wasn't the kind of crying someone helpless and fragile would display, it was the kind of crying someone might exhibit when the weight of where they sat was no longer something they could carry.

Rin sighed. He then mumbled something and a sound similar to a match being struck filled the tunnel. The noise was followed by a green light that filled the space completely.

Sigi looked around wondering if she was dying and now needed to head to the light. What she saw, however, wasn't death beckoning, it was her father standing there holding his staff. The orb on the top glowed a hypnotic green color and bathed the dark walls in a comforting glow.

Rin looked down at his kneeling daughter and the bird in her hand. He smiled, looking proud. He winked at his Sigi as if she were impressed.

The wink was premature and misguided.

Sigi swore and then took two deep breaths before standing up and shouting, "That thing *lights up*?"

Rin took a step back. "I feel like answering that would be an insult to your intelligence, seeing how it's already lit."

"Why didn't you use that before?"

"We didn't have the need."

"Why didn't you tell me that when the phone died we'd have another form of light?" Sigi demanded.

"There's always more light," the wizard said. "You just need to access it when needed. Now, let's help Clark access some."

Sigi was mad, but she held the bird out and Rin leaned his staff forward so that the glowing orb was closer to the silver strip. She stared at the green light while holding the bird. The glow was bright, with a swirling, hypnotic pulse to it. And the color was green, but not like any shade she knew—it felt familiar and foreign at the same time.

"How does that work?" she asked, mesmerized. "Batteries?"

"Please," Rin said with a scoff, "a wizard's staff is a tool powered by magic."

Sigi moved her head around the orb looking for a switch or knob that turned it on.

"Are they LED lights?" she asked.

"I don't know what that is," Rin told her. "So I'm going to assume no."

Clark began to flap his wings as he came to.

"Oh yeah, that's the good stuff," he moaned softly. With a big twitch, his talons went straight and he stood up in Sigi's hands. He shuffled closer to the orb. "Hey, Wizzy, you didn't tell me your twig could glow."

"It's not a twig," Rin said. "It's a staff. We have no time to waste. You were talking about my apprentice before you passed out. You said there was something else."

"His mind is gone," Clark said as he continued to soak in the light. "Also, he kept saying the words 'This must end.' That's not good, right?"

"I'm afraid it isn't." Rin frowned and both Sigi and Clark felt it. The feeling within the space changed with the wizard's expression. "Remember when I said things were happening?"

"Yes," Sigi said. "You've said it about a hundred times."

"Well, then there's no need to say it again."

Rin didn't walk, he ran—farther down the tunnel toward a boy that was very much in need of assistance.

Sigi and Clark followed the speeding light.

CHAPTER FIFTY-FOUR

CAVES ARE HEAVY AND COMPLICATED

Running through the tunnel wasn't easy. The height of the ceiling fluctuated and the ground was uneven, making any form of continually smooth motion almost impossible. Rin held his staff out in front of him lighting the way brilliantly, while Clark circled and flew around the glowing orb. Sigi was right behind her father, reminding him that they would have already caught up with Ozzy if he had just used his stick earlier.

"It's a staff," Rin hollered back.

The narrow tunnel ended in a large, square cavern with an uneven ceiling. The floor was covered with flat stones that jutted up out of the ground. Under the light of Rin's staff, the flat rocks looked like headstones in a psychedelic graveyard.

"Whoa," Clark tweeted. "Ozzy and I didn't make it this far."

The father-daughter-bird combo walked carefully

between the blank headstones and toward the continuation of the tunnel on the other side of the massive room.

"This is like that park," Clark said. "The one in New Mexico."

"That was a cemetery," Sigi said softly. "These are just blank stones."

"So when people die, they're planted under the ground and given a rock to pin them down?" Clark asked.

"Kind of," Sigi answered as she followed her father, "except the rock is a headstone that tells people their name and when they lived. And people aren't planted, they're buried."

"In Quarfelt they're planted," Rin spoke up. "It's a much more hopeful way to phrase it."

"I'm glad I'm immortal," Clark bragged.

"You could always rust—or be blown apart," Rin pointed out.

"If I am blown apart, I'd like every bit of me to be buried separately with a different stone over each piece."

"I don't like to think about stuff like that," Sigi said. "Let's just hurry."

"I don't like to think about it either," Rin admitted. His voice was so soft and serious that he didn't sound like himself.

"What's up with you?" Clark asked.

"Caves bring out the melancholy in me," the wizard answered. "I look at all of this and think of the thousands of things that have died in my life."

"You call people things?" Clark asked.

Rin stopped walking. "Not people. Things."

"Like staplers?"

The wizard looked around. "Not staplers, Clark, just things." As Rin talked, the light from the staff began to soften. "Life used to be so different."

"Pre-wizard?"

Rin nodded.

Sigi looked at her uncharacteristically somber father. "Are you okay, Dad?"

The wizard gazed back at the room full of blank tombstones.

"People always think I've got it easy," he said mournfully. "'Look at the wizard—he has all the power and influence and prestige.' Well, this life requires sacrifice."

"People say that stuff?" Clark asked, confused.

"Things die and sometimes we don't even realize it until it's too late to properly mourn. I think what I miss the most is you and your mother."

"Neither one of us is dead," Sigi reminded him.

"But in certain ways I am."

"Wow," Clark chirped. "This room is really bringing you down."

Rin stood up as tall as he could and tilted his head back to stare at the uneven ceiling. Sigi stood next to him, holding on to his left elbow.

"You know," she said, "some of the stuff you mourn

isn't worth the energy. Life will be full of many other things to distract you and cause worry."

Rin smiled at his daughter. "I can hear the wizard in you."

"Actually," Sigi said, "that's a quote from you. You wrote it on the card you gave me when my cat died years ago."

Rin stared at Sigi—the green light helped him look wiser. "You are ten times better than I will ever be," he said honestly. "But I suppose that some of that greatness is the result of you having to accept me as your father."

"At least 90 percent of it."

"Come on," Rin said, feeling renewed by his own words and the way his daughter had delivered them.

Clark continued to fly circles around the glowing orb as the wizard and his daughter traveled through the tunnel, beneath the surface, and on their quest to find the boy.

CHAPTER FIFTY-FIVE

NO PEOPLE

Ozzy stood at the edge of the ocean. His long, dark hair hung down over his eyes and obscured the view as he stared out at the blank and empty ocean. Waves reached out to grab at his toes, but he kept far enough away for any of them to pull him in.

Ozzy's mind cleared.

Glancing about, he realized that he was alone, standing on a beach and wondering just how he had gotten there. Looking behind himself, he saw the mouth of a cave a hundred feet back.

"What's happening?"

His clear mind whirled and snapped as all the important parts of who he was and what was going on flooded back into his head and washed over his gray matter. He looked back at the cave again, wondering where Sigi and Rin and Clark were.

The sea continued to reach out and call to him.

In the last few days, the decision to enter the ocean had been forced upon him multiple times. At the moment, however, his mind was whole. He found himself wanting to get wet all on his own volition. He stood there staring at the choppy sea, processing the impulse to go in. The ocean meant a lot to him. It had been the place he and Clark had found happiness. It had been the place where he first met Sigi. And aside from the cloaked house, the sea was where he felt the closest to his parents. Now, as he looked out, he felt something indescribable inviting him to partake.

Ozzy pulled off his shirt and shoes.

The sea approved of what he was doing, the waves making a fuss and the water churning.

Running at full speed, Ozzy charged in, his legs pushing against the waves until he was deep enough to lunge forward and swim. The turbulent ocean absorbed him and, for the first time in weeks, he felt better.

Even on his best visits to the beach, he had never felt the charge and warmth he felt now. The cold temperature of the water didn't even register with him. Instead, a syrupy happiness enveloped him.

He swam out until the water was three times as deep as him. He then stopped and bobbed up and down in the wild sea.

Ozzy stared west.

Ahead of him there was nothing but water—the Pacific Ocean stretched out over five thousand miles before it touched the shores of Japan. The distance was far too great to see past, or swim to, but for a moment Ozzy contemplated doing just that. The answers, the closure, the wholeness he sought seemed connected to the wild liquid he was now floating in. There was something out there that he needed to understand.

Ozzy turned to look back toward the beach.

As he spun, an uneasy sensation brushed up against his right ankle. The sensation increased in pressure. It felt as if a thick hose was wrapping itself around his leg and trying to pull him under.

Instantly, the warm feelings he had been experiencing vanished.

Ozzy reached down and frantically pulled at what was holding him. His fingers closed in and he could feel a strong rubbery rope of water coiled around his ankle, wriggling downward. The movement pulled him under.

He squeezed the strange water and it broke up and released him. Needing air, he tried to swim upward, but was stopped when a second strand of liquid moved in and encircled his waist. The lasso of water pulled him down farther. As before, he dug his hands into it and it broke up.

Ozzy kicked fiercely until his head pierced the surface of the sea. He gulped in air, imitating a fish left on land, as four more strands of killer water reached out from below and took ahold of his legs and arms. Ozzy fought the thick vines of sinewy H_2O, but with his arms restrained, he couldn't stop them from dragging him down. Both hands were held tightly by meathooks of liquid. He tried to scream, but that only served as an invitation for a long invisible rope of water to shove itself down his throat.

The strange rubbery strands seemed to have a destructive mind of their own, dragging and pulling him deeper. The ocean churned, and his body, though submerged in water, felt like it was on fire.

Ozzy bucked and kicked, but the fight was futile. The watery ropes only grew stronger the more he struggled. The thought of this caused Ozzy's eyes to flash open as he was being towed farther down.

He blinked calmly in the dark water.

Then, remembering the feeling of security and purpose he had felt only moments before, he instructed his mind and body to relax.

Going limp, his finger buzzed.

The thick water gripping his left hand relaxed and was smothered by the ocean. Ozzy reached his free hand over and touched the wet ropes around his right arm. Immediately they unraveled and joined the greater body of water he was sinking in.

With a calm mind and burning lungs, Ozzy bit down on the liquid in his mouth and throat while tearing methodically at the water holding his legs. The strange strands burst like rubber pipes, releasing the boy.

Ozzy swam up.

He reached the surface without an atom of air left in his lungs. Sucking in oxygen, he bounced up and down in the now-calm ocean. It took a dozen deep breaths for him to feel normal again. He looked up at the cloudless sky.

Ozzy felt no worry or fear—the struggle beneath the water had changed something in him. He wasn't worried about Jon, or the cloaked house, or if anything else was lurking beneath him.

He twisted in the water to face the shore, and in the distance he saw two things worth swimming toward.

CHAPTER FIFTY-SIX

DRAGGED DOWN, BUT NOT UNDER

Clark was the first to see the light. He shot away from the glowing orb and raced through the last stretch of tunnel like an avian bullet. The bird burst out and flew straight up into the cloudy sky.

He shook and twisted in the heavy wind.

Stretching his wings as far as he could, he closed his eyes and rocked up and down on twisting currents of invisible wind. Feeling free from the oppression of the tunnel, Clark chirped loudly before diving back down to earth.

On shore, Rin and Sigi emerged from the tunnel, happy to leave behind the darkness they had just experienced. They shed the oppressive feeling of the cave and filled their lungs with air.

"Where's Ozzy?" Sigi hollered to her father as she surveyed the empty beach.

Rin looked down at the ground and pointed to a set of

footprints. The two of them followed the tracks, running and scanning the ocean ahead of them.

At the water's edge they found Ozzy's shirt and shoes laying on the sand.

"He's in the water?" Sigi asked in disbelief, her voice heavy with fear.

Clark dropped out of the sky and landed on Rin's right shoulder.

"Did you see him?" Sigi asked the bird.

"See who?"

"Ozzy." The wizard pointed at the small pile of clothes. "That's his shirt and shoes."

"Is he still wearing trousers?" Clark tweeted.

"I'm sure he is," Sigi said.

"Good, my pocket is attached to those things," the bird reminded them. "Also, I know how squeamish you humans are about nudity."

"Thanks for understanding us," Sigi said sarcastically, "but pants or no pants, Ozzy's in trouble."

"But it is pants, right?" Clark wanted to clarify. "Not no pants?"

Sigi ignored the bird and began to walk into the water, looking for any sign of the boy who had made her life so crazy.

She pushed quickly through the small waves near shore. There was no sign of him. She walked farther and the ocean appeared to grow bigger and emptier with each step. When the water was at her waist, she stopped. The waves rolled around her, making it hard to stand still. She glanced back at her father on the shore and he waved in a manner more fitting of a family vacation than a missing person case.

Sigi shivered and felt the entire ocean close in around her, causing her to feel like she was only a speck in the vast wet world around her.

"Ozzy!" she hollered into the windless sky.

It had nothing encouraging to say.

The watery sand beneath her feet shifted as each wave thumped up against her and then traveled on to the shore. Locking her knees, she planted herself and gazed with a Sauron-like intensity over the ocean. There was an abundance of water and waves, but no . . . Her eyes locked in on something. It was two hundred feet out and directly in line with where she was standing. At first glance it appeared to be a small circle of seaweed. At second glance, it was something much better. There, coming out of the calm ocean, was a dark head of wet hair.

"Ozzy?" she whispered.

The temporarily lost boy rose out of the water while moving closer. From a distance, only seeing his head, he looked like a different Ozzy than the one she had seen only an hour before. His wet brown hair was pushed back and his wide shoulders broke the surface of the sea like a stone pillar being thrust up from the ocean floor.

Clark came in from behind and landed on Sigi's hair.

Together the two of them stared at the shirtless stranger emerging from the rough sea.

"Oh, my," Clark whistled.

"Same . . ." Sigi managed to say. "I mean, well, . . . same."

Ozzy was slowly getting closer.

Sigi suddenly wasn't sure how to act. She had just seen him in the cave, but the tunnels, and conversation, and everything else she had walked through since then felt like another lifetime. Now, the boy she cared about was wet, shirtless, and staring at her.

"He looks different," Sigi said to Clark.

"Yeah," Clark replied. "Wetter."

Ozzy pushed through the ocean at a steady pace, and in a matter of moments he was fifty feet away from them, the water level just below his waist.

"Oh, good," Clark said. "He's wearing pants."

Sigi felt the wind on her damp, curly hair. She felt Clark jump down from her head and perch on her shoulder. She felt the waves trying to push her over. But more than anything, she felt happy to see Ozzy.

"Are you crying?" Clark asked as he leaned forward to look at her eyes.

"No," Sigi insisted. "It's just spray from the waves."

"Yeah, same here."

Ozzy stopped fewer than five feet from them. He smiled in a way he had not done in quite some time. The look only made him more appealing.

"Are you okay?" Sigi asked.

"I think I am," he replied.

"You look weird," Clark chirped. "Did something sting you? Or were you bitten by a shark? I've heard that those kinds of things can change you for life."

Ozzy smiled at the bird but left the question unanswered. "We need to get to shore."

"Good," Clark said. "Being over water still makes me uneasy. What are we going to do on shore?"

"Get a boat," Ozzy said. "There's something out there, and I need to find it."

Clark complained loudly and with attitude as they returned to the shore. Ozzy let the bird vent as he held hands with Sigi and prepared himself for the fifth challenge.

CHAPTER FIFTY-SEVEN

BOUND AND DETERMINED

"Impressive," Rin said. "I can see from your aura that you've accomplished the fourth task."

"Yeah," Clark twerped. "He does look friendlier."

Ozzy, Sigi, Rin, and Clark were walking north up the shore on their way to find a road, or a ride, that could take them to the marina. The world felt different than when they had last been together. The wizard filled Ozzy in on what he and Sigi had been through in the tunnel. And Ozzy tried his best to describe what had happened to him beneath the sea.

"So your staff can glow?" Ozzy asked Rin.

"Among other things."

"Like what?"

"Like turning stop signs," Rin said.

The sun was giving up and beginning to drop as late afternoon forged on.

"I'm curious about the fourth task I completed," Ozzy said. "What was it?"

"You learned to let go," Rin answered. "What happened beneath the water could have happened less pleasantly. But you let go and calm followed. Congratulations. Only one more task to go."

"Does the last challenge involve him lending you more money?" Sigi asked.

"No. If only it were that easy."

"Whatever it is," Ozzy said, "I just hope I'm aware of it before it happens."

"I'm sure you won't be," Clark said. "Riny will just wait until you do something and then claim it was your test."

"Wizards don't claim things," Ozzy said, defending Rin. "They state them."

"Oh," Clark chirped defensively, "way to throw *me* under the nest. So no more making fun of Mr. Wizard?"

"At least not in public." Ozzy held out his hand and the bird landed on it.

It had been a long day filled with parades, kidnapping, and caves. And they still had a hike to get to the marina.

"Maybe we should call Mom," Sigi said. "She can come pick us up."

"My phone's dead." Rin sounded relieved about his phone's condition.

"Even if we find a road, how far are we from the marina?" Sigi asked.

"Best guess," the wizard mused, "ten miles."

"Ten miles is a long way to walk," Sigi said.

"I wouldn't worry about it," Ozzy suggested. "Somehow we'll end up where we need to."

"Whoa," Clark tweeted, "you sound like a mini-Wiz. That stringy water must have really worked you over."

"Fly ahead," Ozzy said. "Try to find the closest road or building."

"Normally, I like people to say please," the bird told him. "But you sound so sure of what you're saying that I feel compelled to skip the formalities and just—"

"Go!" Ozzy insisted.

Clark shot off the boy's shoulder and up over the trees growing alongside the beach.

Rin stopped walking to smile.

"What?" Ozzy asked.

"I'm just so proud. It takes most apprentices years to boss people around."

They walked farther north for a couple of minutes before the bird returned.

"The only road anywhere is straight through those trees." Clark pointed with his left wing. "It's covered with that stuff . . . what's it called, black ground?"

"Asphalt," Rin answered.

"No need to swear," the bird said. "It's still a road."

They hiked in the direction Clark had pointed. The trees in their path were thick, but in less than half a mile they found the road. It was narrow, with bushes on both sides. They began walking north.

"It's getting dark," Sigi said.

"It's going to get much darker," the wizard replied.

"Maybe we should go home and tell Mom what's happening," Sigi suggested. "She's got to be so worried."

"She knows you two are with me," Rin reminded his daughter.

"Exactly," Sigi replied.

"Besides," the wizard added, "it's not going to take us long to get to the marina."

There was no audible poof or flash of smoke, but like magic, a vehicle could suddenly be heard from behind them.

They turned their heads to see a small white van driving toward them. Rin didn't hesitate for even a second. He stepped into the middle of the road and lifted up his staff.

"Halt," he called out.

The van rolled closer, coming to a stop ten feet away from the wizard. Wide rays of sunlight were bouncing off the windshield, making it hard to see who was driving. The door opened, and before they could react, there was Jon, holding a gun and smiling.

The sight was so shocking that they all froze.

Jon looked far more remarkable than he had when they had first met him. He had scratches on his arms and a big bruise on the side of his face. His clothes were torn in a couple of spots and his messy hair didn't look bland—it looked ridiculous.

"Everyone in the van," he said angrily.

Ozzy looked at Rin and shrugged. He returned his gaze to Jon and said, "Okay."

Jon, Sigi, and Clark all looked surprised—Rin didn't. They had needed a ride and now they had one.

"Okay," Jon said suspiciously, "first I need to lock up your bird."

Clark wanted none of that. He shot up into the sky and disappeared. Jon swore while looking around nervously.

"Don't worry," Ozzy said. "He's not coming back down. He just doesn't want to be locked up."

"That bird is a mess," Jon said. "Drop the stick and let's have all of you turn around with your hands behind your backs."

With no fight or arguing, Rin dropped his staff and they all spun around and put their hands behind their backs. Jon cautiously bound their hands with a roll of packing tape he'd pulled from the van.

"I didn't expect you three to be so agreeable," he said, motioning for them to climb in. "Ray will be pleased to hear that you cooperated."

Rin laughed.

"What's so funny?"

"Your confidence," the wizard replied. "If you knew what this girl and boy are capable of, you'd release us and join our cause."

"You need help," Jon said shaking his head.

"And you have come along to provide it."

The three captives climbed into the back of the van and Jon shut the door. Rin was squeezed tightly between Ozzy and his daughter. Jon put the staff up in the passenger seat and then started the van and drove them all east. Jon held the gun in his right hand and the wheel with his left. He repeatedly looked in the rearview mirror to keep an eye on the three misfits sitting uncomfortably on their bound hands.

"Marina del Damp," Rin called out.

"What about it?" Jon asked.

"That's where we'd like to be dropped off."

"You have no idea how annoying you are."

"That's not true," Rin said kindly. "People tell me all the time."

Jon just wanted this job to be over. He wanted to close the book and never deal with any of his current passengers again.

"Is this a new van?" Rin asked loudly. "I know a bird who's interested in cars."

"Shut up."

Jon pressed on the gas pedal of the van he'd stolen only a half hour before. After he had been pulled out of his beige car, he'd thanked one of the kind Samaritans who'd helped him by taking her vehicle. He knew that the police would be looking for a white van, but he also knew that he'd be finished with it in no time—and then they were welcome to it.

Jon looked up out of the windshield. He wasn't a superstitious man, but he had a couple of wishes he hoped would come true. One was that the helicopter he had arranged was ready and waiting. The other wish was that he would have no further run-ins with any metal birds.

Far, far above the van, two little eyes kept watch on the moving vehicle. Two little eyes attached to one metal bird who was more than ready to ruin any and all of Jon's wishes.

CHAPTER FIFTY-EIGHT

DON'T TRY TO TALK TO ME

Jon kept the gun pointed toward his passengers in the back. His hand swayed slightly with the motion of the car, making it feel that if he did shoot, there was no telling who he would hit.

"You can put the gun down," Rin said kindly, sounding as if he were giving Jon permission. "There's no way for us to do anything with our hands bound."

"Thanks, but I'll keep it where it is just to make sure." Jon growled. "I take it back—I didn't mean thanks."

"My arms are falling asleep," Sigi complained.

"Why are you doing this?" Ozzy asked. "We don't even know."

"You know I work for Ray."

"And that's enough of a reason to force us to go with you against our will?"

"Ozzy," Rin scolded, "he's not forcing us, he's giving us a ride."

"You take the cake," Jon said, shaking his head while looking into the rearview mirror. "I've never met anyone as delusional or out of touch as you are."

"I will take that as a compliment," Rin said.

"I'm sure you will. Where did you escape from? Is there an asylum somewhere that's short a patient?"

"I don't think he's the one who needs to explain himself," Ozzy said with conviction. "You ransacked my lawyer's office, burned down my house, kidnapped Sigi, and now you've kidnapped us. If anyone should be locked up or checked out, it's you."

"I don't know what you're talking about," Jon said. "I didn't ransack any lawyer's office."

"Right."

"He's telling the truth about that," Rin said. "That was me."

For a second, Ozzy and Sigi both looked as shocked as they were uncomfortable.

"*What?*" Ozzy said. "Why would you do that?"

"It's complicated," Rin whispered.

"I'd still like to know," Ozzy whispered back.

The wizard leaned in closer to the boy and continued to whisper. "I was the one who discovered the safety deposit box in Portland. I filed papers to have it released, but they wouldn't give the stuff to me. They insisted on sending it to your lawyer."

"How did you find that?" Sigi asked, doing some whispering of her own.

Jon was watching them in the rearview mirror, but he didn't seem bothered by their telling each other secrets because it meant they weren't talking to him.

"Yeah," Ozzy said, "weren't you in Quarfelt?"

"I haven't completed what you hired me to do," Rin said seriously. "The discovery of your parents being dead seemed like an unfinished job. I've told you I'm still on the clock. So maybe I slipped in and out of Quarfelt to continue my investigation."

"Why did you go through Ryan's office?" Ozzy was confused and his grey eyes showed it. "I would have let you see anything that was in there."

"I couldn't be sure."

"Right," Sigi said. "You just wanted to get what was in there and pretend to be magical about it."

"Is that true?" Ozzy asked.

"No. There's nothing pretend about magic."

The van drove off the paved street and onto a dirt road that turned sharply and continued to head northeast.

"Are you sure you know where Marina del Damp is?" Rin hollered.

"I'm not taking you there," Jon insisted. "I just want to stay off the main roads."

"Smart," the wizard said. "Drive instead on the roads less driven."

Jon shook his head. "Does he always talk like that?"

Sigi wanted to shout yes, but she wasn't going to openly agree with Jon about anything.

"Have you never met a wizard before?" Ozzy asked Jon. "He might be different than you, but at least he works magic with words instead of fire."

"What?"

"You burned my home," Ozzy said with disgust. "I had—"

"Wait," Jon said, "I didn't burn anything. I hate fire. It's too difficult to control."

Both Ozzy and Sigi slowly turned their heads to look at the person sitting between them.

"Well," Rin said, "it wasn't my intention. I accidentally knocked—"

"*You* burned down the cloaked house?" Ozzy couldn't believe what he was hearing. "You . . . you . . . why would—?"

"It's not what you think," Rin said calmly. "There was some spilled gas, and well . . . well, even though wizards have few regrets, I do feel devastated. I'm so sorry."

"Dad, I don't believe it." Sigi looked like a four-year-old who had just been told that Santa had torched her tree and gifts and insulted her looks.

"Magic is complicated," the wizard tried. "Sometimes it's messy."

Ozzy turned away from Rin and looked out the window of the moving van. He took two long shallow breaths and then, like the worry and fear he had left in the ocean, he let go of the confusion and anger he now felt.

He turned back to Rin. "All those books and papers . . . gone."

"I know it seems dark," the wizard said softly, "but you need to trust the promise of a wizard."

"What promise?"

"You called me because you were looking for your parents. I promised I would help you find them."

"They're dead," Ozzy told him. "You did your job. You even warned me that the answers could be painful."

"I'm just not convinced."

"Don't do this," Ozzy said softly. "You know they're gone."

"Sometimes the—"

"Dad, stop it," Sigi begged.

"I thought you came back because you needed me to be your apprentice. It seems like you came back to burn down things and open new wounds."

"Sometimes powerful things rise from the ashes," Rin insisted. "And real strength grows quickest in a garden of hurt. It also produces the most profound results."

"I don't know what to think," Sigi said. "It kind of seems like Ozzy and I should be running from you, not Jon."

"Light always triumphs over darkness," Rin said with power. "You see chaos now, but when the dust settles, it will be blindingly clear what has happened."

The three of them had started their conversation in hushed tones and whispers, but as the discussion had continued, their voices had increased, allowing Jon to hear most of what they were saying.

"You two actually believe the garbage coming out of this man's mouth?" is what Jon would have said if he had any civility. Instead he said just about the same thing, but he substituted a few of the words for ones that were stronger, less flattering, and incredibly offensive. "He's feeding you garbage," Jon continued. "I've never seen a more pathetic case of parenting. You're following this loon around on some journey that involves him putting your lives in danger and making a mockery out of everything in your lives. Pathetic."

Rin looked at Jon. "Do you know where Marina del Damp is?"

"I swear I'm going to hurt you," Jon replied.

"It's a simple question."

Jon used some of the more classic and strong swear words to convey as clearly and harshly as he could that he had no idea where Marina del Damp was.

"That's odd," Rin said. "Because you're driving straight to it."

Jon glanced out the window at the evening sky. He scanned the trees and dirt road in front of him, searching for any sign of what Rin was talking about.

As Jon looked, Rin pushed his feet up against the seat beneath him and with all the strength he had in his legs, he propelled himself forward over the middle seats and up over Jon's head. The wizard's hands were still bound, but his whole body was draped over the driver's seat. His head was touching the steering wheel and his feet were dangling behind the chair. Most of Jon was smashed beneath him. Rin wriggled and bucked like a fish doing the worm. He threw his head back and hit Jon's chin. The surprise caused Jon to drop the gun and grab at the steering wheel and wizard in his lap. The van lurched back and forth as Rin twisted his legs up over the seat so that his entire body was pressed up into the windshield and on top of Jon. The angry driver began to hit and push.

"A little help!" Rin yelled.

The wizard's actions had come as just as much of a surprise to Ozzy and Sigi as they had to Jon. Their hands were tied, but they jumped up and rolled over the middle seat. Ozzy crashed into Sigi and the two of them fell in between the front seats.

Ozzy squirmed his way down where Jon's feet were frantically trying to press the correct pedal and bring the out-of-control van to a stop.

The van ran off the road, moving along the edge of the road inches away from hundreds of trees.

With her hands still tied, Sigi managed to use her legs and push up so that she was sitting in the passenger seat. She aimed her legs at Jon's right side and began kicking wildly. Rin was crammed on top of Jon and Ozzy's head and shoulders were at his feet.

Their once-bland driver wrapped one arm around Rin and grabbed one of Sigi's feet with the other. Rin's shoulder hit the steering wheel and the van jumped away from the trees and back onto the dirt road. It raced toward the other edge, where there was a four-foot drop into the forest.

"Ozzy!" Rin yelled.

Ozzy shoved his head down against the brake and the van came to a screeching halt in the dirt inches from the edge. All four were thrown closer to the windshield and dashboard. The tape around Ozzy's hands caught on a metal edge at the bottom of the passenger seat and tore open. Ozzy pushed up from the floor and scrambled onto his knees. He reached through Rin's legs and Jon's arms to grab the keys from the ignition.

While the wizard was pummeling Jon with his head and shoulders, Ozzy jammed the end of a key into the tape around Rin's wrist.

The tape ripped and Rin screamed as his arms were freed. He grabbed the handle on the driver's door and pulled. The door popped open and Rin, Jon, and Ozzy fell out of the van and onto the ground. Rin sprang up and then came down on Jon, sitting firmly on the back of his shoulders as Ozzy sat on his legs. Jon tried to roll and buck them off, but he had already been worked over and didn't have the energy to lift a wizard and some kid that seemed far too much trouble for anyone to deal with.

Sigi scooted out of the open door legs first, her hands still bound. She stood so that Ozzy could cut the tape without having to get off Jon.

"Yes!" she yelled as the pain of being bound ended.

Sigi found the tape in the van and, with some struggle, they were able to get Jon's hands taped together behind his back. Sigi then took a seat between her father and Ozzy on Jon's bound hands and back. They all rubbed their wrists and tried to catch their breath as the bench they sat on squirmed beneath them, swearing a blue streak.

Sigi turned her head and looked at her father. "In all of the spells that exist for wizards, there isn't one that you could have used to release our wrists from that tape?"

"Who said I didn't?"

"Me," Sigi answered. "Ozzy used a key."

"You think all spells begin and end with *poof*."

"I think you all are out of your minds," Jon screamed from beneath them.

If nighttime had an official crier, he would have stepped out at that moment and officially called the day over and night at hand. Clark fluttered down from up above and landed on Ozzy's right shoulder. His head tilted back and forth as he took in the scene.

"I'm impressed," he said, though still sounding disappointed. "I guess you didn't need me."

"We always need you," Ozzy insisted.

Clark patted the boy on the ear with his wing.

"What now?" Ozzy asked Rin. "Is there something we should ransack or accidentally burn?"

"No," the wizard replied as if Ozzy had just told a joke. "We go to the marina. It's just behind those trees."

Jon cursed a few more times. Together they lifted him so they could tape him to a nearby tree.

"Where were you heading?" Ozzy asked Jon moments before leaving. "I mean you obviously weren't taking us to the marina."

"You three are dead," was Jon's only reply.

"Let's tape his mouth," Rin suggested. "These trees shouldn't have to put up with him saying such things."

"Sorry," Sigi said. "We used it all sticking him to the tree."

They took off, Jon still yelling curses at them. Ozzy led the way with Rin taking up the rear. The wizard looked back at Jon and made eye contact. Without Ozzy or Sigi seeing, he snapped his fingers and their tree-taped captive went temporarily mute.

Jon stared at the wizard, trying to scream obscenities—but no sound came from his mouth. Rin smiled and then slipped away into the trees.

If Jon had had any voice, he would have been speechless.

CHAPTER FIFTY-NINE

AND HOLD SO TIGHTLY

Marina del Damp was less than a quarter mile away from where they had left Jon taped up.

Ozzy was impressed. "It's like he drove us right here."

Clark was not. "Yeah, but he didn't drive you all the way."

It was dark, but the marina was still open. The wizard got the keys to the *Spell Boat* from the attendant on duty. And after the same attendant filled the old wooden boat with fuel, they left the marina and traveled straight out to sea.

The weather was unusually still, and once they were past the breakers, the ocean looked almost like glass. It would have been beautiful but darkness had come on strong and everything felt eerie and odd.

Sigi had a few reservations about them going out on the ocean in the dark. She suggested that it might be smart to call her mother, Patti, for a ride home. Then they could take the boat out exploring in the morning.

Rin had a rather high opinion of his daughter, but he didn't like her suggestion.

Clark shared some of Sigi's concerns. He was worried about heading out into the ocean under the cloak of darkness. There were lanterns on the boat that lit up where they were sitting, and those lights would keep the bird charged, but Rin hadn't told them where they were headed or how long the voyage would be. And unlike Ozzy, the bird had some concerns about the wizard's mental well-being. If Rin was capable of burning down the cloaked house, he could also be capable of leading them all somewhere from which they would never return.

For the most part, Ozzy had been quiet since the van ride. His mind was trying to process the fact that so much of the pain he had felt in the last couple of days had come from Rin—not Ray or Jon. But as hard as he tried to be mad or upset at the wizard, his mind kept reminding him of the feeling he had experienced in the ocean. He was different, and he couldn't deny it. Had he been told that Rin had destroyed the cloaked house earlier in the day, he might have refused to ever speak to the wizard again. But he didn't feel any hate or horror over what had been done. He felt misunderstanding and a will to let it go, not resentment or anger. He also felt a desire to be heading out to sea. For the first time since Rin had returned, Ozzy was committed and filled with purpose—somewhere up ahead the fifth challenge awaited his completion.

The old boat flew forward on the flat water, bouncing and spraying water in its wake.

"You know what you're doing?" Sigi asked her dad for the third time. The first two times she had asked she had gotten nothing but riddles as answers.

"Does the hen know where to store her feathers?"

"Do those who thirst also hunger?"

This time Rin omitted the riddle and gave her a half answer. "Don't worry, Sigi," he said in a kind, fatherly manner. "We are going to a spot that Ozzy was destined to visit."

Rin was standing behind the steering wheel, gazing out into the dark ocean in front of them. The boat was old; there were wooden benches on the deck behind the steering wheel where Ozzy and Sigi sat. The ship had been retrofitted with a motor, but there was still a tall wooden mast sticking up from the middle of the deck. There were no sails on the mast, but various ropes and other rigging hung down and were tied off at intervals along the deck. A short railing lined with wooden boxes adorned the edges. Above the stern there was a small lifeboat in case the old and out-of-shape *Spell Boat* sank.

Sigi was seated on the port side of the boat behind her dad, and Ozzy was on the starboard side near the edge. A string of small white lights was wrapped around the railing of the deck. Ozzy held Clark up against one of the small lights as he sat on the bench.

"Why did you rent such an old boat?" Ozzy asked as they glided over the water.

"Fine," Rin said as if caught. "It's not a rental. Don't tell your mother," he instructed Sigi. "I bought it years ago. Patti didn't want me to, so I figured I'd do her a favor and not tell her that I did. I've worked on it a little, but my time in Quarfelt has delayed most of my improvement plans."

"Why didn't you buy a nicer one?" Sigi asked. "It feels like this one could split apart any second."

"New ones have no character," Rin insisted.

"Can this make it to where we're going?" Sigi asked.

"Of course." Rin was quiet for a moment. "Well, as long as we don't run into something, or a storm blows in, or the engine acts up."

"How far are we going?" Ozzy asked.

"About a half-hour more."

"*Where* are we going?" Sigi asked again.

"I don't know for sure," the wizard spoke, "but I'm fairly certain that it's where Ozzy's fifth challenge lies."

"Good," Ozzy said, looking out into the dark.

"How do you know that, Dad?" Sigi asked, ever the skeptic.

"Ozzy," Rin said, "do you remember that picture of you and your parents that was framed and in the cloaked house? The one where you're wearing that tiny purple suit?"

"The one without me in it?" Clark complained.

Ozzy ignored the bird and nodded. "I remember that picture."

The photo in question had been one of the few Ozzy had of his parents. It was also the one he had looked at every day as he grew up alone in the woods. He thought of the picture and how it had met its end in the fire. His soul wanted to rage, but as quickly as any anger began he brushed it away, refusing to react in a way that would do no good at this point.

"I know that picture too," Sigi said. "Now it's burnt."

"No," Rin said happily, "I saved it. It's back in Otter Rock."

"You saved it?" Ozzy asked. "Why?"

"I was looking around the cloaked house for any clues we might have missed. I know we spent many hours there arranging things and that everything there was familiar. So I looked for other places where something could be hidden. Like the space under the stairs where you found Clark."

"Why?" Ozzy asked.

"I told you—I have a job to finish."

"And I told you that you finished it," Ozzy said. He wanted to be mad, but his newfound personality prevented it.

"Well," Rin said, "you know I'm not the kind of person to pull rank on anyone, but as you are *my* apprentice, I don't think you telling me when or if it's over is your call."

"You pull rank all the time," Clark squawked. "You told that guy at the marina that being a wizard entitled you to have him fill the boat with gas."

"That's different," Rin insisted. "That was a teaching moment."

"What about the picture?" Sigi said as her hair blew and twisted in the wind.

"Right," Rin said with a sigh. "As I was looking around the cloaked house, I accidentally hit the picture with my staff. I was still getting used to the thing," he explained. "The picture fell and the glass shattered."

"You burned down the whole house," Clark said sharply. "And you're worried about a picture that doesn't even have *me* in it?"

"I picked it up and tried to fix it with a spell. But before I zapped it back together, I noticed there was writing on the back of the photo—some numbers."

"Like the date it was taken?" Sigi shouted over the sound of the motor and the wind.

"No," he hollered back. "The numbers were the latitude and longitude for two different locations."

Ozzy leaned forward on the wooden bench with a feeling of great interest growing in him. "What?" he asked excitedly. "What do they match up to?"

"One was the latitude and longitude of the cloaked house."

"And the other?"

"That's where we're heading now."

Ozzy stood up and held onto the wooden mast in the center of the deck. "It's in the middle of the ocean?"

"It's out here," Rin hollered. "It could be the reason you've been pulled this direction."

Clark squawked as Ozzy and Sigi got chills that were intensified by the cool night.

"I was on my way out here earlier when you spotted me from the shore and had Clark get me to turn back," Rin added.

"You're sure about those locations?" Ozzy asked.

"Positive." The wizard held down his hat with his left hand. "Orienteering is in my blood. I was an Eagle Scout, remember?"

"I still don't know what that is," Ozzy said. "Some wizard rank?"

"Pre-wizard," Rin said loudly.

Ozzy's finger buzzed for the first time since being pulled under water. The sensation ran up his left arm and through his body like a hundred thin strings of ice and fire. The buzzing was different than before—it was deeper, and it came with a heavy sadness. He shook as he stood and closed his eyes until the moment was gone.

"Are you okay?" Sigi asked.

Ozzy nodded.

"Good," she added, "because I'm not sure I am. This seems like a bad idea." Sigi looked around at the dark empty sea and sky. "Don't you think it would be better to look for something like this during the day? We might sail right by whatever it is in the dark."

"Caution can stunt or propel," the wizard said. "We will be as cautious as needed—but time is not with us. Everything has been building to this moment."

Sigi pulled a life jacket out of one of the wooden boxes on the deck and put it on.

"Do they have one of those in bird size?" Clark asked.

The four of them kept quiet as the boat raced forward. Ozzy moved over by Sigi and put his right arm around her. With his left hand, he continued to hold Clark up to the light.

"Are we in international waters now?" Ozzy asked. "I learned in one of my classes that if you go more than twelve miles offshore you're in international water."

"All water is international to me," Rin said. "But yes, we are."

"Bad stuff can happen in international water," Ozzy said. "At least that's what I was told."

"We should turn around," Sigi shouted.

"I'm with her," Clark crowed. "This is not a place I want to be stranded."

Ozzy looked at his hands. The purple birthmark on his finger was shaking slightly and his mind was trying to take over. But the ocean seemed to stifle his feelings and leave his brain free to think its own thoughts. Having some control of his will gave him a strange, unjustified confidence in what they were doing.

"Keep going!" he told Rin.

"That's what I like to hear," the wizard said cheerfully, having never had any intention of turning back.

"Maybe this would be better if you had a faster boat," Clark squawked. "We could have been there and back already."

"It's faster than it was before I put the motor in," the wizard said defensively. "Traveling by wind was so tedious."

"Most wizards can travel through a fireplace or dimensions," Sigi told her dad. "You should just summon us to be where we need to be."

Ozzy replied for Rin. "And miss what happens in between the beginnings and ends?"

The bird and girl stared at the boy.

"It's like Rin's a virus," Clark said, spooked. "And you caught it. Why are you talking like that?"

"He's an apprentice," Rin said proudly. "And he's right. This is the part that counts. Life would be unfulfilling if we all just showed up where we need to be with no knowledge or memory of how we got there."

"I'm not saying *all* the time," Sigi argued. "I'm just saying that for life-and-death situations it might be nice to skip the travel time. We've been running all day, I'm exhausted, and the dark is making me crazy."

"Yeah," Clark said. "Can't you just shapeshift into a whale and push us there faster? I'd remember that."

Despite the lack of whale power, their boat moved swiftly on the calm ocean and under the clear, dark sky. Thousands of tiny stars blinked with concern as they alone witnessed the unseaworthy vessel traveling farther than it should.

Rin looked up and pretended to be reading something in the sky. Glancing over at Sigi, he reported, "We're close."

"How can you tell?" Ozzy asked.

"The stars. And this compass by the steering wheel."

The old boat chugged on. The three of them looked ahead into the vast darkness.

"Is there an island out here?" Ozzy asked.

"Not one that's on any maps," Rin replied.

"Then how could a spot in the water have any significance?"

"Each bit of earth and sea matters," Rin told him. "There is a spot of water in Quarfelt that if you are able to find and dip your feet into it, it makes you immune to Pnoversal."

"What's Pnoversal?" Sigi asked.

"It a disease that causes all your spells to come out in reverse. I know a wizard named Flanters who had the affliction. He ruined a lot of lives before he found that spot of water."

"And that's true?" Sigi asked skeptically.

"Unless you think Flanters is a liar."

"I'm not sure Flanters even exists," Sigi said.

Clark stepped off Ozzy's hand and moved closer to one of the small lights. "It's pretty black out here," he tweeted. "Almost as bad as that cave. If I shut down and fall in this water, I'm not going to be happy."

"Me neither," Ozzy said.

Clark cleared his beak.

"Same here," Sigi told him.

"And me too," Rin chimed in. "I know as a wizard I'm not supposed to be impressed by much, but you are a remarkable thing."

Clark nodded humbly. He loved to be called a thing, because it made him sound so much more compatible with the objects he liked.

The old boat kept moving. The lights on the front lit up ten feet immediately in front of them, making it feel as if they were traveling through a dark and endless cave. The calm water was a blessing, but it also came with a heavy dose of eerie. It didn't feel or look like the ocean they knew.

None of them talked for the next few miles, but eventually Rin turned and announced, "We're close."

He pulled back the throttle and set the boat to idle. The boat slowed until it was just bobbing softly on the surface of the ocean. Rin cut the motor and a terrific silence settled over all of them.

"Wow," Sigi whispered.

"Where are we?" Ozzy asked.

Rin pulled up the right sleeve of his robe and read some numbers he had written down in pen. He then looked at the boat's compass to see if the numbers matched.

"We're right where we're supposed to be."

The wizard picked up his staff and it began to glow. The green light lit up a circle of light around them and the boat. He moved the staff slowly, but there was no sign of anything except the ten feet of water directly around them.

"I know I've been pulled to the ocean," Ozzy said quietly, his voice carrying beautifully over the water. "But I don't know why my parents would write this spot down. Maybe it was a mistake, or they transposed the numbers."

"Your parents were brilliant," Sigi said. "They didn't make mistakes."

"They did with the Discipline Serum."

Rin started the boat back up and sailed in a small, tight circle, searching for any indication of anything out of the ordinary. The night was so blindingly dark that they couldn't see anything outside the circle of staff light. Rin shut off the motor once more, and once more a stunning silence filled the air.

"I don't know who my parents were," Ozzy confessed. "I remember I loved them, and that they were kind. But I can't fit those memories with what they created, or what they were thinking when they gave this to me."

Ozzy held up his left hand and looked at his birthmark.

"I also don't know how this has anything to do with me passing the fifth test. My parents are dead. Maybe Quarfelt should be looking for a different apprentice for you."

"You know that's not true."

"I'm pretty sure it is," Ozzy argued. "There must be way more qualified candidates."

"Maybe," Rin said gently, "but I'm not talking about *that* not being true."

Ozzy stared at the wizard as he tried to remember what else he had just said to Rin. His mind whirred and hissed as his finger began to grow warm and uncomfortable. The realization of what Rin was alluding to hit Ozzy in the gut.

"I told you," he insisted, "you shouldn't say stuff like that."

"Like what?" Sigi asked. "What are you two talking about?"

"I hired you to find my parents," Ozzy continued. "You found out they had died. What do you think you're doing now? Are you saying my parents are alive? Because don't . . . just don't."

Rin held his staff forward and closer to Ozzy. Under the green glow, the boy's eyes looked swollen and upset. His jaw was tight and the dark hair on his head hung limp.

"There was more written on the back of that picture," Rin said kindly.

"No," Ozzy insisted, as a painful hope that he had given up on months before began to creep back into his being. "No." He shook his head and stepped back as if Rin were someone to fear.

Clark hopped onto Ozzy's shoulder and glared at Rin like a good guard bird should.

"What's happening?" Sigi asked, confused.

"I wrote down what else Ozzy's parents had written," Rin said.

He handed his daughter his staff and it continued to glow. Then he grabbed the bottom of his left sleeve and pushed it up. Ozzy and Sigi could see the latitude and longitude numbers. The wizard pushed it up even more. There, written sideways but in clear block letters, it read:

NO MATTER WHAT YOU ARE TOLD, WE ARE NOT DEAD.

"Impossible," Ozzy said, not yet willing to believe a word of what Rin was saying.

"I don't think you believe that," Rin said compassionately. "I knew the moment we heard they were dead that there were still reasons to believe. But I'm not the kind of person who throws around hope if there is no cause. I wanted to be certain before I said anything to you."

"You think they're alive?"

"I believe they are, and I've come back to finish the job and bring them home."

Ozzy began to shake and cry. "I . . . I can't let myself even . . . I just can't . . ."

Rin stepped forward and wrapped his arms around Ozzy. He let him cry for a few minutes before speaking.

"This spot may not have offered up any answers yet, but I believe it will. I think you have been drawn this direction because somewhere, your parents are longing for you."

Ozzy shivered and heaved.

"And I will find them," Rin added. "It may take more than a wizard—maybe an apprentice, and a Sigi, and a bird, but I will find them."

Sometimes it's best to let important moments breathe.

CHAPTER SIXTY

THE MOMENT HAS ARRIVED

The dark ocean was void of any light or movement on the sea. Everything felt still and stationary as Ozzy stood on the deck of the *Spell Boat* trying to absorb the things that Rin had just said.

As he stood there, caught up in the emotion of it all, a new voice chimed in.

"I don't know what you are all talking about, but I've come to change your plans."

Ozzy, Rin, Sigi and Clark all spun to see Jon standing on the deck of their boat, pointing yet another gun at them.

"If the bird so much as twitches, I will shoot you all."

Clark froze on Ozzy's shoulder.

"How did you get here?" Sigi asked.

"Do you think I don't know how to get out of being taped up? I got out and followed you to the marina."

"Good," Rin said. "So now you know where it is."

"Shut up," Jon ordered. "I was going to take Ozzy

before you got on your boat, but then it occurred to me—maybe you were heading somewhere we needed to know about. It turns out I was wrong. You were easy to follow from a distance. I just kept my lights off and stayed far enough away. Your long distracting conversation allowed me to quietly glide up to the boat and climb on board. Now, Ozzy needs to come with me. But first—put the bird in that box."

Jon pointed to a small metal toolbox under one of the benches.

"No," Ozzy said, his eyes still looking wounded from the things Rin had revealed to him.

Jon raised the gun and shot into the air. The noise was so startling and so loud that they all jumped a few inches off the deck.

"Put the bird in the box."

"Don't worry," Clark tweeted to Ozzy's left ear. "I'll be fine."

Ozzy reached under the bench and retrieved the toolbox. He set it on the bench and opened the lid. The green light let him see that it was half full of tools.

"Pick the bird off of your shoulder and put him in," Jon said. "Make any sudden or dumb moves and I'll shoot."

Ozzy reached up and put his hand around Clark. He carefully put the bird in the box and closed the lid.

"Lock it."

Ozzy locked the latch and then began to slide the box back under the bench.

"No," Jon barked. "Slide it here."

Ozzy pushed the box as hard as he could and it slid to within two feet of Jon.

"Now, take that rope and tie the loon and his daughter to the mast."

"Just take me," Ozzy bargained. "I'll go without any trouble if you just leave them. If I tie them up, they could die out here."

"I don't care," Jon said. "I should have gotten rid of them both a long time ago. If you want, I can shoot them . . . or you can tie them up and we'll be on our way."

Rin placed his staff between the wooden railing and one of the boxes. It continued to glow like a lamppost. Then he and Sigi stood with their backs to the mast while Ozzy tied them up. He ran the rope around them a number of times before Jon was satisfied. Then Ozzy tied off the end.

"Now, let's have you come with me, Ozzy."

"You might want to wait a moment," Rin said calmly. "The water seems uneasy."

"Right," Jon said. "I've never seen the ocean so still."

"Really?" Rin questioned. "Maybe you should look around."

As the wizard stopped talking, the sound of bubbling and churning water could suddenly be heard. The boat wasn't moving, but all around them the ocean was beginning to foam and churn.

Jon looked up at the sky, but there was no weather and no wind.

Big rings of rising water began to circle the boat and ripple in and out. The rings never dissipated or disappeared, and they were surrounded by large popping bubbles. The bubbles lifted off the surface, burst, and then sprayed big plumes of water into the air. Under the green light, the popping spheres looked otherworldly and sinister. The sound of the roiling ocean was growing to a small roar.

The only person on board who was not frightened by what was happening was Rin. He looked calm as he was tied to the mast.

"What is that?" Jon asked while waving his gun. "What's causing that?"

Rin whispered something and a fog-like mist rose up from the water and drifted over the deck of the *Spell Boat*. The glow from the staff sent sparks of light flashing though the fog like synapses snapping in the brain.

"What are you doing?" Jon yelled.

"The easy answer is magic," Rin said. "The long answer? Well, that might be better told another time."

"Magic?" Jon asked, looking around, his vision blocked by fog and his ears filled with the sound of the uneasy water surrounding them. "If it's magic, then maybe I should just shoot you and put an end to all this."

"With what?" Rin asked.

Jon looked down and the gun was no longer in his

hands. Through the patchy mist he could see that it was now lying on the deck ten feet away from him.

"How did—?" Jon practically screamed.

"You should be careful what you drop," the wizard insisted. He looked through the fog and nodded at Ozzy as if to prompt him into action.

Ozzy understood the nod and lunged at Jon. But Jon was too quick and sidestepped the boy while swinging his right leg into Ozzy's charging feet. Ozzy tripped and flew over the side of the boat and into the torrid water.

Instantly the ocean tried to claim him, the belching waters pushed him up against the side of the boat and tried to drag him down. But Ozzy would have none of it. He reached his left arm out of the water, grabbing for the side of the boat. There, as if expecting Ozzy's hand, Rin was reaching down and he grabbed ahold of the boy. A burst of energy traveled through Ozzy's arm and shot into Rin as the wizard hefted him up and back onto the boat. They both shook until Rin released his grip and the boy fell to the floor of the deck.

The fog thinned.

Ozzy looked up to see Jon holding Sigi, his left arm around her and the gun in his other hand. Jon had used the few moments that Rin had been distracted to grab the wizard's daughter. Sigi was putting up a fight, but her captor was strong and had a weapon while she didn't.

"Nobody move!" Jon screamed. "Freeze where you are or she's done."

Rin froze while standing. Ozzy froze while kneeling, and Sigi stopped struggling.

"I don't know what kind of magic trick you used to slip out of that rope," Jon said nervously. "I saw it just drop to the ground." He was losing it. "And I don't know what's going on with this fog and this water."

As if on cue the sea burped and churned, causing the boat to rock and sway.

"You can't win this," Jon yelled. "I'm just the collector. Do you think Ray will stop if I fail? He won't. He'll stop at nothing. This is his white whale. He will hunt Ozzy down until he has what he wants. Now get in my boat, Ozzy. We're going."

"Let go of my daughter," was all Rin said.

The patches of thinning fog lit up like green pulsating strobe lights.

"I won't harm her if you do as I say," Jon shouted. "Just no more tricks!"

"Let her go." Rin's words were calm but had an edge. He was issuing an ultimatum that felt as frightening as the turbulent water around them. The wizard looked at Ozzy and nodded his head.

For a second Ozzy was unsure what he was communicating, but as his finger began to buzz he knew clearly what Rin wanted. Growing up, he had spent many days trying to figure out if there was anything special about him. Living alone and isolated, he had longed to have an ability that would make his life easier. As his finger buzzed, he could feel Rin's thoughts and for the first time, he felt like his apprentice. Ozzy repeated Rin's simple thoughts in his own head while pointing his finger at Jon.

The flashing patches of green fog grew brighter.

Jon began to tremble as he held onto Sigi. His head shook and his eyes grew wide with fear. He lowered the gun he was holding and then, with one surprising move, he brought his arm up and smashed the gun against the side of his own head. The blow stunned him and caused him to stumble forward. Sigi didn't waste a moment. Spinning on her heels, she threw her right fist up and forward, connecting with the underside of Jon's jaw.

The hired goon fell to the deck, out cold for the third time.

Sigi kicked the gun away and then took a second to stand triumphant over Jon.

"We seem to have a knack for knocking people out," Ozzy said.

"Jon earned that one," Rin said, complimenting Sigi's uppercut. "He'll remember it when he comes to."

Ozzy lowered his hand and the ocean settled. He picked up the toolbox and Rin reached out to hold it so that Ozzy could get Clark out. He got the top open and took out the bird, placing him next to the glowing light.

Clark came to and saw the bits of remaining fog floating around. "Why is the air so wet?"

"It wasn't weather," Ozzy answered. "It was Rin."

The wizard tried to look humble.

"What did he do?" Clark chirped up. "Did he change shapes? What did I miss?"

"It was incredible," Sigi added. "I can't describe it."

"There's only one way I can explain it," Rin said. "I'm a wizard. Oh, and it helps to have an apprentice."

Clark looked down at Jon. "Who took out Blandy?"

Ozzy and Rin pointed to Sigi.

"What do we do now?" she asked, still pumped up with adrenaline.

"I think I know," Ozzy said, looking at Rin. "You're leaving, aren't you?"

"I like this new communication we have," the wizard said seriously. "I *am* leaving. Jon was right, Ray won't stop at this. He'll send another, and another, and another, until he gets what he wants. His actions will put you, Sigi, Patti, and others in constant danger. We must stop him."

Rin was silent for only a moment.

"But," he continued, "there is reason to celebrate. You passed the fifth challenge beautifully. The Cin-Wiz-Com is over and there will be celebrations in Quarfelt tonight. I'd watch the mail for any deliveries of new trousers. What an ability you have, Ozzy—mastery over the minds of others."

"I would give it up in a second if it meant my parents were alive."

"Perhaps you can have both."

"I still don't believe it," Ozzy said seriously.

"Truth exists regardless of what you believe," Rin said kindly. "Now, you two need to climb down into the boat

Jon brought. Take it to shore and get to Patti immediately. I'll be back sooner than you think."

"This is nuts, Dad," Sigi argued. "What are you going to do? Take this boat? What about Jon?"

"I'm not taking this boat," the wizard replied. "Leave Jon where he is. He can wake up and take care of himself. Here." Rin set down the open toolbox and picked up his still-glowing staff. He handed the stick to Ozzy. "Take this and go."

"You can't do this alone," Ozzy said. "Let us come with you."

Rin picked the toolbox back up and looked at both Ozzy and Sigi with an expression of pride.

"You both continue to amaze me, but this next move is for me to do. Now go, you two."

Clark fluttered in front of Rin and cleared his beak. "Two? You know I hate to be excluded from the count."

Rin smiled. "I didn't exclude you. In fact, I was just about to tell them that I wouldn't be traveling alone."

"Wait," Ozzy said nervously. "You—"

Still holding the open toolbox, Rin moved with cat-like reflexes and closed the top down over a fluttering Clark. He then clutched the box to his chest and with a smile, said, "Don't tell Patti about the boat."

Rin leaped off the deck into the dark, still water. Clutching the metal box, he instantly disappeared beneath the surface.

"Dad!" Sig screamed. "Dad!"

Ozzy was screaming as well, but his words did nothing to change what had just happened.

"What do we do?" Sigi yelled frantically.

Ozzy held the staff out over the water trying to see any sign of where Rin had resurfaced or was swimming away.

"I don't believe this," Sigi moaned.

Ozzy laughed in a way that was both happy and sad. "I think that's something we need to stop doing. I can't explain what happened tonight, but I'm kind of thinking that wizards are real."

Sigi was still staring at the water, willing her father to pop back up.

"Yeah," she said. "Me too. So he's okay? He's not going to drown?"

"He's a wizard," Ozzy replied. "And he's got Clark. He knows that if that bird isn't returned to me in perfect working order I will not only decline being his apprentice, but he'll have a new enemy."

Ozzy and Sigi left Jon lying on the deck and climbed down the small wooden ladder attached to the back of the boat. The small white boat that Jon had followed them in was tied to the bottom of the ladder, and much newer and nicer than Rin's *Spell Boat*.

As Ozzy untied the rope that was holding them in place, they heard Jon's voice once again. He was standing on the back of the *Spell Boat* and pointing another gun at them.

"Don't move."

"How many guns do you *have*?" Sigi asked with disgust.

"Where's that wizard?" he demanded. "Where is he? And how did he do those things?"

"If you put the gun down, I'll tell you."

"I'm not putting this down." Jon was terrified and kept looking over his shoulder. "How did he do those things?"

"He's a wizard," Sigi said.

Jon jumped at her answer. "This is insane. But now that he's gone, I can take you to Ray and be done with all of this."

At that moment, the lights on both the boats and the green orb on the top of the staff went dark. The darkness was followed by a terrifying sound of something rushing upward beneath them. In the dark, that something exploded out of the water and made contact with the *Spell Boat*.

The earsplitting noise of wood cracking and Jon screaming filled the air.

The small white boat that Ozzy and Sigi were on was pushed backward and away by a large wake of water.

The green orb began to glow again.

They were now fifty feet from a very different looking *Spell Boat*. It had been split by whatever had surfaced and then disappeared. Both of the remaining halves were beginning to sink. There were pieces of wood all over and they could see Jon hanging off one section of the boat, screaming. He let go of the *Spell Boat* and swam over to its lifeboat, which was loose and floating free.

Jon looked out toward Ozzy and Sigi, but he didn't look mad or angry, just scared. His face was pale and his hands shook as he tried to work the oars in the small boat.

"Go," Sigi said.

Ozzy turned key in the boat's ignition, pushed the throttle forward, and began the trip back to shore.

"What was that?" she yelled as they sped toward the marina. "Something came out of the water."

"I don't know," Ozzy answered. "A whale?"

"Like a real whale? Or did my father finally shape-shift . . ." Sigi couldn't finish the impossible thought.

"If he did, Clark's going to be upset about missing it."

The boat raced for shore in the dark, clear night.

CHAPTER SIXTY-ONE

EVERYTHING IS CONNECTED

Ozzy looked out of his bedroom window. The new glass had been installed the day before and the view was beautiful today—just the right mix of sun and clouds to make the sky interesting. In the distance, the ocean was blue and endless. His finger had not buzzed since the night of the boating accident, but the ocean still called to him. His mind felt in control and stronger than it ever had before.

He put on a red T-shirt and orange shorts. He knew the colors didn't work together, but he brushed aside any concern. That kind of worry was no longer a part of who he was.

He climbed the stairs down from his bedroom and entered the kitchen through the breezeway door. Patti was at the table reading from a tablet and drinking lemon water. Her brown skin and wide smile made her feel like a pleasant surprise whenever Ozzy saw her. She had on red leggings and a black tank top. Her feet were bare and she tapped her toes against the hardwood floors as she sipped her water. She looked up, saw what Ozzy was wearing, and smiled.

"You're going to your house?" she asked nicely.

"What's left of it." It was Saturday, and he and Sigi had plans.

"And you won't be taking the motorcycle, right?"

Ozzy smiled.

There had been a few new rules implemented since Ozzy and Sigi had returned from their trip at sea. When they had gotten back to the marina, the office had been locked up, but they banged on the front door of the closest house until someone opened up and let them call Patti.

Patti was thrilled they were alive, but not thrilled about what had happened. Ozzy and Sigi had told her most of what went down, but there were a few details they left out—like the *Spell Boat* being torn apart by something bursting up out of the sea. Or that Rin had jumped off the boat with a toolbox. Instead, they had let her know that Clark was spending a little time with Rin to help him with some genealogy he was working on.

"I was thinking about Rin," Patti said. "He's never been interested in genealogy before."

Ozzy shrugged, hoping he wouldn't have to add to the lie he and Sigi had told her earlier.

"I'm sure he just wants to see if there are other wizards in his family tree," Patti complained. "I can't believe we were married as long as we were."

Ozzy poured himself a glass of milk and a bowl of cereal, then sat down at the table near Patti. She looked up from her tablet.

"Did you sleep okay?" she asked.

"Yes." Ozzy poured the milk over his cereal. "Sorry about everything I've put you and Sigi through." Patti had never asked for an apology, but Ozzy felt compelled to offer one.

"Don't be sorry," she said kindly. "I'm sorry for all that Rin has put you through."

"Why?" Ozzy said with sincere confusion. "They've been some of the best parts of my life so far."

"You are something."

"I read in books that sometimes people who get divorced get remarried. Do you think that could ever be a possibility with Rin?"

Patti laughed so hard and long that she had to eventually leave the room and compose herself elsewhere.

When Sigi came into the kitchen, Ozzy was alone, eating cereal.

"You'll drive to the train tracks?" he asked her.

"If you'll carry me the rest of the way."

Ozzy knew Sigi was joking, but he would have carried her anywhere.

"I miss Clark," she said, pouring her own cereal.

"Me too. More than anything. Well, maybe not anything."

Sigi brought her cereal over and sat down. They both

knew what the other thing Ozzy missed was. But neither of them talked about it. It was just a heavy thing that weighed on the minds of both of them. Rin had offered Ozzy hope with the news he had given him, but with that hope came the possibility of more pain.

They finished their breakfast and headed out in the small white car that they had once driven to New Mexico. As they pulled out of the driveway, a couple of police cars were parked on the street. They waved at both, and one car followed.

Sheriff Wills had been adamant about keeping a constant eye on Ozzy and Sigi and anyone else associated with 1221 Ocean View Dr. They had had long talks with the police department concerning what had happened and what might happen next. Neither Ozzy nor Sigi had protested being watched over. They knew there was still trouble ahead. They also understood how serious Ray was, which made them more than willing to have their own security keeping an eye on them.

They drove along Mule Pole Highway, arms out the windows, listening to music.

See your head in the fading light,
And through the dark your eyes shine bright.

The clouds drifted above them as the air lifted their hands and arms up and down. A sense of wonder filled the car and permeated their bones.

Sigi looked at Ozzy and smiled. "Any guesses as to when they'll come back?"

"Just at the right moment?"

"It's hard to tell who's more wizardly these days," Sigi said. "You or my dad."

"Well, Rin's not around to argue his case. So I win."

They parked by the train tracks and the police car pulled up and parked behind them. Then they walked the two miles alone to where the cloaked house had once stood. The two of them stood in front of the burnt remains, holding hands as the sun flopped down from above and rested like a giant cat on the ashes.

"I still can't believe it's gone," Sigi said.

"I know," Ozzy said, "but things have to change for us to understand uncertainty. Just think—the next time something burns down it will be easier to deal with."

"That's a dumb thought."

"It won't be my last one."

"I guess there's *one* thing in this world that's certain."

"What do you think Ray's next move will be?" Ozzy asked.

"He'd be a fool to try anything."

A loud squirrel was arguing with a small bird in a tree behind them. The two turned around and looked up into the branches.

"You want to try practicing some more?" Sigi asked.

"Of course," Ozzy said smiling.

He reached out and pointed toward the squirrel with

his purple finger. The noisy rodent's eyes went wide. It turned away from the bird, scurried down the tree, and ran into a dark hole beneath a large bush.

"You're getting good."

"I just don't like to see birds getting picked on."

Sigi's new phone vibrated, and Ozzy looked at his finger, worried.

"It's just my alarm," Sigi told hm. "We need to head back or that cop will come looking for us."

"That's okay," Ozzy said. "The exercise will do him good."

The clouds above Ozzy and Sigi grew fluffier, and the birds began to harmonize, as they spent a few extra minutes alone. There were other things they could worry about, but the smell of the burnt cloaked house, mixed with the hope of what was to come, made them feel that all things are connected, and that every possibility was available.

DISCUSSION QUESTIONS

1. Ozzy accepts an airplane ticket to New York City from Ray, thinking that it's from Rin. Is it possible to be too trusting—or too suspicious? Give an example.
2. Rin acquires a tree branch that is later transformed into a wizard's staff. If you were to use a magical object (a wand, a staff, a magic carpet, or something else), what would it be and why?
3. Sigi finds herself helping Ozzy regain control a few times. Have you ever needed to help a friend in trouble? How did you do that?
4. More than once, Clark is separated from Ozzy, Sigi, and Rin, and has to figure out a way back. If you were far away from someone you love, name three things you would do to reconnect with them.
5. Rin is awarded new plaid trousers when he advances as a wizard. What are some examples of rewards you've received for doing something well? How did the reward

make you feel? Why is it important for people to feel valued or rewarded?

6. Rin asks Ozzy to be an apprentice wizard. What do you think an apprentice wizard does? If you were Rin's apprentice, what would be the best thing about it? What would be the worst?
7. Because of something Rin does, Ozzy loses the cloaked house to a fire. How hard would it be to forgive something like that? What would a friend need to do for him or her to earn your trust again?
8. Ozzy gets some encouraging news about his relatives a couple of times. What's the best news you've ever received? Describe how you felt or how you reacted upon hearing the news.
9. Rin, Ozzy, Sigi, and Clark outwit Jon several times, but he keeps coming back. Do you know anyone who won't take no for an answer? Who? Why was this person so persistent?
10. It seems like Ray will stop at nothing to get his hands on the Discipline Serum. Why do you think it's so important to him?
11. Clark is obsessed with Rin changing shape. Is there something you would like to shapeshift into? What? And why?
12. Sigi and Rin have a complicated history. When they are finally able to say what they feel, things begin to change for the better. Do you ever wish for chances to tell those you love how you are feeling?

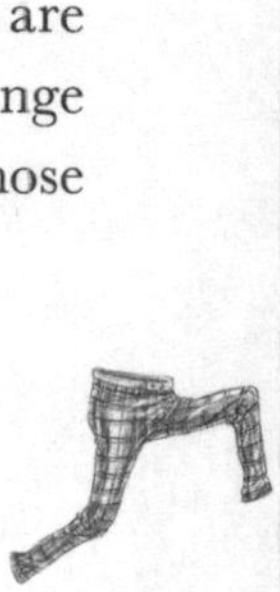